selection of titles by Kathleen Delaney

The Mary McGill and Millie series

PUREBRED DEAD *
CURTAINS FOR MISS PLYM *
BLOOD RED, WHITE AND BLUE *
DRESSED TO KILL *

The Ellen McKenzie series

DYING FOR A CHANGE
GIVE FIRST PLACE TO MURDER
MURDER FOR DESSERT
MURDER HALF-BAKED
MURDER BY SYLLABUB

* available from Severn House

DRESSED T

DRESSED TO KILL

Kathleen Delaney

severn House

This first world edition published 2019
in Great Britain and the USA by
SEVERN HOUSE PUBLISHERS LTD of
Eardley House, 4 Uxbridge Street, London W8 7SY.
Trade paperback edition first published
in Great Britain and the USA 2020 by
SEVERN HOUSE PUBLISHERS LTD.

British Library Cataloguing in Publication Data
A CIP catalogue record for this title is available from the British Library.

ISBN-13: 978-0-7278-8894-5 (cased)
ISBN-13: 978-1-78029-625-8 (trade paper)
ISBN-13: 978-1-4483-0318-2 (e-book)

All Severn House titles are printed on acid-free paper.

Severn House Publishers support the Forest Stewardship Council™ [FSC™],
the leading international forest certification organisation. All our titles that
are printed on FSC certified paper carry the FSC logo.

Typeset by Palimpsest Book Production Ltd.,
Falkirk, Stirlingshire, Scotland.
Printed and bound in Great Britain by
TJ International, Padstow, Cornwall.

ACKNOWLEDGMENTS

No published book is produced by the author alone. It takes a team. Someone to read it while it is in the beginning stages, someone to critique, in a good sense, someone to edit it and someone to say it's ready. I would like to gratefully thank my team.

My wonderful editors at Severn House, Sara Porter, Natasha Bell and Kate Lyall Grant who invariably suggest changes that make the book stronger; my long suffering agent, Dawn Dowdle of Blue Ridge Literary Agency, who is not only my first editor but also keeps me writing and sane while I'm doing it; my brother, Mike, who is my first reader and has no problem telling me when the plot isn't coming together and making suggestions to get it back on track; and finally, my youngest granddaughter, Delaney, who loves to plot with me and comes up with some astonishingly good ideas.

Thank you all.

ONE

The man lurched toward Mary, hands outstretched, white hair encrusted with mud and gore. The slash from his left ear to his jaw was raw and bright red. His eyeball seemed to dangle from his left eye socket and moaning sounds escaped from his lips with each step.

Mary didn't move. She stared as he got nearer and nearer. Millie, Mary's not-so-brave cocker spaniel, peered at him from behind Mary's legs and made a few moaning sounds.

'Your wig is slipping and your moans sound like stomach trouble. Other than that, you look pretty good,' Mary told the apparition, who frowned.

'I told Mom it slipped. It was Grams's when she got breast cancer, and I guess she wanted it big. Mom gave me some hairpins, but they don't work very well.' The apparition sighed. 'Other than that, what do you think?'

'I think it will be dark in the House of Horrors and you'll scare the daylights out of all the girls and some of the boys. Just try to groan a little louder. Think of how you'd feel after eating eight hot dogs.'

A wide grin appeared. 'I'd feel great, but I'll try to make it louder. How's this?'

He let loose with a groan that made Millie howl. Mary laughed. 'I think that will do just fine.'

The apparition nodded and lurched off, practicing as he went.

'Was that Bobby Connors?' Joy Maguire stood beside Mary, watching the retreating figure. 'I hope that's his House of Horrors costume. He'll have all the little ones in hysterics if he keeps wandering around the park like that.'

Mary turned to look at Joy. Millie wagged her stump of a tail.

'Yes, that's Bobby and he'll be in his position in the House of Horrors before people start arriving. Thank goodness the little ones have their own fun house.' She took another look at Joy and nodded. 'You look great. Where'd you get your costume?'

She assumed Joy had whipped it up somehow, but the colonial dress she had on looked authentic. So did the mop cap she wore and the voluminous apron. White stockings and black shoes with buckles completed her ensemble.

'I got the cap and apron when we went to Williamsburg last summer, and I had Victoria Witherspoon make the dress. I showed her a picture, and this is what she came up with. She's pretty good.'

High praise from Joy, who was no stranger to the sewing machine. Mary was surprised, though, that Joy had entrusted the task to someone else, especially someone she had to pay. Joy was notorious for having a tight grip on her family budget. However, the money had been well spent. Joy looked just like the interpreters Mary had seen on her one and only trip to Williamsburg. If she'd known what Joy had in mind, she might have been tempted to try something like that herself. All the other volunteers on Mary's Halloween in the Park committee were dressing up in some way, but Mary had demurred. As chairman she had the right to refuse, she'd said, and besides, she'd be too busy to be bothered with long black witches' skirts, clown pants, or any of the other silly-looking things her committee people were wearing. She'd come as herself, a woman of a certain age, a widowed, retired school-teacher with a dog who wasn't wearing a costume either. Speaking of which . . .

'Is the stage in the gazebo ready for the costume parade? I don't want anyone to trip over the sound equipment the band's going to have, but I do want the music.'

'All taken care of. They know they have to play sort of soft music while the costume contest is going on, especially when it's the little kids, but then they're going to let it rip. I've never heard of even one of the songs they're going to play.'

Mary didn't doubt that for a minute. Joy wouldn't be up on the music the kids of today listened to. She hadn't much liked the music of her own era. Joy had disapproved of Elvis Presley, and he was tame, compared to today's performers. 'Good. I'll stop by and check on them later. Right now, I want to make sure the fun house for the babies is actually fun and safe.'

'It will be. The preschool fathers from St Marks put it together under the watchful eyes of the preschool mothers. I'd better check on the trick and treat bags.'

Mary watched her retreating back with the familiar mix of feelings she always had about Joy, admiration for her competency in organizing just about everything and slight irritation with her joyless attitude at doing it. Joy's mother's optimism about her future attitude toward life when she gave her that name hadn't born fruit.

'Come on, Millie. Let's make sure the little ones' fun area is finished.'

They headed toward the end of the town park that faced the library and the local bank. The other side faced the auto parts store and a newer building filled with attorneys and accountants. That they needed a building for that many still amazed Mary. The town had grown a lot in the last few years, mostly due to the wineries that had appeared and the tourists that visited them. There wouldn't be tourists tonight, however. Halloween was for the children of Santa Louisa and there would be no wine involved. She pulled her sweater closer around her. It was a chilly afternoon, but the sky was clear. It would be a cold night but a beautiful one. It was quiet at this end of the park, which was why Mary had chosen it for the events slated for the aged six and under crowd. The only people on the street were going in and out of the bank. She recognized one of them. Her nephew-in-law, Dan Dunham, entered the bank, followed by someone dressed as a clown. The red, white, and blue suit had a high ruff around the neck, long sleeves with exaggerated ruffles, blue gloves, baggy pants, and oversized shoes. Whoever was under all that had completed the look with the customary red nose and one of those awful rubber masks you pulled on over your head. Once again, she was glad she'd refused to wear anything like that but had to admit it was a well-done costume.

She walked back to view the events. The small slide was decorated with cutouts of black cats, black and orange crepe paper, and a laughing ghost made from a bedsheet and stuffed with pillows at the bottom. The children would slide down almost into its arms. There were small tables holding spray chalk for decorating the sidewalk and big boards set up for painting the witches, goblins, and ghosts that were outlined on them. Small tubs held apples for bobbing, but the rules and safety precautions were different from the ones for the older kids, and so was the fun house. Nothing scary here. Just some fun and surprises – at least Mary hoped so. She stared at it, trying to decide how she felt about it when a loud blast distracted her. It distracted Millie, too, who yelped as if she'd been hit. A firecracker? Then another sounded, and another. They seemed to be coming from around the bank. Some teenager trying to get things started early?

Beyond irritated, she grabbed Millie into her arms and headed for the street at a brisk trot. It seemed empty. The door of the bank flew open and the clown appeared. He had a tote bag in one hand and a small gun in the other.

Mary gasped and tightened her grip on Millie, who yelped again. The clown turned to look at them and raised the gun. He was going to shoot them. Horror and disbelief filled Mary as she stared at the clown. Should she try to shove Millie behind her? Or drop to the grass? She could do neither. Her body seemed frozen in place. Except for her heart. It was beating so hard she thought it might escape. But the clown didn't shoot. He dropped his hand and, with surprising speed, ran down the street and turned the corner toward the parking lot behind the library and disappeared.

What had just happened? She took a deep breath, only now aware she had been holding it. Her brain started functioning again. Had she really seen what she thought she'd seen? A clown with a gun? One who had almost shot them? Oh, dear God. Those weren't firecrackers she'd heard. They were gunshots. What had that man been doing? Robbing the bank, the unfrozen part of her brain answered. Had he shot someone? Before she could react, sirens screamed, and a lone police car careened to a stop in front of the bank. Gary, a policeman she knew well, jumped out, gun drawn.

'Mrs McGill, get down. Get out of the way. Move!' He looked around somewhat wildly, gun drawn.

'He went into the library parking lot,' she yelled back. 'He's dressed as a clown.'

Gary paused to stare at her, mouth agape. 'He's what?'

'Dressed like a clown. In a Halloween costume. He's in the library or in the parking lot.'

'Stay there,' Gary yelled back and started for the parking lot.

Mary watched, but only for a second. Shots. Gun. Someone might be hurt. She dropped Millie on the grass and, keeping a tight grip on her leash, dashed with her at her side across to the bank. The door seemed unusually heavy, but she finally got it open and rushed in.

A woman lay on the floor, a pool of blood slowly expanding around her, one of the tellers kneeling at her side, crying. Little old Minnie Myers stood by the table that held the banking supplies, holding onto it as if, if she let go, she'd fall to the floor as well. Glen Manning, the bank president and Mary's good friend, stood in the doorway of his office, staring at the floor. There was no sign of the other two bank employees. Behind the counter? But that thought was fleeting. Mary had caught sight of what Minnie, Glen, and now Millie stared at. The woman wasn't the only body on the floor. There was another one. A man. Aghast, Mary stopped. She didn't feel Millie crash into her legs. The policemen and EMTs who rushed in barely registered.

It was Dan. Lying on the floor outside Glen's office, blood slowly stained the shoulder of his blue shirt. Dan, who had practically grown up in her kitchen, who had married her beloved niece, Ellen, who . . . Cold enveloped her and, for the first time in her life, Mary felt her knees give out.

TWO

Mary squirmed in her chair, trying to get comfortable. She'd been sitting too long, and her legs were going to sleep. She looked around. None of the chairs in this small hospital waiting room looked any more comfortable. It wasn't the chair that caused her distress. She felt useless and miserable as well. How could she have fainted? She'd come to as they were wheeling Dan out on a gurney and trying to get her on one as well. As if she needed something like that! It was momentary shock, that was all. She just needed a minute . . . she'd had plenty since then. How many, she didn't know. But it had been several hours, she was sure.

She watched Ellen, her niece, as she paced the floor in this small, enclosed room. She wove in and out of the chairs, barely missing the small table set up with a water pitcher and paper cups and the chair containing Glen Manning. Mary wasn't sure she even saw him.

Glen sat with his head buried in his hands, not saying a word. None of them said anything. They were talked out. Now they waited. Dan was in the operating room, getting only God and the attending surgeon knew what done to him, and the suspense was almost intolerable.

The door leading to the hall opened and everyone turned, holding their breath, expecting, hoping, to see the doctor. Instead, it was Pat and Karl Bennington, the local small animal veterinarian and Mary's close friends. Disappointment washed over Mary, but a little relief as well. She'd been worrying about Millie. They would know where and how she was.

'Where's Millie?' she asked before they could ask about Dan.

'She and Morgan are safe at our house. I didn't want to put them in a kennel at the vet clinic. I just admitted a dog with kennel cough,' Pat explained.

Mary wasn't sure what kennel cough was and right now didn't care. She did care that Millie and Morgan, Dan and Ellen's dog, were safe and probably happy, sitting on Pat's living-room sofa instead of being locked up in crates at the clinic. She watched as Pat walked over to Ellen, took her by the arm, and guided her back to the chair next to Mary's.

Karl went directly to Glen, sat beside him, and forced him to look up. 'What happened?'

It took a moment for Glen to respond. He didn't look at Karl. Instead, he stared across the room. His hands were in his lap, tightly folded, presumably to keep them from shaking.

'Dan and I were talking in my office,' he said finally. 'He'd just sat down. I hadn't paid any attention to the clown, just another customer in costume, until we heard a gasp and a scream. Then there was a shot. I started to get up, but Dan said to stay put. He was on his feet and had his gun out before I knew what was happening. He went to the door and looked around it. I don't know what he saw, but he raised his gun and shouted for someone to get down, then he said, "Police, drop the gun,", or something like that, then there were more shots and he dropped to the floor. I had already hit the alarm, so I rushed over to him in time to see the damn clown go through the front door with a sort of tote bag. How much he got away with, I don't know, but it wasn't nearly enough to pay for what he's done.'

'Who was he shouting at to get down?' Karl looked a little white and Pat squeezed Ellen's hand.

'Minnie, I think. She was the only other customer in the bank.'

Mary let her mind flash back to what she'd seen when she and Millie came through the bank door. Minnie stood at the bank table, holding onto it. Could she have blocked Dan's view of the gunman? It didn't matter. What did matter was how badly Dan was hurt.

'Who was the woman he shot?' Pat asked, not letting go of Ellen's hand. 'All we've been able to learn was she died, but not who she was.'

'Victoria Witherspoon.' Those were the first words Mary had heard Ellen speak since they'd taken Dan into the operating room.

'Oh, no,' gasped Pat. 'Not that nice woman. She was so talented. Why did . . .'

Glen shrugged. 'I don't know. I think the police are questioning my tellers, but I'm not sure what happened. Or where the blasted clown went. The cops that came with the EMTs said there was no sign of him. I don't know what's happened since.'

Karl shook his head. 'I don't think they've found him. At least not that we've heard. He just disappeared.'

How could he have, dressed like that? Somehow, Mary

couldn't seem to focus on the clown. She shook herself a little, trying to make her brain work, but it didn't want to function just yet. All she could think about was Dan.

The door opened again. This time the man who appeared wore green hospital scrubs and a face mask hung around his neck. A large grin spread across his face. 'He's out in the recovery room and is going to be all right.' He walked over and dropped into the chair beside Glen Manning, put his arm around him and pulled his close. 'He got hit in the shoulder and is going to be pretty sore for a while, and he'll be in the hospital for a few days. It'll be fun for us when he comes out of the anesthetic trying to keep him in bed and quiet, but he'll be fine.' He addressed that to all of them, then turned to Glen. 'It wasn't your fault, so stop tearing yourself apart. You couldn't possibly have known that clown was going to rob your bank and that he had a gun and wasn't afraid to use it. The thing to do now is find the SOB. I guess our guys called the San Louis Obispo Homicide people to help them, but I'm sure Dan will want in on this as soon as he's awake and sitting up.'

Everyone gathered around John Lavorino, all asking questions at once.

'Wait.' He held up his free hand, keeping his arm around Glen. 'The doctor will talk to Ellen in a few minutes. She can go into recovery with him, but only her. That's about all I know, at least for now. I don't know a thing about what happened, only what we saw in the operating room, which was surprisingly good considering the cannon that blasted clown has, whoever he is.'

'When can I see him?' A little color had come back into Ellen's face and a little life back into her eyes.

'Now,' John told her. He patted Glen on the shoulder and stood. 'I'll take you in. The rest of you might as well go home. You can probably see him tomorrow.'

'Wait,' Mary said. 'Ellen, do you have a car here? How are you going to get home?'

'It's in the parking lot. I may spend the night, if they'll let me. Can you look after Morgan?'

Karl interrupted. 'We'll keep Morgan until you can come

get him. We'll take Mary to pick up Millie and then take her home.'

'Oh, no. I have to get to the park and make sure everything is going smoothly.' Mary grabbed her purse and started looking through it, trying to find her phone. 'What time is it, anyway?'

'Nine. The park is shutting down. Joy was there with your clipboard, making sure it all went off like clockwork.' Pat had let go of Ellen to put her arm around Mary's shoulders. 'You had things so well organized, it was all perfect. Even that blasted corn husk maze that took up half the park didn't swallow up anyone. All who went in came out again. So, you're going home with Millie.'

'I'd better go back to the bank.' Glen looked a little stronger. His hands were no longer clenched, and his voice was steady. 'I'm sure they locked up fine, but I never thought to call or anything. I just left and followed the ambulance over here. I'll need to check the drawers to see how much money is missing. I hope the girls are all right. I never even thought to ask about them, either.' He sounded distraught again, and his hands made fists.

'The girls are fine.' An unfamiliar voice spoke up from the doorway leading into the hall. A tall, balding man with black-rimmed glasses stood there, surveying them all. 'They're a little shook up, understandably, but we made sure they got home safely and there's someone with each of them. We'll question them again in the morning. I assume you're Glen Manning and we do need you at the bank. We'll need your help with a number of things.'

'Who are you?' There was more than a little hostility and suspicion in John's voice.

'Detective Sean Ryan, San Louis Obispo Homicide. Your police department called us in. Which one of you is Mary McGill?'

'I am.' Mary stepped forward. What could this man want with her? Then she remembered. She'd seen the clown. She'd seen his gun. He'd pointed it at her and Millie. She felt a little weak in the knees again and sat back down.

'Mary, are you all right?' Pat knelt by her chair. 'Are you going to faint? Someone bring her some water.'

Mary had no intention of fainting. Why she had in the bank, she had no idea, but it wasn't going to happen again.

'I'm fine. Just a little . . . How can I help?'

Detective Ryan hadn't moved. Now he walked into the room, glanced at John, passed over Glen, studied Pat and Karl Bennington for a moment, and looked long and hard at Ellen.

'You're . . .?'

'Mrs Dunham.'

Dismissively, he nodded and snapped at Mary. 'One of the patrolmen said you saw the clown exit the bank. Is that true?'

'Yes.' Mary wasn't impressed with this detective. He came across as rude and certainly insensitive. He hadn't asked about Dan. He had shown no courtesy to Ellen. However, she wanted the man who had done all this caught. She wouldn't give this detective her middle schoolteacher stare. Not this time, anyway. 'I saw him go into the bank but other than thinking his costume was great, never gave him another thought. Then I heard the shots and Millie and I ran to the sidewalk just in time to see him come out. He pointed his gun at me. For a minute, I thought he was going to shoot, but he ran for the corner and disappeared. Then Gary came. I told him where the clown had gone, and he went after him. I went into the bank and found . . .' That was as far as she could go.

Detective Ryan looked up from his phone where he had evidently been making notes. 'Did you recognize him?'

Startled, Mary responded crisply. 'How could I? He was covered completely by that costume and the mask. Besides, it all happened so fast . . .'

'Right.' He closed his phone and looked around. 'Who's Millie?'

'My dog.' Mary knew her tone was crisp, but the man was seriously irritating her. Dan would never conduct an interview with such discourtesy. 'She's not here.' She gestured to the people who were. 'You've met Glen Manning, the bank president. The couple next to him are Dr and Mrs Bennington. He's our local veterinarian. The man in the bloody scrubs holding Mr Manning's hand is John Lavorino, head surgical nurse. Glen and John also own Furry Friends, our local pet shop. And, of course, Mrs Dunham. None of them, except Mr Manning, saw anything.'

The expression on Detective Ryan's face changed. Annoyance? Possible. His tone of voice didn't show any. It was all business.

'I'd appreciate it if Mr Manning would return with me to the bank. There are a number of questions we need to ask.'

Glen nodded and started to stand but turned to John. 'When do you get off?'

John looked at the wall clock. 'Another hour. Did our dogs get fed?'

Glen nodded. 'Krissie ran over and took care of them. She closed the shop, too. Not sure what she did about the cash register, but you can check that tomorrow. You're off, aren't you?'

John nodded. 'Do you want me to go home and wait for you or should I come to the bank when I'm through here? I want to make sure Dan is settled in for the night and has all his meds, and Ellen said she'd like to stay with him. I need to arrange that.'

'I have no idea how long I'll be. Why don't you stop by before you go home?'

Detective Ryan had taken note of the conversation. His expression didn't change, but his eyelids flicked. 'Shouldn't take more than an hour, but we'll need you to come in and give a formal statement, probably tomorrow. Can't be sure you'll be able to open the bank, though. Don't know when forensics will be finished.'

Glen looked startled and not at all pleased, but he didn't say anything.

Karl did. 'Is there anything we can do?' he asked John. 'You said we can't see him but he's out of danger?'

John nodded. 'He came through fine. His shoulder will take a while to heal, and he's got some extensive therapy ahead, but, for tonight, I think you all should go home. Get some sleep.'

Mary thought sleep wouldn't come easy tonight but going home sounded good. If she could just talk Karl into dropping by the park so she could make sure . . .

'In that case,' Karl said, 'we'll be going. I think we're going to have to stop by the park on our way. Mary won't sleep a wink if she thinks anything got left undone.' He smiled at her and pulled her to her feet and looked over at Ellen. 'We'll keep Morgan for you. I just hope he doesn't like to sleep on the bed.'

'Well . . .' Ellen looked embarrassed but grateful. 'Thank you.'

'I'll feed Jake, too.' Pat put her hand out. 'That cat likes his dinner on time. His time. Want to give me the key?'

'I didn't lock the back door. After I got the call about Dan, I rushed out.'

'In that case, I'll lock it when I leave. You do have your keys?'

Ellen nodded, and Karl ushered Pat and Mary out the door. Mary thought Glen and Detective Ryan were probably right behind them. She was afraid it would be quite some time before Glen saw his bed.

THREE

'**M**illie, move over.'

Mary surveyed the sleeping dog, stretched sideways on the bed. She had made herself a cup of tea, fortified with a little something soothing, and had taken a hot bath. She hoped that would help her to sleep, but it wasn't helping her get into bed. The dog didn't want to move.

'How such a small dog can take up so much room, I don't know.' She pushed at her.

Finally, Millie moved to the end of the bed, where she belonged. Mary put out the light and crawled in, but sleep evaded her. All had been well at the park. Joy had done a marvelous job, as had all her volunteers. Even though the bank was still cordoned off with crime-scene tape and the robbery and shootings had been the chief topic of at least the adult conversations, it seemed everyone had had a good time. None of the babies had freaked out, the teenagers had loved the bob for apples tub, and had even eaten some of them, and the band was a big hit. Also, a loud one. The line to try to find your way through the corn maze had been long, but everyone who'd tried came out the other end. By the time Mary arrived, her volunteers were tearing down what had to be done that night. They would be back in the morning to finish. She was told, in no uncertain terms, to go home and rest. Millie had been overwhelmed with joy when she saw Mary and tried to climb into her arms, which was a bit awkward but flattering as well. Morgan kept looking at the door, as if he expected Dan or Ellen to come through any minute, but he knew Karl and Pat well, so would be fine overnight.

Mary lay in bed, trying to relax after what had been a seriously taxing day, but she couldn't shut out the pictures that kept returning. Everything had happened so fast she hadn't had time to let the horror of it in, but it came back now, clearly. She squeezed her eyes closed, hoping that would erase the pictures that ran through her mind like a newsreel, but it just made them more vivid. Dan going through the bank door, the clown close behind him, looking a little awkward in those oversized red shoes. Then the shots, clutching Millie as they watched the clown come back out, hesitate, raise the gun, then turn, running faster than she'd thought he could down the street. Her eyes flew open and she sat straight up in bed. The clown running. No. That wasn't it. It was something else. A flash of light as he turned. From the gun? From the front of his clown suit. What, she had no idea. What would be on a clown costume that reflected light? There was something else. Something about him was familiar. Something she couldn't put her finger on. Mary hugged herself tightly. Did that mean she knew the clown? No. She couldn't. Surely no one she knew would do such a terrible thing. Only, there was something . . . what, she wasn't sure. She had to think. Maybe those ridiculous clown shoes reminded her of someone. But she didn't really believe that. She felt a little sick. If she was right, that meant the clown was someone who lived in her town. Someone who had worn that elaborate costume because he'd be recognized. Did he think she'd recognized him? No. He'd have shot her. But he shot Victoria. Why? She knew why he shot Dan. But Victoria . . .

Mary lay back down, her eyes wide open, thinking. It was almost dawn before her eyes closed and her thoughts disappeared behind a curtain of sleep.

FOUR

T he sun shone through Mary's window much earlier than necessary, in Mary's opinion. Millie didn't share that thought. She wanted breakfast. Yawning broadly, Mary eased herself out of bed and headed for the broom closet, where she kept the dog food. Maybe she'd go back to bed, but one glance at the kitchen clock changed her mind. What she needed was coffee. She filled her Mr Coffee and urged it to finish quickly before she fell back asleep sitting at the kitchen table. Only, she wouldn't. The events of yesterday were back to haunt her, and there was no way she could avoid them. A trip downtown was in her near future. Not only did she want to see Dan, but she needed to talk to Glen. She wanted a firsthand account of what had happened in the bank. Had he seen the clown? She thought he'd said he'd watched him leave. Had he, too, thought the man looked familiar? Had the clown said anything to the tellers? Had one of them recognized his voice? Had Minnie? Where was Minnie?

Where was Detective Ryan? He'd said he wanted her statement but hadn't said where or when. She didn't mind giving one, not in the least, but she wasn't going to sit around waiting for him to contact her. The coffeepot had stopped gurgling. About time. She got up, pulled her favorite blue and white Chinese pattern mug out of the cupboard, filled it to the brim, and opened the back door for Millie. She stood in the doorway, staring at the yard but not really seeing it as she sipped her coffee and thought. The clown had disappeared awfully fast. Where had he gone? Not into a car, at least not one parked behind the library. According to Agnes, who manned the front desk of their small police department, Gary had seen two vehicles drive out of the parking lot – one a pickup, the other a sedan. He didn't get a good look at the drivers but didn't think either wore a clown mask. They were both gone before he could flag them down. Mary wondered who they were and what they were doing there. Dropping off library books? In the drive-by box? She could think of several more questions that should be asked, if the police could find them. Probably more than she'd thought of. But she'd like to know who they were. She wondered if anyone in the park had seen the clown. There were several people setting up a food booth just opposite the corner of the parking lot where he'd disappeared. Had any of them seen him?

She took another sip, but her cup was empty. She looked at it with disapproval then went back into the yard. Millie had finished and was headed for the stairs. She stood aside to let her in. 'I'm going to take a shower, then we're going downtown. There are a few people we need to see, even if it's not our job to ask questions. That Detective Ryan doesn't know the people in this town. We do. They'll talk to us, and then we'll talk to Dan. A hurt shoulder won't have affected his mental process one bit.'

She washed out her cup and started toward the bathroom.

FIVE

C rime-scene tape was strung up around the bank door like Christmas decorations, only there was nothing joyous about this tape, nor decorative. Mary sighed, and she and Millie resumed their tour of the remains of the Halloween celebration. Most of it was already gone, but the Kiwanis were taking down the last of their House of Horrors and loading everything in the back of a pickup. The Lions had finished taking down their display and were helping the city crew clean up the mess left by the half-eaten apples, the spilled candy and soda, and the thousands of cookie crumbs.

Phil Goforth caught up with her. 'Hey, Mary.' He paused and smiled. 'Hi, Millie. You're looking good.'

Millie wagged her stub of a tail.

Phil turned to Mary. 'We're actually ahead of schedule. This was another huge success, Mary. Thanks to you and your committee of by now experts. You sure know how to whip these volunteers into shape.' He paused, and the smile turned tentative. 'Just one thing, though.'

Mary waited. There was always just one thing. It didn't take long.

Phil put his hands on his hips and said in a disgusted tone of voice, 'Marty Evans said he can't get over here to take down that blasted maze until after the weekend. That's a whole week of having it up in the park. I told him it was a liability. Some little kid could get lost in there, but he said he's going to a conference and won't be back to do it until Monday. He's going to put up a couple of doors, which means nail a couple of boards across the entrance and the exit, but that's the best he can do.' He paused again and scratched his head. 'What should we do?'

A wave of impatience washed over Mary. She had been against that maze from the beginning. It took up too much room in the park and she'd been afraid of fire. However, the fire department had OK'd it and most of the men wanted it, so she'd given in. She hadn't expected it to become a permanent feature. 'Can any of you take it apart and return it to Marty's farm?'

'He says not to touch it until he gets here. Something about all the dust from the corn stalks or something. He said he's sorry, but he'll get to it as soon as he can.'

Thoroughly annoyed, Mary responded with uncustomary tartness. 'He must have known he'd be gone. Why didn't he let any of us know?'

Phil shrugged.

'Have you contacted the fire department yet, or the city manager?'

Phil smiled a rather sheepish smile. 'Thought I'd talk to you first.'

There went her visit to Dan, or at least it did right now. 'All right. I'll take care of it. Somehow.'

Phil beamed. 'I knew you would.' He turned on his heel and left.

Mary watched him go, grinding her teeth as he disappeared behind a half-dismantled food booth. 'Damn.'

Millie looked up at her, surprised by the tone in her voice. 'You don't have to look so disapproving, you know.'

The little dog cocked her head.

'That man is a coward, that's what he is, and he stuck me with all the dirty work.' She ground her teeth again. 'No point putting it off. We'll let Kevin over at the fire department know first. He's the one that must provide fire protection for that thing. Then we'll visit Max. As city manager, he's responsible for the liability if some kid gets hurt trying to break in, or out of it. Why I let them talk me into something as stupid as a maze in a public park . . .' She tightened up Millie's leash and they headed for the fire department.

SIX

Mary pushed open the door to Furry Friends, the only pet shop in town, in no better mood than when she'd left Phil. It had gotten worse after her conversation with the fire chief. Just exactly what he expected her to do about providing fire protection for the blasted maze she didn't know. That was his job. He was one of the enthusiastic supporters of it when it was proposed. He'd have to think of something. Max Whittaker wasn't going to be much help. All he'd done was say over and over that the thing was a lawsuit waiting to happen. He hadn't worried about that when he voted for it at their Halloween in the Park planning meeting. She'd thought, when she retired from teaching middle school, that life was going to be uncomplicated and quiet. But she'd managed to become the 'go to' person for every civic event and fundraiser in town. Well, she was sick of it.

'That's it. I'm calling it quits. I'm never doing this ever again.'

John Lavorino was behind the desk, talking with a tall,
nice-looking lady who Mary knew slightly. A black Labrador
dog sat quietly beside her. Millie pulled at her leash, her tail
going a mile a minute as she strained to reach the other dog.

Mary let her go and addressed the dog. 'Good morning,
Zoe, or I guess it's afternoon.' She nodded to Zoe's owner,
searching her memory for her name. Janelle Tucker, that was
it. But it was John's question that caught her attention.

'What are you never going to do again?'

'Chair any more committees. Organize any more holiday
celebrations or fundraisers. I'm done. That's final.'

'What happened?' John sounded more resigned than surprised.

'You're not going to . . . why?' Glen Manning appeared
from someplace in the back, carrying a small hamster. He put
it into a hamster run that sat on a table next to the checkout
desk and turned to Mary. 'What happened this time?'

She told them. 'I can't believe we're going to have to contend
with that maze for another five days because Marty Evans
didn't tell anyone he was going to be out of town.'

'I can't believe I can't get into my own bank,' Glen said.
'I can't believe Victoria is dead and Dan's in the hospital. I
do believe you're so upset about those same things that the
maze was the last straw.' He paused then smiled. 'No pun
intended.'

'I guess you're right,' Mary admitted a little ruefully. 'I
didn't sleep much last night and that always makes me grouchy.
I couldn't even get to the hospital because of all that maze
nonsense.' She turned to John. 'How is he this morning?'

'Still groggy. He was in surgery for some time and we're
giving him pain medicine, but he's going to be all right. He's
barking orders right and left. Wants to know what's going on,
what happened, and if we found the clown. Then he gets
another shot and goes back to sleep. By tomorrow he'll really
be a pain in the you know where.'

Mary laughed. Yep. Dan was going to be all right. 'Have
you talked to Ellen this morning?'

'She's fine as well. She went home to take a shower, then
she's going back to the hospital. I told her she didn't need to
come back right away, but I don't think she even heard me.'

'She heard you all right. She just didn't want to listen.'

Krissie, the dog groomer at Furry Friends, came through the doorway, followed by an almost equally as tall blond young woman. Mary was struck once again at the contrast they made, one with beautiful dark brown skin and short black hair that showed up her huge brown eyes and high cheekbones, the other with long pale blond hair let loose to frame a porcelain completion and blazingly blue eyes.

Krissie bent down to give Millie a quick scratch behind her ears then reached for Zoe's leash. 'You must be Zoe. Ready for your bath, love?'

Zoe wagged her tail so hard her whole behind wagged. Krissie laughed and addressed the lady, who up to now had said nothing.

'I'm sorry if I kept you waiting.' She waved the hand not holding the leash in the air and addressed them all in a more than exasperated tone. 'We were trying to find out something about Victoria, what is going to happen to her shop, if the cops are going to search it or something, and when we can get in.'

Everyone looked at her with blank expressions. Why would they want access into Victoria's shop? That seemed inappropriate in the extreme, then Mary remembered. 'The wedding. Oh, my, she was making Pamela's wedding dress.'

Pamela nodded. 'She was also making Krissie's bridesmaid dress, Luke's mother's, and the flower girl's. I know it seems callous to worry about dresses in an awful moment like this, but that's the whole wedding party. The wedding is two weeks from Sunday. This is Tuesday. There's no time to get other dresses. For anyone. If I can't get in to get the dresses, I'll have to get married in my jeans.'

The tragic note in her voice made Mary smile. She knew it wasn't funny, none of it was, but somehow the drama written all over Pamela's face made her think of Melodrama Theater they used to frequent as kids. It also made her want to do something to help. 'I'm sure we'll be able to get you into the shop. Who have you talked to?'

'That Detective Ryan. He wouldn't say if they were going to search the shop or what they were going to do. I can't

imagine why they would want to. She was shot in the middle
of a robbery that had nothing to do with her. It doesn't
make sense.'

Mary agreed. It didn't. 'I'll talk to Dan.'

'You sound as if you all know both victims well.' Janelle
Tucker looked from one of them to the other, curiosity in her
voice.

'Dan Dunham is my nephew-in-law.' Mary kept her voice
carefully neutral. Janelle hadn't lived in Santa Louisa long
enough to know about relationships and friendships. The rest
of them had lived here all their lives.

Janelle's mouth made a small 'oh' and she shook her head.
'No, I didn't know.'

Mary gave a small nod and went on. 'Glen is the president
of our local bank, but he and John are also the owners of Furry
Friends.' She waved her hand around to indicate the shop,
then stopped to include Pamela. 'Pamela will be managing the
shop for them after she gets back from her honeymoon. She's
marrying Luke, our head librarian. John and Glen have other
jobs. Krissie, as you've probably guessed, is the dog groomer
here.'

Janelle watched each of them carefully. 'Oh,' was all she
said. 'So all of you know – knew – both? It was a terrible
thing.'

'Understatement of the year.' Krissie scowled, anger in her
voice. 'No one seems to have any idea who he was and where
he went. He's disappeared like smoke.'

'Yes. He seemed to.' Janelle turned to Glen. 'I understand
you were in the bank. Did you recognize him?'

Glen shook his head, the expression on his face a little wary.
'He wore one of those masks that you pull on over your head
and that clown suit covered the rest of him. I think he did it
on Halloween because no one would think twice about
someone in costume.' Glen paused, his eyes narrowed, and
fury flashed across his face. 'He didn't hesitate to put a bullet
in Victoria. Tammy thinks Victoria recognized him.'

Janelle stiffened a little. 'That's horrible. Who's Tammy and
what made her think that?'

'She's the teller. He passed her a note which said to empty

her cash drawer into his bag and she wouldn't be hurt, then showed her his gun.' He paused and glanced at Mary, then at John. 'I've told what I know to the police. I'm not sure how much I'm supposed to discuss this.'

Janelle smiled. 'I am the police. I started work for the Santa Louisa Police Department a couple months ago. I also have an account at your bank, but I don't yet know the names of the tellers.'

No one said anything. They stared at Janelle then looked at each other. Mary had known Dan had a new hire and she was a woman, but she hadn't realized she was her new neighbor.

'My goodness,' Mary finally said. 'Welcome to Santa Louisa. We certainly gave you a tragic beginning. I'm sure you know Dan is going to be fine. Grumpy but fine. Are you working with Detective Ryan?'

Janelle nodded, the small smile gone, her face devoid of expression. 'I'm supposed to be off today but got called in. Everyone's working on this. I had the appointment for Zoe, so I thought I'd bring her in on my lunch hour. She's been going to doggy day care and is beginning to smell.'

Janelle kept her gaze on Glen. 'I assume someone has asked you exactly what happened.'

Glen nodded. 'Yes, I'm supposed to go in this afternoon to sign a statement.'

Janelle nodded. 'I'll bet I'll be the one taking it. Did you get a good look at the guy?'

'No. I wish I had, but the whole thing was such a shock. It all happened so fast. I'd hit the alarm under my desk and was trying to see if Dan was all right. I didn't even notice poor Victoria or little old Minnie for a few moments. Then the EMTs came in and I moved away and saw Tammy sitting beside Victoria, crying.'

Mary nodded. She had seen Tammy as well. A sight she wouldn't forget for a long time.

'Did Tammy say anything? Did she recognize him?' Janelle seemed to be pushing. Wouldn't she get all this when she took his statement tomorrow?

Glen answered immediately. 'No. He just pushed a note at her saying this was a stick up and to empty her drawer in his bag, but she said something else. Something I haven't told Ryan yet, because I didn't know it until today. Tammy thinks Victoria recognized him. How, I don't know, but she came out of the safe deposit room about the time he was holding the gun on Tammy. I guess Victoria said something like, "What are you doing? You can't do that." That's when he turned and shot her.'

All eyes were on Glen, even the dogs.

This was the first Mary had heard Victoria might have recognized him, but it fit with everything she knew. 'Did he ever speak?' She held a forlorn hope Tammy might have recognized his voice, but if she had, that meant the clown was someone local. That, she didn't want.

'I don't think so. About then Dan appeared in the doorway to my office, I heard him shout "get down", then "police, drop the gun". The next thing I knew, he was on the ground and I caught a glimpse of the clown running out the door. You all know the rest.'

'We know he disappeared. No one seems to know who he is or where he went. Gary saw two cars leaving but he doesn't think either of them was the clown.' Janelle sounded frustrated but also a little disapproving. 'I hoped maybe you might have seen something helpful.'

Glen shook his head. 'Sorry. I wish I had.'

'We've all been too busy worrying about Dan to think much about where the blasted robber went.' John's voice was a little strained. 'Finding him is your job. I know we're a small force, but they're all trained well and they're pretty fond of their chief.' He got up. 'I guess I'd better get started on those reptile cages. Pamela, do you want to do the fish tanks?'

Janelle showed nothing as she watched John. 'Yes, finding him is our job, but we need all the help we can get from citizens like all of you. I'm sure Gary did his best and the rest of them got there as fast as they could. I guess I'm still getting adjusted to a small force, but I assure you, I think they're a great bunch and Chief Dunham has done an excellent job putting it together. I'd better go.' She turned to Krissie. 'Can

I pick her up around five?' She fumbled in her purse for a minute, took out her keys, and promptly dropped them on the floor. 'Damn,' she almost whispered.

Zoe was on her feet and on the keys almost in one motion. Krissie let the leash slip through her fingers as they all watched the dog gather the keys in her mouth and turn and hand them to Janelle. 'Thank you,' she told the dog and patted her on the head. 'About five?' she asked Krissie, who nodded. Without another word, she walked out of the shop.

'I hope I didn't insult her.' John sighed. 'But we do have a good police department. Dan's made it that way. I hope she doesn't think because we're small our people don't know what they're doing. Where did she come from, anyway? She must have police experience or Dan wouldn't have hired her. If he wasn't in the hospital, we'd have that blasted clown in jail.' He ran his fingers through his long, black hair.

'I've never seen a dog do that.' Mary stared at Millie, who looked the other way.

'She's a certified service dog,' Krissie said. 'Ms Tucker told me when she called in to make the appointment. She was her mother's dog, but when she died, the place where they got her said she was too old to take on another client, so she kept her. Really a special dog, aren't you, Zoe?'

Zoe wagged her back end, but not with much enthusiasm.

'Too old?' John bent down to take a better look at Zoe. 'Odd. By looking at her, I'd say she was a young dog. Krissie, Pamela, you know dogs. What do you think?'

'She doesn't look more than four to me,' Krissie said.

Pamela walked toward the dog, put out her hand, ran it over the dog's head, pulled up an eyelid, looked in her mouth, then sat back on her own haunches. 'I'd say Krissie's right. About four. She should have several more years of service in her before retiring. But then, there could be health problems we don't know about.'

'Humm. I suppose so.' John didn't sound convinced.

Mary didn't really care how old Zoe was. If the organization who had placed her with Janelle's mother didn't want her back, that was the end of it. She had more immediate things on her mind.

'I want to go see Dan. Can Millie stay here while I'm gone? I won't be long.'

Glen put his arm around Mary and hugged her. 'You won't be satisfied until you see for yourself he's all right, will you?' He and John smiled at each other. 'Of course she can stay here. We'll be here all day. I'm off and Glen can't get back in the bank yet. We're using today to sort of break Pamela in.'

'What a lovely idea.' Mary smiled at Pamela. 'You couldn't have better bosses, and you'll be right across the park from the library and Luke.'

She smiled then immediately frowned. 'Mary, could you ask Dan if we can get into Victoria's shop? I don't want to make too big an issue about this, but she doesn't have any family that I know of, and she didn't have a partner or anything, so how we go about this, I have no idea.'

'Are the dresses finished?'

'As good as. We were to go in for one more fitting today, but she said that was just to make sure nothing needed to be changed. She's got the veil and everything. If I can't get that dress, I'll . . . I'll . . .'

'Don't get yourself in a snit. I'll talk to Dan if he's able. If not, I'll think of something.'

What, Mary didn't know, but the wedding had to go on, even though the murder would put a damper on the festivities. But Luke, from the library, was a popular figure in this small town. Pamela had lived here all her life and had a large family as well as tons of friends. The wedding was going to be one of the social highlights of the year, so that dress, all the dresses, had to be rescued. 'I'll tell you what I find out when I pick up Millie.'

SEVEN

Dan was going to live. Mary could tell by the glower on his face as the nurse tried to take his blood pressure.

'Chief Dunham,' she said, clearly as exasperated as he was,

'I'm never going to get this right unless you lie still. Relax your arm and let me get your vitals. If you don't, I'm going to enter you don't have any.'

Dan started to say something tart, but Ellen interrupted. 'Dan, let the poor woman take your blood pressure.' She sounded exasperated as well.

Dan looked at her, then at Mary as she came in the door, laid back on his pillow, and muttered something under his breath Mary thought she was better off not hearing.

The nurse stuck a thermometer in his mouth, recorded whatever the blood pressure machine read on her computer terminal, grabbed the thermometer out of his mouth, and took the oxygen count gizmo off his finger. 'You'll live.' She mouthed her thanks to Ellen, nodded at Mary, and rolled her computer out the door.

'Mary,' Dan called out, 'just the person I want to see.'

Mary dragged a chair up close to the bed, on the opposite side from Ellen. She studied him for a minute. He didn't look too bad, all things considered, but his left arm was heavy with bandages, all his left side seemed to be. It was immobilized by an elaborate sling that seemed to operate with pulleys. He was propped up in bed, a pillow behind his head, the movable tray table across his knees. At least he could pick up his water, eat, and write. Someone had brought him a pen and pad of paper and it looked as if he had put them to use. She watched as he tried to turn to see her better. A look of pain washed across his face, his eyes squinted, and a groan escaped.

'Damn,' he whispered.

Ellen covered his hand with hers, careful to avoid the intravenous drip line inserted into his arm. She blinked rapidly but a tear escaped, despite her efforts. 'You're almost due for another pain shot.'

'Then I'd better talk to Mary quickly. Once they give me that stuff, I'm good for nothing but sleep. OK, Mary. They tell me you were there. What happened?'

'How much do you remember?'

'Not much. I heard a shot and a scream, went to Glen's office door, looked around but only saw Minnie and someone dressed like a clown. Like an idiot, I stepped into the room.

Minnie was sort of blocking the clown, so I didn't see the gun until too late. That's all I remember. Tell me, what did you see?'

She told him. Unfortunately, it didn't give him much additional information, except that Tammy thought Victoria had recognized the clown.

'Gary ran around the library into the parking lot but no sign of him?'

'Not that I've heard. Supposedly Gary hunted all through the library and the city offices, but nothing. I can't imagine how he did it.'

Dan looked thoughtful then tried to change his position. A groan he couldn't suppress escaped. Ellen was up and out of her chair, hovering over him.

'I'm fine.' He returned to his original position. 'Just fine.'

She lifted a water glass up to his lips and he sipped a little through the straw then waved it away.

'OK. What else? Has anyone done anything about contacting Victoria's people? She doesn't have any family in town I've heard about. And Minnie. How is she? Was anyone there besides Tammy? Is she all right? Did she see anything, recognize anything about that blasted clown?'

Even in pain, the policeman in Dan rose to the occasion. Mary almost smiled, but it wasn't amusing. It was awful. Victoria. The shop.

'Dan, Pamela's wedding dress is in Victoria's shop and no one knows if we can get to it. The wedding is a week from Sunday and Pamela's torn between feeling selfish and thinking she'll have to get married in jeans.'

For the first time, Dan smiled. 'She'd look cute in jeans, but we can probably work something out. Ellen, how about your wedding dress? It's only two years old. Don't you have it packed away? Can you loan it to her?'

'Yes, I do and no, I can't. Pamela is a good two inches taller than I am and a little, well, rounder in certain areas. We could get Pat Bennington to let it out in the chest, maybe, but she can't let down a hem that isn't there. Susannah may want to wear it this summer when she and Neil get married, so that won't do.'

Mary doubted that her great-niece would want to. Susannah and her mother were very different types and didn't have the same taste in clothes. She thought Susannah would want her own. But one never knew.

'OK.' That came out a little weak and sounded painful. Strain was starting to show on Dan's face. 'Listen. Both of you. Go tell Agnes I said to let the two of you in the shop. The shop isn't evidence, but Sean Ryan doesn't seem to know what is and what isn't. He's trying to handle my case, and he doesn't have a clue how to start. This isn't some big city drive-by shooting. You two go find the dress then go through the shop. If Victoria knew who that clown was, there might be something in the shop that will point us the right way. Then go see Minnie. See if she's all right and if she saw anything we missed. And Tammy. Quiz her especially on what Victoria said. Ryan will push her, and either scare her to death or make her so nervous she won't be able to think straight. Talk to her. Give her time to think about what happened without pressuring her. Then come back and tell me what you learn. In the meantime . . .'

The door opened, and the same nurse walked in, pushing a mobile drug dispenser. A male nurse entered behind her. 'Time for your painkiller, Chief. We're going to change your position as well. Maybe you ladies would like to step out for a moment?'

'Actually, we just got our marching orders.' Ellen smiled at the nurse. She leaned over and kissed Dan on the forehead. 'Be good. I'll be back soon.'

'Wait.' Dan waved his good hand at them. 'Do either of you know how my recruit is doing? She seemed competent, but I hate to leave her in Ryan's clutches. He doesn't have any idea how this town works and will ride roughshod over everyone. Janelle's quiet. She was a cop in the city, so she should be able to hold her own, but you never know.'

'I just saw her at Furry Friends. She seemed fine.' Mary wasn't sure that was truthful, but then, Janelle wasn't falling apart, so she guessed she was all right.

Dan grinned. 'Good. Looking forward to hearing what you find. Take notes.'

'Take notes on what?' The male nurse looked interested as he pushed back the chair Mary had been sitting in.

Mary and Ellen ignored him.

'Get some rest,' Ellen told Dan. 'We'll be back.'

They heard a distinctive yelp as the door closed, followed by a string of words Mary rarely heard Dan utter. She ignored them as she and her niece walked down the hallway and out of the hospital.

EIGHT

Agnes looked at them in horror. 'You want me to do what? I don't have the key to Victoria's shop and couldn't give it to you if I did. Why, Dan would have my scalp if I did something like that.'

'Dan's the one who told us to come to you.' Ellen's tone was mild, but her eyes said Agnes had better not give them any grief.

She was the office manager for the Santa Louisa Police Department, but no one, including Dan, was quite sure why. Agnes wasn't very good at managing anything. She, on the other hand, thought she was enlisted personnel. She wore a light blue shirt and dark navy pants to work, held up with a thick black belt. Her shoes were black and her tie was almost the same color as the ones the patrolmen wore. However, she was forbidden to carry a gun or any knife sharper than a butter knife. Mary thought this time she had a point. How was she supposed to let them into a shop she had no key to, had probably never been in, and knew the owner only by sight? Agnes had little need or interest in custom-made dresses.

'Where are Victoria's personal effects?' Ellen's narrowed eyes said Agnes better give her a straight answer.

'What effects?'

Mary knew Ellen had little patience with Agnes at the best of times, and now wasn't one of those times. 'Did she have a purse?'

Agnes nodded.

'Where is it?'

'In a paper bag in the evidence room.'

'What is it evidence of? She was a victim. Shot in the bank. What do you expect to find in her purse?'

Agnes looked blank. 'Don't know.'

Evidence room was a very grand title for the small room reserved for items that might be evidence in ongoing cases in far-from-crime-ridden Santa Louisa.

'Go get it. Her keys should be in it. Dan wants us to look in her shop and that's what we're going to do. You can ask him later if it's all right with him, but you can't call him now. He just had a pain shot and is asleep. At least, I hope so. The keys, Agnes. We have a whole list of things Dan wants us to do and not much time to do them.'

Agnes looked around the empty front office, at the closed door to Dan's office, and down the hall to the one interrogation room and the closed and locked door that opened onto the two holding cells and sighed. 'OK, but if that Detective Ryan ever finds out, I'm going to tell him you made me.'

'Do that,' Ellen replied.

Agnes slowly pushed herself out of her swivel chair and disappeared down the hallway. It didn't take her long. But instead of handing over a ring of keys, she handed Ellen a quilted bag. 'It's her purse. Take it. I don't know what's in it and if I get in trouble . . .'

'You won't. Thanks, Agnes. Come on, Mary. We have to get moving.'

They stood outside the police station on the sidewalk and stared at each other.

'That was easy,' Mary finally said.

Ellen started to laugh. 'Poor Agnes. We did bully her a little.'

Mary smiled. 'Maybe a little, but I can't imagine why Detective Ryan would want to go through Victoria's purse or her shop, and Pamela and Krissie need those dresses. Where do you want to go first? Minnie's or should we tackle the shop?'

Ellen pulled out her cell and checked the time. 'Minnie's.

I have to go into the office. I have a client coming tomorrow, and I haven't begun to prepare. They're first-time home buyers and understandably nervous. I need to concentrate on what they need and what they can do. Do you know where Minnie lives?'

Mary did. Minnie had a tiny one-bedroom house on a half lot not far from the police station. They could walk. In no time, they were climbing the slightly crooked front stairs that led to Minnie's faded red front door. As they waited for someone to answer the bell, Mary looked around. The porch needed a good sweeping. Autumn leaves had piled up around the rungs of a white wicker rocker. A Boston fern gasped its last breath in a basket that hung from one of the porch roof's rafters, as much from lack of water as from the increasingly chilly nights. Minnie had always prided herself on how well she kept her house up, but it didn't look that way now.

The door opened a crack. 'Oh, it's you.' Minnie opened it wide. 'Come in, come in. I've been nervous since that awful thing happened at the bank. Just jumping out of my skin if the door rings or the phone sounds. Ellen, how is Dan? Is he all right? Mary Louise Webber said he was, but she doesn't always hear things right. I know poor Victoria—' She broke off and sniffed into a wadded-up handkerchief. 'Would you like something? I can fix coffee . . .' She looked somewhat vaguely toward the kitchen, as if she wondered if the coffeemaker was still there.

Both Mary and Ellen assured her they were fine and, without asking, sat down on the lumpy-looking sofa.

Mary motioned for Minnie to sit as well. 'We've just come from Dan. He's doing fine, but he'll be in the hospital for a while. He asked us to talk to you. He thought you might have gotten a good look at the clown.'

The platform rocker Minnie sank into looked as if it had been used a lot. Judging from the slightly sticky small table that sat beside it, the half-full glass of water, the empty plate, and the wire-rimmed spectacles, it seemed safe to assume it was where Minnie spent much of her time. She squirmed around, pushing a small pillow behind her back before she gave her attention to them. 'It all happened so fast. I was trying to fill out the little slip so I could deposit my retirement check and wasn't paying much attention. Then Victoria came out of the room where they keep the boxes and I wanted to speak to her. I have some dresses that don't fit. They seem too long; I think I've gotten shorter.' She gave a wheezy kind of laugh and seemed to lose her train of thought.

'Right.' Ellen gently nudged Minnie back on track. 'You were filling out the deposit form, then what?'

'Oh. Yes. Well, Victoria didn't see me, at least I don't think she did. She stared at the clown as if she knew him. How she could have, I don't know. He was covered from head to toe with that frilly-looking collar and that baggy suit. But then I saw the gun. I couldn't believe it. I thought I was going to faint dead away, but I didn't. Then he shot her. Poor thing. She gasped and fell right down. I saw the blood. Then someone shouted, "Get down, police," and I turned to look. It was Dan.' She smiled brightly. 'You know he's the chief of police. Such a nice man.' She looked at Ellen. 'Do you know him? I hope he's all right.'

Ellen and Mary looked at each other.

Ellen shrugged. 'Minnie, do you remember what happened then?'

'Oh, yes,' she said brightly. 'I thought I'd go to Dan, where I'd be safe, but Dan fell down too. Then the clown turned to me. I thought he was going to shoot me. He still held that gun, but he didn't. He grabbed a bag the teller gave him and ran out the door.' She didn't say anything for a moment or so.

Neither did Mary or Ellen. They waited, wondering if there was more. There was.

'He had red eyes.'

'Who had red eyes?' Ellen sat forward on the sofa, intent on what Minnie was saying.

'The clown?' Mary felt a little stir of excitement, which was quickly overcome with doubt.

'Of course, the clown. I saw his eyes through the slits in his mask when he was looking at me. They were ringed around with red. Like the devil. It made me so scared, I had to hold onto the table so I wouldn't fall down. Then the police came and the ambulance and someone took me home. I haven't left since. Do you think he's still around? The clown, I mean.'

Ellen shook her head and mouthed, *Say something*.

Mary wasn't sure what, but she had to try. 'Ah, no, we don't think he is. He seems to have gone. Minnie, when was the last time Bob came to see you? Has he been here since yesterday?'

Minnie looked around as if Bob, her son, might appear at any minute. 'Bob? He was here, oh, not so long ago.'

'How about Estelle? Has she been to see you lately?'

Mouth slightly open, Minnie seemed to be searching her memory. 'Estelle?'

'Your daughter-in-law, Bob's wife. Has she been here?'

'Oh, that Estelle. Why, she was here . . . she lives in this town . . .' The rest of the sentence drifted away.

Ellen jerked her head at Mary, indicating they needed to go. Mary was reluctant. Minnie needed someone with her. She clearly wasn't doing well and shouldn't be in the kitchen without supervision. But neither of them could sit with her.

'We're going to leave now,' she told Minnie. 'Thank you for talking with us. Will you be all right?'

'Oh, yes. I'll be fine.' She peered at Mary with uncertainty. 'Do you live in this town? I'm glad you both came. I don't get many visitors anymore. You must visit our town again. It's nice here.' She looked at Ellen as if she'd never seen her before. 'What did you say your name was?'

'Ellen.'

'Such a pretty name. My grandmother's name was Ellen. Don't you think it's a pretty name?' She stared at Mary, as if trying to remember who she was, then looked at her folded hands.

Was it embarrassment at forgetfulness or not knowing she was forgetting? Mary wasn't sure, but she was alarmed.

'Ellen, why don't you get Minnie a glass of water before we leave and some cookies or something? I'll find her TV remote.'

Minnie brightened up. 'Cookies?'

Mary hoped there were some. She picked up the magazine that lay on the table then handed Ellen an empty plate and glass. The remote must be here somewhere. It was. Under a newspaper that had been thrown on the floor. She handed it to Minnie. 'Why don't you turn the TV on? Make sure it works?'

They left Minnie happily munching on Oreos and watching some game show.

'I'm not sure she even knows we left.'

Ellen's face was grim. 'I don't think she'll remember we were there. How long has she been like this?'

Mary looked back at the house, reluctant to leave but knowing they had to. 'I don't know. I haven't seen her for a while. Maybe the robbery and seeing Victoria and Dan shot did something to her.'

'Maybe,' Ellen replied, 'but I think one of us needs to call Bob. I think it's time Minnie moved to Shady Acres.' She too looked back at the house. 'It's odd. She seemed to remember what happened at the bank. But that stuff about the red eyes, that was bizarre.'

Neither of them said anything as they hurried toward town. They paused on the corner.

'I'll call Bob.' Mary was happy to take the moment and catch her breath. 'He runs Sam's old insurance company, so getting ahold of him will be easy.'

'Don't you still own the insurance company?' There was curiosity in Ellen's voice. 'You never talk about it.'

Mary nodded. 'I own it, but I don't run it. I never had anything to do with it when Sam was alive, and I didn't want to start after he had the heart attack. Anyway, I'll either stop by or give Bob a call, then I think I'll call Pat Bennington.' She glanced at her watch, wondering if she was the only one left in town who wore one. It was easier than trying to find her cell in her purse. 'She can help me go through the shop. I don't expect to find anything useful, but we can at least pick up the dresses and see if anything is left to do on them.'

'Can you ask Pat to drop Morgan off at your house? I'll pick him up after I see Dan one more time before I go home.'

Mary nodded, watched Ellen cross the street to the real estate office, and then pushed open the door to Furry Friends.

NINE

Mary and Pat Bennington stood in front of Victoria's small shop, staring at the board that hung over the doorway announcing the name, A Stitch in Time.

'Clever,' Pat murmured.

'You think?' Mary asked.

Millie and Morgan sat between them. They also looked at the shop but said nothing.

'You do have the keys, don't you?'

Mary held up a key ring with only three keys on it. One a car key, another a safe deposit key, and a third one. 'It won't take long to figure out which one we need.'

Pat gave a soft laugh. 'OK. Let's see if we can guess. By the way, what are we looking for?'

Mary sighed. 'I'm not sure, but Dan said to look around. And I've been thinking.'

'Uh oh.'

'Seriously. Tammy said Victoria acted as if she recognized the clown.'

'Who's Tammy?'

'The bank teller. But I got to thinking, how could she? He was covered up with a costume and wore a full-face mask. There's only one way I can think she could have.'

That caught Pat's interest. She turned to stare at Mary. 'OK. I give up. How?'

'She recognized the clown suit because she made it.'

Pat didn't move or say anything for a long minute, long enough for Morgan to begin to whine. 'How do you do that?' Pat finally asked.

'Do what?' Mary gathered up Millie's leash. She moved to the door and tried the third key in the lock. It turned immediately. 'I hope there's no alarm on in there. I really don't want to explain this to our police.'

'I don't either.' Pat tightened her hold on Morgan's leash

and joined Mary, who tentatively pushed the door open and paused. The shop remained quiet. Relieved, they walked in, closed and locked the door behind them, and looked around.

'Is there a shade on that door?' Pat asked. 'It's dark in here and if we turn on the lights, we'll be advertising our presence as loudly as if we hired a band.'

There was a blind on the door and a black curtain that closed off the window display from the shop. Pat closed them both and Mary, who had found the light switch in the dim interior of the shop, turned on the lights.

'This is the first time I've been here.' Pat started to slowly move around. 'Not too big, is it?'

It wasn't. A table close to the front window held picture albums, one of which showed an elaborate wedding party. Mary hoped Pamela had chosen something a little less dramatic. The bride's dress had a full skirt and a train long enough to stretch halfway down the aisle in St Mark's. The top barely managed to cover the relevant parts of the bride. Well, they'd find out what Pamela had chosen soon enough. She looked around, wondering where the dresses were. One side of the shop was covered with shelves that held bolts of uncut cloth. Lots of bolts. A low table with three chairs sat in the middle of the room. Floor-to-ceiling mirrors covered the opposite wall. That area could be closed off with hanging curtains. A small platform sat in front of the mirrors. For the bride, or debutante, to stand on to see the dress from collar to hem? Probably, but it was the bolts of cloth that had her attention. She walked closer, drawn by one bold print. Red and blue balloons of all sizes danced on the white cloth, looking as if they could take off at any minute. She stared at it, sure she recognized it. This was the pattern on the clown's costume, she was sure. Pretty sure. She hadn't really looked at the costume when he stood across the street from her, pointing a gun at her and Millie, but this felt right. Could she swear to it in court? She thought about that. She didn't think so, but it was a start. It made sense to think Victoria had made the costume and recognized the pattern and the person wearing it. But it wasn't enough.

'Mary, come see this.'

Mary turned to see Pat coming through the curtains that hid the back part of the shop.

'What have you found?'

'The dresses.' Pat motioned to her.

Mary walked through the curtains to where the business of dressmaking took place. Four or five garments hung on a rack, each covered in light plastic wrap. There was filmy wrap on the floor, keeping the hems of the two long dresses clean. A commercial sewing machine took up most of the space along the far wall. A large flat table scrubbed clean filled the middle of the room. Tubs on rollers fit under it. One appeared to be full of thread, all color coated, with trims of all kinds. Another was stuffed with patterns.

Mary, a retired home economics teacher, nodded her approval of the clean, efficiently arranged workspace.

Pat stood beside the rack of dresses, moving them slowly along the pole they hung from. 'Which one of these is Pamela's?'

'I have no idea. Aren't they marked?'

'If they are, I can't see a name. No, wait. I think these are initials. What's Pamela's last name. What's Krissie's?'

'Pruitt. Pamela Pruitt. I think Krissie's is Kramer.'

'That fits. There's a tag on the hanger of each of these dresses, but all it has on it is initials and a date. But this one has PP on it. Besides, it's the only wedding gown. This one' – she pulled a beautiful soft green full-length dress off the rack and spread it out on the table – 'is marked KK.'

'Sounds like you found them. Are they finished?'

Pat pulled the covering off the dress and started to examine the seams, then the beading on the bodice. 'Looks like it. Unless there's fitting left to do, I'd say they're good to go. What are we going to do with them?'

'We need to leave them here for tonight. I'll call Pamela in the morning and tell her she can get them tomorrow. The girls need to try them on. If they need anything, can you do it?'

'Depends. You can if I can't.'

Mary almost laughed. 'I taught home ec. That meant making aprons and hemming tea towels. Women don't do that anymore, and I neither do I. We'll keep our fingers crossed they fit.' She looked around. 'Where do you suppose she keeps her logbook?'

'Her what?'

'Logbook. Where she writes down what she makes and who for, their measurements, if they paid or owe money. That kind of thing.'

'Oh. A logbook. I've no idea. What are you doing now?'

'Looking at these patterns. If I'm right . . . I thought so. Look at this.'

Mary pulled one of the rolling tubs out from under the table and thumbed through its contents. She held up an envelope clearly marked *clown costume.*

Pat took it, turned it over, and ran her finger down the picture of a clown wearing a baggy two-piece costume topped with a huge fluffy ruff. 'Looks like she made the costume he was wearing. You think his name might be in Victoria's logbook?'

'I think it's quite possible. There's a bolt of cloth in the front room that may be the material she used. I couldn't swear that was what I saw and, even if it was, it doesn't get us any closer to knowing who wore it.'

'But you think the logbook might.'

Mary shrugged. 'I think it's worth taking a look.'

Pat nodded and looked around the room once more. 'All we have to do is find it. If she even had one.'

'I don't see a desk or anyplace where she might keep her business records.' Mary started to slowly walk around the room, closely followed by Millie. There were two doors at the far end, both closed. She opened one. 'Bathroom.' She reached out to open the other when Millie started to growl, then bark. A loud, sharp bark. She was answered by a yowl, long and plaintiff. Mary let go of the handle and jumped back. 'What on earth was that?'

'Sounds like a very upset cat.' Pat inched closer to the door, pulling a reluctant Morgan after her. 'We get a lot of cats in the vet office who don't want any part of being there. That's the howl of protest they make.' Cautiously, she opened the door a crack, peeked around the corner, then pushed it wider. 'How did you get in here?'

A black and white cat stalked out, looked at Mary and Pat, then at the dogs and yowled again.

'That is the scruffiest cat I've ever seen.' Mary had a good hold on Millie's leash.

The cat wasn't only scruffy but huge, and the way he studied the dogs made her sure he wouldn't mind taking a swipe at them if they even considered coming closer.

'I've seen scruffier, but this one looks as if he's been in a fight or two. Look at that ear. It's half gone.'

The cat seemed to have taken offense at their comments. He yowled again, turned around, and walked back through the doorway, pausing to look over his shoulder, as if he wanted them to follow.

'He wants something,' Mary said, 'but what?'

'Probably food. He probably lives here. No one's been around for a couple of days to refill his dinner dish.' Pat started through the doorway, dragging an even more reluctant Morgan. 'Come on, the cat's not going to eat you. Or scratch you.'

Morgan didn't seem convinced, and Mary didn't blame him. The cat looked as if he'd been in more than one fight, and he wasn't even slightly afraid of Morgan or Millie. Or them, for that matter. He didn't have to be. He was in charge and knew it. She also entered the doorway. The cat was already halfway up a short flight of stairs, Pat and Morgan following. Morgan took the stairs slowly, setting his front paws on a stair then hopping up with his remaining back leg. He had been hit by a car when he was a puppy, abandoned by the side of the road. Karl Bennington had been able to save his life, but not his leg. Morgan didn't seem to even notice but there were times when it did slow him down a little. Pat didn't hurry him, letting him set the pace. Mary and Millie waited until they were safely on the landing before starting up.

'What's up there?' she called out to Pat.

'Victoria's living quarters. Also, an empty food and water dish.' The sound of running water told Mary that at least was being filled. She and Millie reached the landing, and she walked into a small but efficient combination living room/office.

'This is darling. So cozy.'

'So efficient.' Pat pointed toward the desk that sat at the far end of the room. 'Look on the desk, or in the filing cabinet, while I take care of the cat.'

Mary hesitated a moment, watching Morgan and Millie, who had eyes for nothing but the cat. She walked over to the desk. A closed laptop sat in the middle, a small printer in the top left corner. The rest was littered with papers, most of which looked like bills. She sorted through them, feeling like an interloper but hoping to find something, anything, that might prove Victoria had made the clown costume and that she had, indeed, recognized the killer because she recognized her own creation. Only, just what she didn't know. She picked up a library book, open and lying face down on a small table beside the only comfortable-looking chair in the room. She noted that it was a popular thriller and started to close it when she was startled by a loud hissing sound and a sharp bark. The cat was warning Morgan not to get any closer.

'That cat is getting upset,' Pat said. 'Keep Millie and Morgan away from him while I fill his dinner dish and then we'd better get out of here. He's not the only one who wants his dinner.'

Mary glanced at her watch. It was getting close to their dinnertime as well.

'I need to get back to the clinic. Have you found anything?'

Mary called Millie to her and grabbed Morgan's leash, then set the book back down on the small table and, for the first time, noticed a closed small black notebook. It must have been under the thriller. Was this Victoria's logbook? Victoria's desk forgotten, she tucked Morgan's leash under her arm, picked it up and opened it to the first page. She had no idea what she was looking at. The page was carefully ruled off into columns, which were filled with initials. Some kind of code? At least she could read the dates. These were almost a year ago. She flipped through it until she got to the last page. It started the first of October. The first column held the date, the next one two initials, the third one more letters and the last column seemed to be payment information. They were all in ink, but none of them was done too legibly.

'Pat, come look at this.'

'What have you got?' Pat stuffed the cat food back in a

cupboard and walked over. She took the notebook Mary handed her and stared at it. 'What is all this?'

'I'm not sure.' Mary took the notebook back and laid it on the desk, open to the last page so they could both see it. 'This first column is the date, but I don't know if that means the day someone picked up whatever she made or the date they ordered it. I think the next column might be the initials of the person who ordered whatever it was.'

'Look,' Pat exclaimed. 'There. KK. Could that be Krissie Kramer? And the next column, BD. That must be the brides-maid dress. And the last one. PIF. The dress is paid for. Yes, look at this one. $200. I'll bet that means that's how much whoever this is owes. Who do you think PC is? Or MB?'

'I've no idea.' Mary continued to run her finger down the page. 'Look here. This one has a C in the column that describes the garment, here's another, and another, and . . .' She flipped the page back. 'Here's another one dated late August. Do you suppose all of these are clown costumes she made?'

'If that's what they mean, how are we supposed to know who these people are who bought one when all we have to go on are initials? Blurry ones at that.'

Pat pulled her cell phone out of her pocket and checked the time. 'Mary, I have to go. Karl will be seeing his last patient about now and the girls will start the evening chores, feeding, cleaning cages. I always do the meds. Why don't you take that thing home and see if you can find out anything more? Tell Pamela and Krissie to come try on their dresses tomorrow. We'll meet them here. If they need anything, I'll see if I can do it.'

Mary nodded and stuffed the notebook in her purse. She turned to Millie, who still stared at the cat. He had jumped up on the kitchen counter and was calmly licking his front. 'What about him? Can we just leave him?'

Pat sighed. 'We can for tonight, but we're going to have to do something about him tomorrow. Can you take him for a few days while we figure out what to do with him?'

'Me? Take that cat? No.'

'Why not? Just until we find him a home. If we turn him over to the Humane Society, he won't make it. They only keep them a few days then put them down. We're working on a no-kill shelter but haven't gotten there yet. I have no room at the clinic, so if you could just for a few days . . . Ellen can't. She has Jake, and they'll fight, and she has Dan to worry over so . . . I really need you to.' She looked expectantly at Mary and waited.

Mary looked at Millie, who looked at the cat and then back at Mary as much as to say she was OK with it.

Sighing, pretty sure she'd live to regret this, Mary nodded. 'All right. But only for a few days.'

Pat smiled. 'Good. I'll bring a cat carrier tomorrow and we can pick him up when the girls come for their dresses. Can you make it around noon? We close from twelve to one so that works best for me.'

The cat watched as they walked down the stairs, but he didn't follow. Full water dish and food dishes seemed to have satisfied him. They closed the door, made sure the lock was engaged, and went their separate ways.

TEN

Mary threw her purse on the kitchen table, walked over to the broom closet where she kept the dog food, grabbed Millie's dish, filled it, and then turned to face the dog, holding the filled dish.

Millie sat, watching Mary expectantly.

'Well, you got your wish. You've been pestering me for a cat for ages. Every time we go into Furry Friends you make a beeline for the kittens. I doubt this cat is what you had in mind.' She glared at Millie and her tone of voice was sharp and accusing.

Millie looked at her at first with alarm then with confusion. She crouched down, her little stub of a tail trying to get between her back legs, her head down. A soft whine came from her before she rolled over on her back, submission in every move, seemingly begging for forgiveness for she knew not what.

'Oh.' Mary squatted down and gathered Millie onto her lap. 'How could I? None of this is your fault. You don't even know what's been happening and here I am, blaming you. You probably don't want that cat any more than I do.' A tear fell from her eye onto Millie's nose and a small grunt escaped Millie as Mary held her closer. 'It's just this whole thing is getting to me. Victoria dead, Dan shot, a murderer running around loose, and I'm almost certain it's someone we know. It's upsetting.' She paused, considering her last sentence. 'That's tame for how I feel, but it's not your fault and what you feel is hungry. Move over.' Mary got to her feet with the aid of the kitchen counter and pushed Millie's dinner onto the place mat reserved for her dish.

Millie hesitated, looking at Mary as if not quite sure what to do.

'Go. It's your dinner. I'm sorry I yelled at you. Eat.'

Millie took her at her word and immediately applied herself to finishing off her food before someone else could get it. Mary didn't think Millie had thought out who that might be, but she wasn't taking any chances. After that big, tough-looking cat came, she might have good reason to worry.

Mary watched for a minute then sighed. She was going to need some dinner as well, but what she didn't know. She didn't feel like cooking anything. She should have stopped at the Yum Yum on her way home and picked up a salad. Could she make one? She was staring into the refrigerator, contemplating her options, when the phone rang.

'Bob, thanks for calling me back. Yes, Ellen and I did visit Minnie this afternoon and we were worried.'

Bob Myers was more than Minnie's son. Mary had known him since he was in middle school. He'd been one of the first group of boys who had taken her home ec class, declaring they wanted to learn to cook. The boys had proven to be twice the work the girls were, but by the time she got through with them, most of them could get a meal on the table, and, in many cases, it was edible. Even the boys who never quite mastered boiling water went away with a greater appreciation of what getting a meal together took. Or that it took an effort to make a decent sandwich. Bob had gone away to college, majored in business, and come home to work and eventually run Samuel's insurance agency. What she would have done without him after Sam died, she didn't know. Tonight, she didn't want to talk about insurance. She wanted to talk about Minnie. Bob was way ahead of her.

'Estelle and I realize how bad she's gotten and this business at the bank was the last straw. We've wanted to move her into Shady Acres for some time, but she won't go. However, we've decided. She's going to move into one of their small apartments next week. It's in the wing for . . . forgetful older people.'

Which meant Bob and Estelle thought Minnie was a victim of dementia.

Mary thought they were right. 'I'm so relieved. She seemed to know us when we came in, but that didn't last long. Neither Ellen nor I thought it safe to leave her, but we didn't have much choice. Is there anything I can do to help before you make the move, or do you need help packing her up or anything?'

'Mary, you're a jewel. I think we have it covered, but I'm sure we'll have a lot of donations for the next St Mark's rummage sale. You'll need to let us know where to bring them.'

She assured him she would and was ready to hang up.

'Your new neighbor came to see me the other day. Do you remember her?'

She'd had her eye on the wine bottle. It was after five, and she was tired physically and emotionally. Wine forgotten, she gave him her full attention. 'Who? Do you mean Janelle Tucker?'

'Yes. I must admit, I was surprised to see her. I never thought in a million years she'd show up in this town again, but there she was, wanting renter's insurance. She's gone to work for Dan as a police officer. Guess she was working in southern California. That's where she went to the police academy, but she didn't say why she came back here.' He waited, as if expecting a reaction from Mary.

Mary didn't know what to say. 'Came back? What do you mean?'

'You don't remember her, do you?'

'Should I? You said something about her not wanting to come back to this town. What did you mean by that? When was she here?'

'It's been almost twenty years, but you usually remember people longer than that. The altercation with Mrs Tucker happened about the time Sam had his heart attack, so I don't think you got involved.'

'Involved in what?' Mary decided she needed to get that glass of wine. This was getting complicated, and, after the last couple of days, one more complicated thing was more than she could handle. Phone in hand, she walked across the kitchen and filled a wineglass half full. 'What are you talking about?'

The sigh Bob heaved came through the phone line loud and clear. 'The Tucker family moved here a little over twenty years ago. Mr Tucker, I don't remember his first name, wanted to raise wine grapes. He didn't know a thing about them or about farming, but that's what he'd decided to do. He, his wife, and their two girls bought forty acres with a beat-up mobile home on it north of town, and he planted vines. He didn't ask anyone, or hire anyone who knew what they were doing, so the vines didn't . . . do very well. Then one day, they found him dead, sitting on his tractor. Heart attack, the doc said. Maybe it was. However, he was in debt up to his eyebrows and the grapes were failing. Mrs Tucker had hysterics when she found out. She made all kinds of wild accusations. She even included us for not writing enough insurance to cover them. What she wanted covered, I've no idea. Anyway, they packed up and left town. I'm not sure if they got any money out of the land or not. I never heard from them again. Janelle was around ten then, too young to be in one of your classes, and the other sister was older, college age or so. The little one, Janelle, was devoted to the mother. I thought the older one wasn't so much, but, as I say, they just up and left. So, when I realized who Janelle was, I was really surprised.'

So was Mary. She took a small sip of the wine and was sure she could feel it relaxing her. She smiled and Millie, who had finished her dinner, looked at her inquiringly. 'Did she say why she came back?'

'Sort of.' Bob seemed a little hesitant. 'She said she'd always liked this town and she'd had enough of the city, traffic, high rents, gangs, all those things, and saw there was an opening on our police force. She thought she'd see if it was like she remembered it. Said it's changed a lot, but she likes it and thinks she'll stay a while.'

'Oh.' Mary couldn't think of anything else to say. Or maybe she could. 'Bob, did she say anything about the dog?'

'What dog?'

'She has a black dog who supposedly is a trained service dog. Evidently, she's leaving the dog at doggy day care, but it's not working out. I wondered if she'd mentioned it.'

'No. She didn't. Can't think where else she could leave the dog. Anyway, we're on our way to Mother's. Estelle wants to make sure she doesn't try to cook anything, so I'll talk to you tomorrow. I'll let you know how we get along with getting her moved.' He hung up.

Mary sat and stared out the kitchen window while she sipped her wine. Her yard was preparing itself for winter. The grass was full of leaves, her summer flowers gone, and the foliage of many of her plants were folding their leaves in preparation for the cold nights ahead. Santa Louisa, inland from central California's coastline, could, and often did, dip below freezing. But what had her attention was the clown, gun pointed at her and Millie. She blinked, but the vision remained, the sun shining down, reflecting off the gun and off . . . something else. What? It had all happened so fast and she had been frozen by shock, but there was something she was missing. It would come to her. Sighing, she put down her half-finished glass and got up to heat some soup.

ELEVEN

'This is the book you mentioned to Ellen?' Dan was propped up higher in bed than he had been yesterday, but he still couldn't move his left arm or shoulder. Mary sat on his right side so he wouldn't have to twist to see her and spread the notebook out on his moveable tray. 'I'm sure she described it. But it's easier if you can see. This column has the date. We think it's either the date the garment was picked up or was supposed to be ready. See? This is Pamela's wedding dress. It has her initials here.' She ran her finger down the second column, which was nothing but initials. 'The third one seems to indicate what the garment is. Beside Pamela's is WD. Wedding dress. Then the next column says PIF. Paid in full. Using that as a guide, it appears she made four clown costumes in the last month. All of them were picked up. But that's all the info we have. No full names, no addresses or phone numbers. Just this. So, all we have to do is find out who the people are who bought the costumes and we'll be able to figure out which one shot you.'

'That's all we have to do?' Dan pulled the book closer to him and bent down as much as he was able to look at the initials alongside the Cs. 'First, we don't know for sure that the C indicates a clown costume. It seems possible, but it's not proof. Then the initials could be anyone's. Do you know how many people in this town's initials are PC? I can think of a couple off the top of my head. Pete Campbell and Phil Connors, for starters. I can't see either of them as a bank robber. Pete hates guns and Phil, well, he's a great guy with a good job and a loving wife. Not the usual description of a bank robber.'

'That's only two. There are others with those initials. We just have to . . .' Mary's voice trailed off.

'Let's say we came across someone who really might be the clown. How do we go about proving it? If whoever this guy is has a lick of sense, that costume is long gone. We're going to need a hell of a lot more than a clown costume to prove someone guilty of this.'

Mary thought about that and nodded. 'I guess you're right. We can hardly go up to Phil or whoever we turn up and say, "I hear you bought a clown costume from Victoria. Were you wearing it Halloween afternoon?"'

'Not if you don't want to get shot, you can't.'

The door opened, and John and Glen walked in.

'Who would want to shoot Mary? You, I can understand. You're a cop and get downright testy when people do things like rob banks. But Mary . . .' John walked behind Mary's chair, leaned over, and gave her a hug.

'Shows how things get really messed up when people eavesdrop. No one's going to shoot Mary because she's not going sleuthing like she's done before.' Dan didn't exactly glare at her, but the look he gave her made his meaning clear. 'If she gets any brilliant flashes, this time she's going to bring them to me and let the police do the dirty work.'

'Did you have a brilliant flash?' Glen looked at Mary with a trace of a grin. 'Or did you turn up some vital piece of evidence? Again.'

Heat crept up the sides of Mary's face. 'Just because I was able to figure out what happened to poor Miss Plym . . .'

'And who killed Jerry Lowell and why and . . .' John squeezed her again. 'Dan's right. Keep out of this. The police will figure out who that guy is, and they'll get him.'

'Sean Ryan will never figure it out. He doesn't know anyone in this town. He's a San Louis person through and through. Dan's the one who knows the people here.' Mary didn't want to be stubborn, but she felt her idea had merit. She was almost sure the material in Victoria's shop had been used to make the clown costume. Minnie wouldn't remember, of course, but Tammy might. It would be hard to remember details like the design on a costume when you had a gun stuck in your face, but she could ask her. If she could establish that, then the initials of who had a costume made would be more important. If they could figure out who they were.

'Sean Ryan didn't make a very good first impression on you, did he?' Dan grinned for the first time since he'd ended up in the hospital.

'No.' She knew her reply was cryptic, but he hadn't.

'He's supposed to be a good detective.' There was reservation in Glen's voice.

'He has a good reputation, but he's also known as a bit of a bully.' Dan's frown deepened into a scowl as he picked up the notebook again. 'I'm going to have to turn this over to him, but I'd like to look at it a little more thoroughly.'

John leaned over the bed and took the notebook from him. 'What's this?'

Glen moved in to look as well. 'Is this something Mary's come up with? Evidence of some sort?'

'Don't know if it's evidence, but it's thought-provoking.' Dan took the notebook back but opened it on his tray and explained what they thought it meant. 'So, if either of you can come up with a name to put with these initials, I'd be grateful.'

Glen ran his finger down the list. It stopped at one set of initials. He traced across the page. There was a large C under type of garment made. His face visibly paled. 'Here. These initials. TT. I wonder . . . no . . . it couldn't be.'

'Couldn't be who?' Dan had gone into police mode. Still with a soft voice, but there was an edge to it now, an insistence on an answer.

Glen looked miserable. 'Troy Turnbull.'

'Troy . . . isn't that the kid you turned down for a house loan?' John asked.

Glen nodded. 'I felt terrible, but he didn't begin to qualify. Poor kids, expecting their first baby and want to buy a house in the worst way, but Troy's only held the job he's got for a short time, she isn't working, and they have late payments for their car. Plus, they don't have a down payment. There was no way I could qualify them.'

'Didn't you say he got pretty belligerent?' John's voice was more insistent than Dan's, if such a thing was possible. 'You said that night he was almost threatening.'

Dan pushed himself higher in the bed and looked from one to the other, like someone watching a tennis match. 'Did he really threaten you?'

Glen shook his head. 'Not really. Just stormed out, saying I'd be sorry. He closed out his account the next day. I wasn't sorry about that. I love to see young people start out in their own home, but there was no way I could help those two. I tried to counsel him, but he was having none of it. I've never seen him since.'

'Do you remember where he works?' Dan's eyes were bright with interest. 'Or where he lives?'

Mary felt a little sick. She knew Troy. 'If he's the same one I remember, I think he still lives out at Meadow View Trailer Park.'

All three men stared at her.

Dan asked, 'You know him?'

She knew almost everyone in town.

Mary didn't answer right away. 'Glen, is he a scrawny-looking guy, probably somewhere in is mid-twenties now, long greasy blond hair?'

'Yeah. Has a tattoo on his left bicep.'

'He didn't when I knew him, but I'm not surprised.'

'Where did you know him?' Dan sat up so straight Mary was afraid for his shoulder, but he didn't seem to notice. His entire attention was on her.

'He worked for Ruthie at the Yum Yum last summer. He was supposed to bus tables, work in the kitchen, do a lot of the jobs no one likes, but he could have worked his way up. Ruthie's wait staff gets some pretty good tips, but his temper was terrible, and she finally let him go. I don't know where he works now.'

'Why?' Dan's gaze bored into her.

'You'll have to ask her.'

'We will. I'd like to have one of my guys talk to this Troy before Sean Ryan does. I wonder . . .' He picked up the notebook and turned to the last page. 'I sure wish I could hang onto this for a while.'

'You can't, but . . .' Mary smiled at him sweetly.

His scowl turned to suspicious to hope. 'What have you done?'

'Made copies. Would you like a set?'

All three men laughed out loud.

'Why am I not surprised,' Dan muttered. 'When can you bring it in?'

Mary looked at her watch. 'Not until later this afternoon. I'm meeting Pat Bennington and Krissie and Pamela at Victoria's shop at noon, and I need to get Millie from Furry Friends before then. Pat's going to make sure their dresses fit.'

'And you're going to do a little more snooping.'

Mary ignored Dan's statement. 'Glen, did you get any indication Troy might do something violent, like rob the bank?'

Glen shook his head. 'Just the opposite. He has a short fuse, that's for sure, but I got the impression it was all talk. He sure hated me, though.'

Mary nodded slowly. 'That fits with what I remember about him. I think he's the kind to carry a grudge. Do you think he might have robbed the bank as much to get back at you as to get the money? He could hardly have used it as a down payment on a house.'

Dan answered her. 'Bank robberies are rarely, if ever, personal. Just some idiot who thinks it's his ticket to instant riches.'

'If it was riches this idiot was after, he was disappointed. There's never much cash in the tellers' drawers at that time of day. We replace it as needed, but they don't have thousands in front of them all the time.' Glen's tone was full of disgust.

Mary didn't say anything, but there was something about this robbery that seemed different from others she had read about or seen in the movies. She couldn't quite place why she felt that way, but it made her wonder. Maybe Troy Turnbull had wanted to get back at the bank that had refused him a loan. Had that humiliated him? Made him mad enough to resort to robbery and ultimately murder? Right now, all they had was speculation. She glanced at her watch once more.

'I have to go. Krissie should be through giving Millie a bath by now. Then we're going to Victoria's. I'll be back later and will bring the copy. It will be interesting to hear what Detective Ryan has to say about our theory.' She picked up her purse and turned to John and Glen. 'I'll see you both later?'

They nodded. Mary heard the hum of conversation start as she let the door swing shut.

TWELVE

Millie sat in the middle of Victoria's shop, staring into the bank of mirrors that showed every side of the person who stood in front of them. Mary wasn't sure if she was admiring the bright red bows she wore on each ear or the train on Pamela's wedding dress. Both were impressive.

'Thank goodness she'd finished.' Pat had examined the dress from the inside out and pronounced it ready to go down the aisle. It was a simple but elegant gown that showed off Pamela's slender figure. The veil she had picked out was short. The train wasn't.

'Let's get this dress off you and back on the hanger. I don't want dog prints on that train.' Mary started to gather it up while Pat started on the small, fabric-covered buttons that ran down the back of the dress.

'You look beautiful,' Krissie told Pamela. 'Just beautiful. Luke's going to be speechless when he sees you.'

'I hope not so speechless he can't say "I do".' She smiled as she stepped out of the dress. 'You look pretty spectacular yourself. That mint green on you is great, and so is the dress. Victoria was really talented.'

Mary paused a moment, her arms full, her eyes threatening to leak tears. What a waste! Victoria had been a good person, kind as well as talented. Ellen and her daughter, Susannah, had been talking to her about making Susannah's wedding dress as well as the bridesmaid and the mother of the bride dress. Now . . . but there was no use crying over what was not to be. And Susannah's wedding wasn't until July. Finding out who killed Victoria and why needed to be done now.

'Did either of you happen to see a clown costume that Victoria was making when you came for your fittings?' Her words were a little muffled as she struggled to tie the train up on the hanger, but evidently, they heard her because Krissie said, 'I did. She had one hanging up out front. I think it was ready for whoever ordered it because she had it in plastic wrap, but you could see what it was.'

The train almost slipped out of Mary's hand. 'Would you recognize it? I mean, the pattern of the material . . .?'

'Sure. It had balloons all over it. All colors. Very gaudy but probably appropriate for what it was.'

The dress, its train finally safely secured, went on the rack and Mary turned to face Krissie. 'Would you recognize the material if you saw it again?'

'Sure. She's got a bolt of it on the shelf in the front. Why?'

Mary was at a loss to answer that one. 'I saw the material and wondered what she used it for.'

She knew it was a lame answer, but it was the best she could think of. Krissie looked dubious, but she let it go. She walked over to her dress, lifted the skirt, and let it drop. 'I love the way this thing hangs on me. It's beautiful. Can we take them home?'

'I don't see why not,' Mary answered.

Pat nodded her approval. 'Did you bring a car?'

Krissie grinned. 'I even brought a sheet and spread it out on the back seat. Can you help us? I don't want the cat to get out.' She looked around the shop. 'I hadn't thought about him until now. He's usually down here, supervising, sitting on things he shouldn't, and batting thread around. I hope he's all right.'

'You would worry about that cat.' Pamela tried to lift her dress off the rack. 'Wow. This is heavy. That cat can take care of himself.'

'He can't open a bag of cat food or fill his water dish,' Krissie said a little testily. 'Or clean his own cat box.'

'Don't worry about the cat,' Pat said hurriedly. 'Mary and I checked on him yesterday and he's fine. He's going home to stay with Mary until we can find him a permanent one.'

'I should have known you two wouldn't let him down.' Krissie's grin was wide and her tone a bit relieved. Because she didn't have to assume responsibility for the cat? Mary could hardly blame her. She didn't think the cat was going to be easy.

Between the four of them they got the dresses successfully into the car. Pat Bennington, Mary, and Millie watched as the girls drove off.

'Are you going to the wedding?' Mary turned to Pat.

'Karl and I wouldn't miss it for the world. I've known Pamela since she and Neil were in grade school. Hard to believe they're both so grown up.'

'Yes.' Mary felt that way a lot. She'd taught home ec for many years in Santa Louisa's middle school and had seen many of her pupils into middle age. She sighed, then wondered why. For all the years that had passed so quickly? Maybe, but now wasn't the time for sentimental rumination. 'Are we going to get the cat?'

It wasn't that she wanted the cat, but she did have other things to do, so this was one chore she wanted to get behind her. 'You go get him in the cat carrier. I'll be right up.'

'What are you going to do?' Pat sounded suspicious and not very happy. 'I may need you to help me.'

'I'll be right there. I just want to get a piece of material.'

'What material? Why? Oh.' She watched Mary take the bolt of balloon-covered material down from the shelf and lay it out on the cutting table. 'What are you going to do with . . . never mind. I don't want to know. Come up as soon as you can.'

She left Mary cutting off a substantial piece of the material and went up the stairs to try to coax the large and opinionated-looking cat into the carrier she'd brought.

THIRTEEN

'Now what do we do?'
Pat sat the cat carrier on Mary's kitchen floor and took the food and water dish out of her hands. 'Leave him in there while I get the rest of his stuff, then we'll decide.'

Mary and Millie waited while Pat collected the cat box and food. They both stared at the carrier, Mary with trepidation, Millie seemingly with curiosity. Mary noticed one bow was missing from Millie's ear, but she was too busy trying to figure out where to put the cat's equipment to care.

Pat staggered a little under the bulky weight of all the bundles she tried to navigate through Mary's back door. Mary relieved her of the box of cat litter and closed the screen tight behind her. 'I have no idea where to put this stuff. I've never had a cat.'

'You never had a dog, either, until you got Millie. That's worked out pretty well.'

It had, but Mary doubted the cat planned on being as

cooperative as Millie had been. 'Well, we'd better get it settled. I have to go out again.'

Pat set the cat food in the broom closet on top of the dog food, turned, and stared at Mary. 'Where are you going?'

'I have to go to the bank and then return a library book.'

Pat frowned. 'Translated, that means you want to talk to Tammy, show her that material, and see if she recognizes it, then you want to talk to Luke. Why Luke?'

'I have a library book I've finished and want to check out another one. So, what are we going to do with the cat?'

Pat looked at her hard then shook her head. 'Please don't do anything that will get you and Millie shot.'

'I'm certainly not planning to,' Mary said with as much dignity as she could muster. 'Now, about the cat.'

'Right. How about we set him up in the guest room for now? We can put his litter box in the bathroom and his carrier, with the door open, and his food and water just outside of it. Then you can close the door until he seems to have settled in a little before you let him explore the rest of the house.'

Mary thought about what she had in the room the cat could destroy. Her computer, for one thing. But if she closed it down and pushed everything to the back . . . 'All right. Let's try it. I won't be on my computer until tomorrow and, by that time, he should be more comfortable. I hope.'

It didn't take long to cat-proof the room and to set up his litter box and food and water dishes. The cat started to yowl while they worked, banging his claws at the door of the carrier, obviously determined to get out.

Mary put her fingers in her ears. 'If he keeps that up all night, I'm bringing him over to your house and depositing him on your front porch.'

Pat put the food dishes on the old plastic tray Mary found, filled them both, stood back, and surveyed the room. 'I think we're ready to let Mr Cat out to take stock of his new home.'

Mary glared at her.

'Temporary home. Why don't you and Millie leave? I'll let him out.'

'Will he stop yowling?' Mary picked up Millie and left the room, half shutting the door.

Soon Pat hastily closed the door and they waited. They heard nothing. The yowls stopped. A strong, pungent odor replaced them, creeping through the cracks in the door.

'What's that smell?' Mary looked at Pat with alarm, wondering what the cat could have gotten into so soon and what it might be.

'He needed to use the litter box,' Pat said. 'I think he'll settle down now.'

He might, but Mary wasn't sure she could. She was glad she and Millie were going out.

Pat gathered her things and left, saying she'd call Mary in the morning to see how he was doing. Mary crept up to the bedroom door and listened. No yowls. The smell was largely gone. No rustling noises, no noises of any kind. Relief flooded her. Whatever was going on in that room didn't seem to be something she had to deal with, at least not right now. There were other things to take care of.

'Come on, Millie.' She gathered up her purse and Millie's leash. 'We're going to see if Tammy can identify this material and then we're going to talk to Luke. And it won't be about his impending nuptials.'

FOURTEEN

Mary walked out of the library into the atrium that separated it from the city offices, carrying a new library book but no new information. Luke said he'd had no idea anything was happening until the police showed up in the library, guns drawn, while they searched it for any sign of the robber. He'd told them he was sure he'd have noticed if a clown had come in, especially one with a satchel of money and a smoking gun. They searched anyway and found nothing, except an upset mother and a couple of very entertained kids. He'd thanked her for helping Pamela get the gowns and said he'd be glad when the wedding was over. Everyone was a nervous wreck over it and should he cut off his ponytail?

Mary couldn't remember ever seeing Luke without his long blond ponytail and his diamond stud earing. 'What does Pamela say?'

'She says she likes me just like I am.'

Mary laughed at that and told him he already had his answer. She, however, didn't have hers.

'We're going to the bank,' she told Millie, who was right by her side. 'Let's hope Tammy's there. If she recognizes this material, that puts us another step forward in finding out who killed Victoria and almost killed Dan.' At least she thought it did. If they could prove Victoria made the clown costume and that she was shot because she'd recognized the person behind the clown mask, didn't that put them further along? She hoped so. She was so absorbed in her thoughts she almost didn't hear Janelle Tucker call out to her.

'Mrs McGill. Just the person I wanted to see. Do you have a minute?'

Janelle had a smile on her face as she greeted Mary. Zoe had a wagging tail and pricked ears as she greeted Millie.

'Of course. How nice to see you.'

They watched the dogs for a minute then Janelle said, 'I wanted to know if you've seen Chief Dunham. Detective Ryan said he's out of danger and doing well. Is that correct?'

Mary could barely make out her expression behind lightly tinted sunglasses, but she thought her tone expressed real concern. 'He's going to be fine. He may even go home in a couple of days.'

'That is good news. The whole thing was such a shock, I'm sure your bank has never experienced anything like that before. A nice, respectable small-town bank like that. It could seriously affect confidence in its safety.'

Mary hadn't thought about her bank in those terms and briefly wondered if there was a hint of insincerity in Janelle's voice. If so, she wouldn't be the first. People who came here from the city loved to say how charming the town was, how quaint, how they loved visiting, but were just as quick to point out its shortcomings, like no Macy's or nationwide bank. Besides, Janelle might be right.

'I don't think it ever has been robbed. At least not at

gunpoint. However, I don't think the robbery will make anyone afraid to bank there. Everyone in town trusts Glen Manning completely.'

'What about that old man who used to run the bank? Did the people around here trust him?'

It took Mary a minute to think who she might be talking about. 'Do you mean Chet Bradley? Chet had gotten a little . . . vague before Glen Manning took over. He retired shortly after that, but a more honest man never lived. How do you know about Chet?'

'My mother told me. We lived here for a short time when I was little. I don't remember him, of course, but evidently that bank held the mortgage on our land. It was a big shock when, after my father died, the bank told her the loan was in default. But she managed to sell the land and we moved.'

Mary didn't know what to say. Janelle seemed pretty matter of fact about the whole thing, but she'd been little, and it had been close to twenty years ago. 'It must have been hard on you and your sister as well.'

Janelle hesitated. 'Not too much for me. I missed my dad, of course, the school and running around in the vineyard, but I guess I was too young to realize how hard things were for my mom. My sister never talked about it. She got married and moved away a long time ago.' She sighed and looked down the street at the bank building looking imposing and important in the glow of the afternoon sun. 'That must be a new building. I seem to remember a much smaller, sort of dark building that always smelled dusty . . .' She seemed to brighten and smiled at Mary. 'Whatever happened to . . . Chet, did you say his name was?'

'Chet's in Shady Acres, a very nice retirement home in the hills on the west side of town. They have a unit for people who have memory problems.' She paused, thinking of Chet the last time she'd seen him. He hadn't known her. He hadn't known his daughter, either. She sighed. 'He's over ninety now, and pretty frail.' Determined to change the subject, she said, 'How do you like working for our police department?'

Janelle seemed caught off guard by the abrupt change but smiled. 'I like it very much. I get to do a little of everything here, and I've already learned a lot. I do hope Chief Dunham is able to get back to work soon. He's a smart man.'

Mary smiled. She completely agreed. Dan was smart, and he was a good man. A fair man. She was glad Janelle realized that. Had Janelle compared Dan to Sean Ryan and Ryan had come up short? *How unfair.* She didn't know Ryan. Maybe she was leaping to conclusions because she hadn't liked him right off, and maybe because Dan was so dear to her. She shook herself a little. Janelle had said something, and Mary had let her mind wander. 'I'm sorry. I missed that.'

'I asked you how long Mr Manning had been with the bank. He seems young to be a manager or is he president?'

'He's the president now. Glen knows what he's doing. He came to work after graduating from Cal Poly down in San Louis Obispo. He and John liked it here, so they both took jobs that would have paid more if they'd gone back to LA, but it's worked out. Glen must have started not too long after your family left. He's built the bank from a small local farmer's bank to a first-class enterprise. A couple of the big banks opened branches when so many wineries moved here, but the wineries prefer Mission Oaks, just like all of us who live here.'

'He worked for Chet Bradley?'

'Chet was a sort of mentor for him at first, but as Chet started to fade, well, Glen took over and the bank took off.' Mary chuckled slightly at her phrasing, but Janelle didn't seem to find it amusing. She shrugged and once again, changed the subject. 'Have you decided what to do with Zoe?'

That seemed to catch Janelle completely off guard. 'Zoe?'

At the sound of her name, the dog abandoned Millie and turned to Janelle, her face upturned, her expression eager, ready for whatever Janelle wanted. Janelle wanted nothing. She waved her hand at the dog, which seemed to confuse her. Zoe looked around then sat in front of Janelle and waited.

'I didn't call you,' Janelle told the dog, who pricked her ears. 'I don't need you to do anything. Go back and talk to Millie.'

Zoe didn't move. Janelle sighed. 'This dog seems to think she should be on duty twenty-four-seven. It drives me nuts. I don't need a service dog, but she was Mother's. I miss her and Zoe comforts me somehow.'

Mary watched Janelle's face closely, as if she'd said more than she had intended. 'I have an idea for what you might do with Zoe while you're at work. I don't have time to explain it now, but if you aren't busy, could you stop by my house say about five this evening? I need to get to the bank and then to the hospital. I have something I promised Dan I'd take care of. Can you do that?'

Janelle hesitated, seemingly a little embarrassed by sharing her feelings, but curiosity, or maybe the offer of friendship, seemed to move her. 'Yes. I'll be glad to. Thanks.'

She walked toward the library door, Zoe beside her. She paused to glance back at Mary and Millie. Mary smiled at her then hurried out the atrium doors toward the bank and, hopefully, to talk to Tammy.

FIFTEEN

Mary and Millie parked in the back of the bank and went into the little hallway that led to Glen's office. The sign on the front door said only service dogs were allowed and Millie clearly didn't qualify. Mary didn't want to walk her through the lobby, but Glen always welcomed her into his office. Today was no exception.

'Hey, you two. What are you doing here?'

'I want to speak to Tammy, if she's not busy, and I don't want to do it out there.' She nodded toward the lobby, where the tellers could be seen through the glass window that enabled Glen to watch whatever went on. 'Can we use your office?'

Mary settled in the chair opposite Glen's desk. Millie walked around and put her front paws on his knees, waiting for her ears to be scratched.

'This is about the robbery, isn't it?' All traces of a smile had left Glen's face. 'I thought Dan told you to keep out of it.'

'All I want to do is ask her a couple of questions. I'm not getting involved, but, Glen, that man almost killed Dan. If there's any little thing I can do to help, well, I want to. This is personal. If I think I've found out anything, I'll tell Dan right away.'

A faint trace of a smile appeared while Glen rubbed Millie's ears. 'Not Sean Ryan? Just Dan?'

Mary didn't smile. 'I doubt if Detective Ryan would listen to me. Now, I'll tell you what I'm thinking, and then you can decide if we talk to Tammy or not.' She waited.

Finally, Glen nodded. 'If this is about those initials, we've already been over that. We don't know if Victoria made that costume or not.'

Mary leaned forward in her chair and rested her arms on Glen's desk. She used her best middle school teacher stare to make him focus on what she was saying. 'If Tammy sees a piece of material and recognizes it as the same material the clown was wearing, then do you think the initials would be important? Then do you think Victoria might have been shot because she recognized the costume she had made and knew who was wearing it?'

Glen sighed. 'How are you planning on doing this? I don't want to traumatize Tammy in any way. She's been through a lot.'

Mary agreed. 'She certainly has. I thought I'd just spread the piece I happen to have out on your desk and ask if she's ever seen it before. She's been through so much she may not remember the pattern on the clown costume, but it's worth a try.'

Glen didn't say anything for a moment, then he set Millie's paws down from his knees and pushed back his chair. 'I'm probably going to regret this,' he said as he walked to his office door.

Mary twisted in her chair so she, too, could see the bank floor. It was almost empty. Glen stepped out his doorway and beckoned to Tammy, who didn't have a customer. She smiled at him and started toward his office.

'Why, Mrs McGill. And Millie.' Tammy hesitated, surprise and worry taking the place of her smile. 'Did I do something . . .?'

'No. Of course not,' Mary answered. 'I just have a couple

of questions I wanted to ask you and Glen said it's all right with him, if it's all right with you.'

Tammy stared at Mary for a moment then looked over at Glen, as if for reassurance.

'No reason to be alarmed. Mrs McGill only wants to ask you a couple of questions about the day of the robbery. She was here, as you know, and wants to get some things straight in her own mind. If you don't want to talk about it, you don't have to.'

Tammy pulled out the other chair in front of Glen's desk and dropped down in it. Millie sat next to her and nudged her knee with her nose. Tammy absently let her hand drop down and started to rub Millie's ears. The dog leaned in closer.

'I told the police everything I could remember. But if you want to hear it, I guess that's OK.'

Mary glanced over at Glen then quietly asked Tammy, 'Can you start with him coming in the bank? When did you notice him?'

'I guess when he sneezed. I was finishing up with something and looked up. A sneeze in that mask had to be uncomfortable, but he didn't do anything. He stepped up to my station. I sort of laughed and said something about spring and fall and how we could count on our allergies to flare up. That's when he pushed the note toward me.'

'What note?'

'It said, in bold black letters, "This is a robbery. Don't scream or I'll shoot you. Put all your cash in this bag." Then he pushed an open canvas tote bag at me.' She paused, took a deep breath. 'He almost dropped it because of those blue gloves he had on.' Then, in almost a whisper, she said, 'That's when he showed me the gun.'

'What did you do?' Mary sounded a little breathless, but she felt a little breathless. Just hearing about it made the hairs on the back of her neck tingle. Tammy must have been petrified with fear.

'At first, nothing. I stood there, with my mouth open, staring at him. I couldn't believe what was happening. He pushed the note closer and let me see the gun again, and I started to fill the bag with the cash in my drawer. Then he waved the gun toward Lisa, gesturing like she should put her money in. Her customer was going out the door and the only person left was Minnie. I handed Lisa the note and she did what I'd done. She just stood there, frozen. I sort of pushed her and whispered for her to start emptying her cash drawer. That's when Victoria Witherspoon came out of the safe deposit room. I didn't see her at first, not until she got close.'

Glen leaned forward. 'Did she say anything?'

Tammy looked away from Mary. 'She stared at first, then her face flushed, like she was really mad. She said something like, "What are you doing?" Then she saw the bag with the money and she said, sort of loud, "You son of a bitch. You can't do that." I remember that because I was so surprised. She said something else, but I couldn't hear it because that's when he shot her. He turned, looked straight at her, and shot her. Twice, I think. He turned back and grabbed Lisa's money tray, dumped what was left in his bag while Lisa fled out the back. That's when Dan came out of Glen's office. He raised his gun and shouted, "Police" and something else, then he shouted, "Get down" at Minnie, but she was on the move. She was crying and screaming and started toward Dan. That blasted clown raised his gun and shot him. Cool as could be, just stood there and shot him. How he missed Minnie, I don't know. Then he turned and ran out.'

No one said anything. They couldn't. This was the first Mary had heard of the coldness of the robber and the deliberate way he'd gone about shooting Victoria and then Dan. That somehow changed things. 'Tammy, was there anything you can remember about him that was familiar? Anything that could help us identify him?'

Tammy looked at Glen with what seemed to Mary to be trepidation. Finally, she spoke. 'He reminded me of John.'

Glen's head jerked up. 'What?'

'It wasn't John, of course,' Tammy assured Glen hastily, 'but he's built like John. About the same height and has broad shoulders like him.' She stopped and examined Glen's face before she went on. 'He runs like him, too. Like John does when he's showing your dogs. Head up and going for it. That's really all I could see under that bulky costume. I wish I could tell you something more but . . ." . . .' She let her voice trail off, her expression one of misery as she stared at Glen.

'I think you did a good job.' Mary reached over and patted Tammy's hand. 'I doubt if I would have noticed anything but the gun. Just to clarify, this man, this clown, didn't seem nervous? Scared? What about when he saw Victoria? Did that seem to throw him in any way?'

Tammy shook her head. 'I've never seen less emotion. I think that's what scared me most. He pushed that note toward me like it was a deposit slip. The only thing I heard him say was when Victoria accosted him. And that was only one word.'

'What was that?' Glen asked. He appeared a bit ashen-faced but his voice was steady.

'Damn.' Tammy took a deep breath. 'He whispered it. If I hadn't been so close, I wouldn't have heard it. But it didn't throw him. He just turned and shot her. He seemed in complete control, not nervous or anything. Like he knew exactly what he was doing the whole time.'

Glen threw himself back in his chair. 'I knew it. Didn't I tell you? That bastard had this whole thing planned right down to the last detail. He's got to be someone local, only who?'

Tammy watched Glen, her eyes wide. Tears threatened to escape, and she raised her hand to wipe them away. Mary didn't want her to cry. She needed to ask her the most important question.

'Tammy, I want to show you a piece of material. All you need to say is if you have ever seen it before. Is that all right?'

Tammy tore her gaze away from Glen's scowl and nodded. She wiped her eyes on the tissue Mary handed her then watched as Mary unrolled the piece of material she had brought on Glen's desk.

'Does this look familiar to you?'

Tammy gasped. Her hand shook a little as she pulled the material closer, smoothing it. 'The balloons. This is the same material as the clown's costume.'

Those were the words Mary had been hoping to hear, but it had been a terrifying experience for Tammy so she wanted her to be certain. 'Are you sure?'

'Yes. I remember because I thought the balloons were cute.

That was right before he handed me that note, but those are the same balloons. I'm sure.'

Mary sat back and sighed. She looked at Glen, he looked at her.

'I think we need to go to the hospital and have a talk with Dan,' Mary said.

SIXTEEN

D an already had company.

Sean Ryan stood next to the bed, Victoria's notebook in his hand. He looked up when Glen and Mary entered the room and scowled. 'Mrs McGill. Mr Manning. I understand you' – he nodded at Mary – 'found this notebook when you searched Victoria's workshop and home yesterday.' Glen, he ignored.

'Good afternoon to you, also, Detective Ryan. I didn't search her place. I went over to see if Pamela Pruitt's wedding dress and Krissie Kramer's bridesmaid dress were ready and if not, what could be done to finish them in time. While Mrs Bennington and I were there, we took care of the cat, who is now at my house, and found that notebook. Of course, we looked at it and formed some ideas, which we immediately brought to Chief Dunham. I think that covers it.'

She sat in the chair that was still pulled up beside Dan's bed and laid her purse on the floor beside her and looked around. 'Where's Ellen?'

Dan seemed to be fighting a grin, but he managed a straight face answering her question. 'She has a client that's put a bid on a house. She's out presenting the offer. She'll be back around dinnertime.'

Which wasn't that far off. Mary nodded and turned slightly toward Detective Ryan. 'If you have any questions about the notebook, I'll try to answer them. We think, Pat Bennington and I, we've figured out what most of the initials stand for, but we may be wrong.'

Ryan's face looked a little redder and he shook the notebook, not exactly in her face but close. 'Who gave you permission to go into that building? That was a potential crime scene.'

'Really, Ryan?' The words were mild, but the anger in Dan's voice was unmistakable. 'How's that? Victoria was shot in the bank. How does that make her shop a crime scene? I gave Mary permission to go there. We couldn't have little Pamela going up the aisle in her jeans, now could we? And what about the cat? You didn't want it to starve to death while you got around to checking out the shop, did you? I may be in this blasted hospital, but I'm still chief of my department, and I'm glad she and Mrs Bennington went over there. You should be as well. They saved you a lot of time.'

Ryan whipped around to stare at Dan. 'How do you figure that?'

'You saw the initials. They figured out the big C means the clown costume. The other initials are for whoever ordered one and the last two columns are the date they were ordered or ready to pick up and the amount paid. You'll see PIF in quite a few columns. We think that means paid in full.'

'That must have been tough to figure out.' Sarcasm dripped from every word.

Ryan was using it on the wrong person. Dan had spent too many years in the San Francisco Homicide unit to show any reaction to it, but Mary bet he wouldn't forget it. This was, after all, his town and his case. If he could just get back to it.

'Anything else you'd like to share?' Ryan couldn't seem to let it go. His ears looked like they were on fire.

Why so much anger? They should be working together, but Ryan acted like a dog with an especially juicy bone that someone was trying to get from him. She wondered if that was how he felt. He was a young man, not too many bank robberies or murders up here on the central coast. San Louis Obispo was a college town. The rest of the communities were devoted to tourists or wineries and acres of wine grapes. The opportunities to shine as a homicide detective were scarce. Maybe he didn't want anyone stepping on his case. If that was so, he wasn't going about it the right way. She wondered how

much more Dan would tell him about their theories. She didn't
have to wait long to find out.

'There are a couple of initials there you might find interesting.' Dan settled back on his pillows, lowering his arm a
little and stuffing the pillow it lay on under it more securely.
He was no longer in the sling. He was getting better.

Ryan didn't say anything at first, but he looked interested.
'How so?'

'The initials TT. We think they may belong to Troy Turnbull.
Seems Troy was denied a loan by Glen and was very upset. If
we can determine if Troy did indeed order a clown costume,
it would be worth giving him a closer look.'

Ryan stared at Dan, at the composed, bland look on his
face and sneered. 'Now, how do I go about finding out if this
guy, Troy, bought a clown costume from our victim? Short of
waltzing up to him and asking.'

Mary could think of several ways but didn't think any of
them were open to Ryan and the one that was, he'd just
stomped on. She also thought she'd keep quiet and see where
this went.

'Well,' Dan said, in that false drawl he sometimes used
when his patience was stretched to the breaking point, 'you
might try finding out where he works and ask around there.
People talk to each other about stuff like that. Especially in
small towns like this one. You might also talk to some of the
volunteers who put up the events Halloween night. Most of
them wore costumes of some sort. I'll bet they took note of
what everyone else was wearing. Someone just might have
noticed Troy.'

Ryan looked at Dan for what seemed like a long time,
then he glanced at the notebook. 'You think there were four
costumes made. Any idea who the rest of the initials
belong to?'

Dan shrugged, or at least he tried to. Ryan looked at Mary
then Glen, but neither of them said anything.

'How am I supposed to know who bought a costume if all
I've got to go on is initials?' Ryan sounded irritated.

'Try the phone book,' Dan said.

Ryan glared at him and the lobes of his ears turned an

unbecoming shade of pink. He snapped the notebook closed and tucked it under his arm. 'I'll check back with you later.'

Mary and Glen said nothing until he'd gone and the door closed behind him.

Then Mary shuffled in the chair beside Dan and reached into her carryall. 'Here.'

Dan took the papers she handed him, opened them, and smiled.

'Glen and I have something to tell you.'

'I'd hoped you might. What?'

'Tammy, the teller who was on duty when the robbery occurred, recognized the material. She's sure the clown suit had balloons all over it and that it's the same as the material in Victoria's shop.'

She watched Dan think about that.

He nodded, then winced. 'Damn thing.'

Mary was sure it was his shoulder he addressed, not the clown suit. She was certain when he went on.

'Sounds as if it might be one Victoria made, but there's bound to be stores around here that carry that pattern. We can't be positive.'

'Unless Walmart carries it, no one north of San Louis Obispo will have it. No one sews anymore, so fabric shops are far and few between. Don't split hairs, Dan. This makes it almost certain.'

He grinned at her, nodded, then grimaced. 'Wish this thing would heal. It's a royal pain in the—'

'You're lucky to be alive. Your shoulder will heal. It's already better. Now study that list and see if you have any ideas who the other three might be. We're going to need to know because Troy didn't do it.'

Dan's head jerked up and he frowned at Mary. 'You sound pretty certain about that.'

'I am.'

'I agree with her.' Glen leaned forward and gave a nod in Mary's direction.

'You mind telling me what piece of evidence you two have come up with that clears our young friend, Troy?'

'It's not exactly evidence, like the kind you take into court, but it's enough. Troy isn't a deliberate kind of person. He gets excited and flies off the handle. The killer didn't. According to Tammy, when he knew Victoria had recognized him, he raised his gun and shot her. Two times. He wasn't nervous about it. He just did it. Then when you appeared, he shot you the same way, just missing Minnie, who was on the move. That's why you didn't fire. She was coming toward you.' Mary paused, waiting for his reaction.

Dan frowned and nodded. 'I remember that part.'

Mary went on. 'Then, according to Tammy, the clown grabbed Lisa's tray, dumped it in his bag, turned, and left. He never said anything except a soft "damn" when he saw Victoria come at him. Troy would never have kept his cool through all that.'

'Mary's right.' Glen also watched Dan's reaction as he backed her up. 'Troy threw a hissy fit when he realized he wasn't getting the loan and that wasn't nearly as stressful as robbing a bank and shooting someone.' Glen paused, and a tiny smile played over his lips. 'At least I don't think it is. Since I've never robbed a bank, I can't say for sure.' All traces of a smile vanished. 'Another thing. Troy is a good kid who's about to become a father. The stress is getting to him. Money's tight. He's working two jobs because right now, she can't. I can't imagine him paying to have a costume made.'

'Unless he thought it would make him money.' Cynicism was ripe in Dan's voice. 'I don't really know this kid. I know who he is and know he doesn't have a record, but I also know stress does funny things. I don't think we can entirely rule him out.'

'Maybe not.' Mary looked at her watch to check the time. 'However, I think we need to find out who the other three clown suits belong to, and we need to confirm if Troy owns the fourth.'

'Then we'd better copy down the initials of the other three.' Glen rummaged in his inside suit pocket, but nothing seemed to be there. 'Dan, do you have a pen or pencil and maybe some paper? I seem to have left my notebook somewhere.'

Dan started to laugh then stopped. 'Oh, it hurts to do that. Glen, you won't be needing them. Mary's made copies for each of us. Sean may get the notebook but she wasn't going to let it go until we all had the information.' He looked at Mary with a huge grin.

Mary dug in her purse and pulled out another couple of stapled-together papers. 'I thought you could check these against bank records. Most of the people in this town bank at Mission Oaks Bank. Poor old Chet almost ran it into the ground, but they trust you.'

'They won't.' Glen looked at the papers, sighed, and slipped them into his inside pocket. 'There is such a thing as a privacy policy. I think I can see if any of our depositors have these initials, but that's all. I can't tell you anything about deposits, transactions, or financial positions. I can't even tell you if anyone wrote a check to Victoria. At least, I don't think so. Even the police would need a warrant.'

'You're forgetting something,' Dan told him. 'I am the police. If those initials fit anyone, all I need is the name and I'll take it from there.' He turned to face Mary, or turned as well as he could, then groaned. 'You know practically everyone in town, so see if any of those initials ring a bell with you as well, but that's all. I'll do the rest.'

'Of course,' Mary told him in a sincere voice.

Dan sighed. 'Please don't do anything that will get you shot.'

'Don't be silly.' She glanced again at her watch. 'Glen, we've got to go, or at least I do. I have to get Millie from Furry Friends and then I think I'll stop by the Yum Yum and get something for dinner. Janelle is coming over around five and, by the time she leaves, I won't feel like fixing anything.'

'Janelle Tucker?' There was surprise and curiosity both in Dan's voice. 'Why is she coming?'

'She has her mother's service dog, Zoe. She doesn't need her, and now that she's working for you, the dog is left alone all day. She had her in doggy daycare, but, for some reason, it didn't work out. I thought, maybe, Robbie Gallagher might like the dog to spend the day with him.'

'Who's Robbie Gallagher?' Glen stood and offered Mary a hand, which she accepted.

'He's the eight-year-old son of one of my officers.' Dan's voice softened as he stared at Mary. 'He has cerebral palsy. How Mary knew that . . . do you think she would? That kid needs a service dog in the worst way. His mother could use the help, too.'

'I plan on asking her after I ply her with a glass of our local Chardonnay.' Mary started toward the door. 'Is Ellen coming tonight?'

Dan nodded. 'As soon as she can. Susannah is coming home from school for the weekend, and I guess Neil is driving down from Davis. I told them not to, but they're coming anyway. Midterms aren't until mid-November, and I guess they both want to see for themselves I'm still alive.'

'Susannah wants to make sure you're going to be fit to walk her down the aisle this summer and Neil, well, I imagine he wants to make sure his father is building the equine clinic to his specifications as well as getting a chance to see Susannah. They're going to be a great couple.'

Dan beamed. He was Susannah's stepfather but much closer to her than her own father. She had asked him to walk her down the aisle, much to the delight of Ellen, her mother. Neil, the Bennington's only son, was about to graduate from veterinary school, and the young couple would settle in Santa Louisa, much to the delight of everyone.

'We're having a rash of weddings.' Glen held the door open for Mary and called back to Dan. 'Take it easy and get out of here as soon as you can. Luke and Pamela won't like it one bit if you're not at theirs. That gives you almost two weeks to heal.' He laughed softly and let the door swing shut behind him.

SEVENTEEN

The alley behind the Yum Yum was empty. All of the delivery trucks that often blocked the now-open back door had come and gone and just a few late lunch customers' cars were evident. The Yum Yum wasn't open for dinner and was officially closed. Ruthie would have a few minutes to talk.

Ruthie greeted them as they came in the door with a huge smile for Millie and a mug of hot black coffee for Mary. 'You need a little caffeine after what you've been through the last few days.'

She motioned toward the jaunty red table she used as a desk and pulled out a purple and black ladder-back chair for herself. A white carton box sat on the table. 'Just so happens I made your favorite quiche for lunch today. Thought you might like some. Put a small salad in, as well.' She gestured toward the box, picked up her own coffee mug, and wiggled a little to settle herself. 'All right, tell me what's going on.'

Mary set her mug on the table, pulled out the striped green and yellow Windsor style chair that was opposite Ruthie, and waited until Millie had crawled under it.

'I don't know where to start. It's all so awful.'

Ruthie nodded, setting the yellow curls that always circled her head bobbing. 'Start with what happened in the bank. All I know is that some idiot dressed as a clown tried to rob it and, in the process, he managed to shoot Victoria dead and wounded Dan. I know you were there, so what happened? Do they know any more about who this guy is and how is Dan?'

Mary moved her foot so Millie had more room and stared into her coffee. How much should she tell Ruthie? It wasn't as if she had privileged information, and it certainly wasn't as if rumors weren't already spreading faster than a California wildfire. Ruthie might be able to help. So, with some careful editing, she told her about the wedding and the dresses and they thought the clown costume had been made by Victoria. 'We think that's why he shot her. She recognized the costume and maybe the man wearing it. Now, if we can just find out who she made the costume for . . .'

'You can figure out who the idiot was who killed her.' Ruthie paused and took a large swallow of her by-now lukewarm coffee. 'Did she leave any records of any kind? Anything that would identify who the clown suit was made for?'

'She did, but she had a sort of code. The only thing we

have been able to identify is Pamela's wedding dress and Krissie's bridesmaid dress. Pat Bennington and I were able to take the girls over to the shop and they confirmed them.' Mary grinned. 'Good thing we were able to. Pamela was certain she would have to walk down the aisle in her jeans.'

Ruthie laughed but immediately the smile faded. 'How were you able to identify them, other than the girls telling you?'

Mary hesitated again, but Ruthie wasn't a gossip. She overheard a lot of conversations in her busy restaurant. Some of them contained information those involved wouldn't want made public. Ruthie never did. She wouldn't this time, either, if Mary asked her not to.

'This is confidential.' She watched Ruthie's face. 'Dan is still trying to work this out and right now, we're guessing.'

The 'we' didn't go over Ruthie's head. She was aware Mary had been more than helpful in solving other crimes in their little town, and she understood the relationship Mary had with her nephew-in-law. She nodded she understood.

'Victoria labeled everything with initials. No full names. We need to find out who owns those costume. Did anyone in a clown costume come in here on Halloween that you remember?'

Ruthie shook her head, letting her curls bob. 'We had a lot of people in here that day, but lots were picking up lunch for the volunteers. I don't remember a clown. Bo Peep, I remember. Alice Ferguson doesn't look good in ruffles.'

Mary had to smile. Ruthie was right, but she didn't comment. 'What else do you remember about that day?'

Ruthie paused and seemed to be searching her memory. 'I remember it was pretty darn busy. There were a lot of people in the park setting up and a lot of guys working on that stupid maze, a couple of them came in for sandwiches and water. Just about cleaned me out of bottled water. No clowns, though.'

'Who was working for you that day? Do you remember?'

'Of course I do. Why?'

Mary sighed. 'Just trust me on this. And remember, we're searching for information, not accusing anyone of anything. At least not yet. Was Troy Turnbull working for you?'

Ruthie let out a little gasp. 'Troy? You suspect Troy?'

'No. Remember what I said. We're going to eliminate more people than we will have as suspects. I'd like to eliminate him so, was he working for you?'

Ruthie shook her head. 'No. He quit some time ago. Went to work for Safe Auto Garage. They pay him more and he has more hours than I could give him. But he was a good worker. A little volatile, but he'll do better with cars. They won't frustrate him as much as people evidently do.' She pushed her mug aside and leaned forward on the table. 'Mary, that kid is no murderer. He's married and is going to be a father. He wouldn't do something like that.'

Mary wasn't convinced. Troy needed money. He wouldn't be the first to try something stupid and have it end in disaster. However, she remembered what Tammy said. The robber was cool and collected. Troy was anything but. Ruthie knew him a lot better than she did, so if she also trusted him, she'd withhold judgment. That didn't mean she wouldn't try to find out more about him.

'How long did he work for you?'

Ruthie furrowed her brow. 'A couple of years, at least. Started part-time bussing tables. Moved up to helping in the kitchen. He would have made a good cook, but he got frustrated easily. He likes to do things with his hands and he knows about cars. He also knows some construction. He's going to help me with the remodel I'm planning.'

Mary had been about to stand. It was four thirty and Janelle would be coming soon, but that sat her back in her chair. 'What remodel?'

Ruthie grinned. 'I've decided it's time to get rid of those cute little wood chickens and the ruffled curtains and stuff. Cute pictures of small children, ribbons and bows on everything, and pastel colors. I'm so sick of pale pink and blue I could puke. So, I'm going technicolor.'

Stunned, Mary could do nothing but stare, first at Ruthie then at the bright red table they sat at and the vividly colored chairs. Was this the way Ruthie was going? She wasn't too fond of the chickens herself, but she was used to them. They'd been around for years. So had the fake flowers on every table and the pots on each side of the cash register counter. Maybe it was time for a facelift, but this one sounded severe. Before she could ask Ruthie any more questions, she got more information, equally stunning.

'I thought I'd get a cat. One who'd like to live in the storage room and could sleep in the window sometimes. Remember that trip I took to France last year? Well, they had cats every-where – dogs too. I've looked up the health laws and, while I can't have an animal in the kitchen or the dining room, I can in the storage area, and I think I can in the window if I can close that off. So, if you happen to hear of anyone . . .'

Thoughts of the cat pushed aside all thoughts of murder. 'I have just the one.'

Surprise showed clearly on Ruthie's face. 'How does Millie feel about that?'

'She hasn't had time to find out.'

'What's the cat like?'

'Big, beat up, but friendly. I think. He's in my spare room right now. He was Victoria's and now that she's gone, I need to find him a home. He's used to being around a shop and people. Come meet him any time you want.'

A thoughtful look passed over Ruthie's face. 'Maybe tomorrow?'

Mary beamed. 'I'll call you. And pay you for this then.' She glanced at her watch. 'We have to go. Janelle Tucker is coming over around five and I need to be there.'

'Janelle Tucker? What's she coming over for?'

Mary detected a little surprise in Ruthie's voice. 'Do you know her?'

'I knew her mother. A very difficult woman. I haven't seen Janelle since she was a little girl, but she idolized her mother. In Janelle's eyes, her mother could do no wrong. Her sister wasn't like that at all. But then, she was about ten years older than Janelle. I can't remember the sister's name, but I think she got married before the father died and all that fuss occurred. I heard Janelle was back in town, but why she came back here, with all the memories she must have, I don't know. I sure never would have dreamed she'd end up as a policeman. Woman.'

Again, Mary glanced at her watch. 'Well, she seems nice

enough, and Dan says so far she's worked out fine. I'm going to try to see if I can get her to loan Zoe, her service dog, to Robbie during the day. I'll see you tomorrow?'

'A service dog? Why does she need a service dog?'

'The dog was her mother's. For some reason, she held onto her. The dog looks bored to death, and I thought this might be good for both the dog and Robbie and solve a problem for Janelle.'

Ruthie nodded. 'I'll call you.' She headed back toward the kitchen, Mary picked up the box containing her dinner and she and Millie headed for their car.

EIGHTEEN

Mary drove into her garage and hit the button to lower the door. She waited for it to hit the concrete before opening the car door, picking up the white box containing her dinner, and letting Millie out.

She walked into the kitchen, leaving Millie to explore the backyard. Janelle should be along soon. Should she offer her a glass of wine? It was a little early, but it also was a little chilly for iced tea or lemonade. Coffee? She'd fill the coffee maker, and if she didn't use it, it would be ready for breakfast. She was filling the carafe with water when she heard the yowl and something hit the bedroom door with a thud. The cat wanted out.

Reluctantly she approached the door, glancing behind to make sure Millie wasn't in yet. She wasn't. She stood in front of the door, wondering what to do. What if Millie attacked the cat? What if the cat attacked Millie? The cat yowled again, and the door shook. Mary sighed and opened it. The cat stalked out on stiff legs, his tail majestically straight up. He turned and examined Mary for a moment then started to move slowly through the living room toward the kitchen. He appeared to be on high alert. Fight or flight mode? She was pretty sure with this cat it wouldn't be flight. All she could do was hope

Millie stayed outside until the cat had finished his exploring and Janelle would be late. Only Millie came in and Janelle wasn't. The doorbell rang, and Millie appeared at the kitchen doorway at the same time. The cat caught sight of Millie and the hair on his back immediately stood up straight and his back curled like a Halloween cat, which seemed appropriate but scary.

Mary wasn't sure what to do. Answer the door or stay and protect Millie? She hollered out, 'Just a minute,' and, telling Millie to stay, edged her way around the cat toward the door.

Janelle stood in the doorway, Zoe by her side. 'I hope you don't mind I brought Zoe, but I hated to leave her at home. She gets depressed.'

Mary didn't mind in the least, but this wasn't a good time for an extra dog. At least Zoe was on a leash. 'Come in but keep ahold of her. We have a visiting cat, and I'm not sure how he feels about dogs.' She swung the door wide, waited until Janelle and Zoe were barely across the threshold, and closed it shut with a decided thump. She turned to face Janelle, who studied her curiously. 'They're in here.'

Mary hurried into the dining room, intent on rescuing Millie from what she was certain would be a horrible death by talons, but she and the cat were standing about a yard apart, studying each other. The cat no longer had an arched back or bristled hair and the soft growl Millie had uttered earlier had faded. Each eyed the other with suspicion, but battle lines weren't drawn. Mary heaved a huge sigh of relief and turned to Janelle and Zoe. Now if Zoe would only restrain herself . . . Zoe did. She looked at the cat then up at Janelle.

'Leave it,' Janelle commanded, motioning toward the cat.

Zoe immediately sat down and looked away from the cat. She even ignored Millie.

'My, she is so well behaved. I've never seen a dog obey like that.'

Mary thought about how she disciplined Millie. Maybe that wasn't the right word. Millie was rarely not at Mary's side and she was easy to take places because she was obedient. Most of the time. But Mary knew if she said to leave something Millie wanted to investigate, they would discuss it. Mary would eventually win, but not before Millie tried to convince her otherwise. Zoe had obeyed instantly. She still hadn't looked at the cat, who wasn't nearly as well behaved. He started to move again. Slowly, warily, his gaze never entirely off either dogs or humans, he made his way around the dining room table, hesitated as if he couldn't make up his mind which way to go next, then he turned his back on the kitchen and decided to explore the living room. They all watched as he went from the sofa to sniff the legs of the coffee table. Then he crossed the room, glanced at the fireplace, jumped up on the table that sat beside Mary's favorite reading chair, wound his way around the lamp, stepped over the library book, avoided the family pictures, and landed in the middle of the chair. He kneaded the seat a little, turned around in several circles, settled down on the chair pillow, and closed his eyes.

'Ruthie better take that animal and she better take him tomorrow.' Mary stared at the napping cat. 'Of all the nerve.'

She could almost hear Janelle trying not to laugh. 'Oreo. He seems to have made himself right at home.'

Surprised, Mary turned toward Janelle. 'You know this cat?'

Janelle shook her head. 'No, never saw him before. It's just that he looks like an Oreo, don't you think?

Mary stared at the cat, who opened one eye, looked at her, and closed it again. He didn't look like a cookie to her.

'Who does he belong to?' Janelle asked. 'It must be a close friend.'

'He belonged to that woman who got killed in the bank robbery the other day. Victoria. The dressmaker.'

'Oh.' The word seemed to come out on a soft breath. 'Yes. The robbery. That's all they're talking about at the station. Poor woman.'

Mary thought she was going to say more but Janelle started to sneeze. She dug a tissue out of her jacket pocket, wiped her nose and eyes, and stuffed it back. 'Sorry. Cats always spark my allergies. I've never had allergies like this, though. The guys at the station laughed, said wait until spring and the almond trees bloom. I'm not looking forward to that.' She sniffed a little and resettled her tinted glasses. 'You said you wanted to talk to me about Zoe?'

'Yes. I have an idea. Let's go in the kitchen,' Mary said. 'The dogs can go outside to play, and we can have a little something while we talk. Do you like wine? I have a nice Chardonnay from one of our local wineries and wondered if . . .'

Janelle's enthusiastic nod told Mary she wouldn't need to make the coffee until morning. Janelle followed her into the kitchen and set her purse on the old table under the window that faced the backyard.

'We can keep an eye on them while we talk.' Mary held the back door open for the dogs.

Millie bounded out, but Zoe held back, looking at Janelle as if for guidance or permission. She unsnapped her leash and the dog raced down the stairs after Millie.

Janelle watched them for a moment. They had found a tug of war toy on the lawn and Zoe was pulling Millie all over, both growling and making all kinds of playing dog noises.

'I haven't seen her play like that in a long time,' Janelle said softly. She accepted the glass Mary offered her and pulled out the chair and sat, still watching the dogs.

Mary pulled out the chair opposite and settled in it. She watched the dogs for a minute as well, smiling at the fun they were having. 'Millie will sleep well tonight.' She took her first sip of wine.

'This is good for Zoe.' Janelle took a sip from her glass. She looked over the rim of it at Mary and smiled. 'Poor dog. I think she's bored and she's getting anxious. She's lost her job.'

'She was your mother's service dog, isn't that what you said?'

Janelle nodded. 'Mom had a stroke a little over a year ago. We applied for a service dog and got Zoe. The dog was great, but Mom had a hard time letting the dog help. She never really liked dogs much, and I don't think she trusted her.' She sighed, raised her glass as if to take a sip, then put it down. 'Then about six months ago she had another stroke. This time we didn't get her to the hospital in time.'

Sadness flooded her face. Janelle blinked a couple of times, then cast her eyes down, fixing on her wine. The slight tint still evident on her glasses effectively hid any expression in them.

'I'm so sorry,' Mary murmured. 'This must be hard for you, coming back here with all the memories of the hard times your family had.'

'Actually,' Janelle looked up from her glass, glanced at Mary, then stared out the window at the dogs. 'I think coming back here will put some of those memories to rest. I was only ten when we left. My sister was the one who had to deal with everything. Mother wasn't capable of dealing with anything. Margot told me to take care of her, and I did. Margot took care of the money, what was left of it, getting us moved, setting us up in a new life, and she moved on. I liked it here, liked school here, and when I saw the advertisement for the job, one I knew how to do well, I thought it was a good time to see if what I remember is real, if the memories I have of living here are mine.' Abruptly, she changed the subject. 'I love the little house I'm renting. The owners did a great job updating it. It's still a twenties house, but with all the amenities we expect today. Even Wi-Fi. I couldn't live there, or work there, if that wasn't true.'

'Do you work from home? I didn't know you could.' Mary was a little surprised. She didn't know what kind of work a policeman could do at home.

'I'll be able to do reports and that kind of thing from home part of the time, but most of my time will be spent in the car. I'd love to take Zoe with me, but I don't think that's going to be possible. She's a service dog, not a trained police dog, but she needs a job.' Her face hardened as she watched the two dogs. They had finished their game of keep away and were lying side by side under the old oak tree that shaded much of Mary's backyard.

'I've got an idea,' Mary said, 'but I need to ask you a few questions before I tell it to you. Is that all right?'

Janelle turned to study Mary. She looked interested but also a little suspicious, as if the idea of answering questions wasn't a pleasing prospect.

'What kind of questions?' Janelle wasn't smiling as she took another sip of her wine.

'About the dog. What she's been trained to do.' *Does Janelle think I'm trying to pry into her private life? Why would she think that?*

'What about the dog?'

'You said your mother had a stroke. What was the dog supposed to do for her?'

Janelle said nothing for a minute. She looked out the window at the dogs, glanced at Mary, then sighed and started to run her fingers up and down the stem of her wineglass. 'Simple things. She'd pick up things my mother dropped and bring them to her or bring her things she was asked to. She could carry her glasses case, for instance, when my mother had left it on a table where she couldn't reach it. She could open the refrigerator door or the screen door so mother could get through in her wheelchair. She could turn lights on and off and pull-down bed covers. Mother could even get her to pull the chair if she felt too weak. Things like that.' She paused, thinking, then gave a little laugh. 'They told us Mother could read to the dog out loud. Evidently, it helps with people who have speech problems, like kids with MS, or older people with a stroke that leaves their speech impaired. Gives the speaker confidence. Often people with speech problems don't talk because they have a hard time forming their words. Mother wouldn't do it.' The sigh she heaved this time was longer and somehow bitter. 'There were a lot of things Mother wouldn't do. She made me do them instead.' Her head came up and she looked at Mary directly, seemingly startled at what she had said. 'I didn't mean she wasn't a wonderful woman. She was. I couldn't have asked for a better mother. But, after everything that happened here, father dying, the troubles with money, she was never the same. She brooded.' She looked down again, into her glass sitting almost full in front of her. 'I did as much for her as I could.' She looked up. 'Have I answered your questions about Zoe?'

Mary nodded and smiled. 'I think I have the perfect solution for Zoe. We have a little boy in town, he's not quite eight, with cerebral palsy. He could use a service dog, and the reading aloud thing is particularly important. Robbie needs confidence in his ability to speak. Reading to Zoe would be a great help.

I thought she could spend the day with him, and you could pick her up on your way home. That way she could help Robbie's mother, who has a smaller child to care for as well, but you'd have her back with you when you're at home. Do you think that could work?'

That Janelle was surprised by the idea was an understatement. A series of emotions seemed to pass over her face before she said anything and then she didn't seem sure. 'What you're saying is I'd sort of lend them Zoe for the day? I'm not sure how that would work out. These dogs need to feel they're never off-duty, that they're responsible for their person. It might confuse the dog, and it might confuse the child as well. I don't know. It would solve the problem of her being alone all day, but I'm not sure.'

'Why don't you think about it?' Mary pushed back her chair and walked to the back door at the sound of a sharp bark. 'Millie wants in and I suppose Zoe does as well.'

She turned to Janelle as both dogs bounded into the kitchen. 'We could try it for a day or so and see how it works out. I don't want the child disappointed, either, but he needs help and so does his mother. So, I thought we might take Zoe over tomorrow and introduce her to Robbie and see how they get along.'

That Janelle was uneasy with the idea was visible, but what to do with the dog was still a problem. Finally, after taking another large swallow of her wine, she stood and nodded. 'I'm on duty first thing in the morning. Can I drop Zoe off here? You can take her over and see how it goes. I guess it's better than leaving her in the house all day by herself.'

Mary knew she was beaming but didn't care. She was sure this was going to work out. 'What time will you leave?'

'About eight. Is that too early?'

'Not at all,' Mary said. 'Not at all.'

Janelle placed her half-full glass on the drain board and snapped the leash back on Zoe's collar. 'We'd better be going. Thanks for the wine and the idea. We'll see you tomorrow.'

Mary and Millie followed them to the front door and watched as they walked down the street. Millie seemed reluctant to have Zoe leave, but Mary decided she wasn't reluctant to see

Janelle go. She seemed nice enough, friendly even, but there seemed to be a thin veneer over what she really felt. Unhappiness lay close to the surface. But then, the woman had just lost her mother, who had evidently meant a great deal to her. The death of someone close to you meant you had to reshape your life, start again. Not an easy thing to do.

Mary thought about Samuel's death and how hard it had been for her to accept it and to reshape her life. 'We'll have to give her time, Millie. It's only been six months and she's not only lost her mother but moved to a strange town and taken a new job. That's a lot to adjust to.'

Millie gave a sharp bark that Mary thought had more to do with her empty dinner dish than Janelle's adjustment to life in Santa Louisa.

She filled Millie's dish on auto pilot, setting it on her dish mat and then reaching for the phone. If she was going to set up Robbie with a dog, she'd better run the idea by his mother first.

NINETEEN

Robbie's mother, Nancy, was thrilled. At least, at first. 'The dog would go home every night? I'm not sure how Robbie would feel about that. I'm afraid he'd get attached to it and then something would happen. Janelle would move, or she'd think of a way to keep the dog with her every day, and Robbie would be devastated. I don't know, Mary. Robbie's life is hard enough. I don't want to set him up for a disappointment.'

Mary thought Nancy had a point, but it seemed a good way to find out if a service dog could help him. 'Why don't we introduce them, see if they like each other, and if they do, then let's call the organization where Janelle's mother got the dog and ask them if this is a good idea. Robbie may even qualify for a dog of his own.'

There was a pause before Nancy answered. Mary could feel

her uncertainty over the phone and she waited. 'I'll talk it over with Mike, see what he says. If he thinks it's all right, we'll give it a try.'

Mary smiled as she hung up the phone. The dog needed a job and Robbie needed help. If nothing more happened than the child read aloud to the dog, that was something. At least she thought it was. She glanced at the clock. Time for the evening news. She would have her quiche and a glass of wine while she watched it, but somehow it didn't hold her attention. It felt strange sitting on the couch, not in her usual large chair. The cat sill claimed it, and she wasn't sure how to dislodge it. She turned off the TV, scowled at the cat, who ignored her, carried her empty plate into the kitchen, and stared out the window. She thought about the last few days, the Halloween celebration in the park and all the volunteers, the robbery and the tragedy it had turned into. Dan. At least, he was going to be all right. She trembled a little as she thought of what might have happened. But it hadn't. Something terrible could have happened to her and Millie, but it didn't. She wondered why. That awful man, that clown, had most certainly aimed his gun at them. Why hadn't he shot them? Because he didn't think she recognized him? Because he was afraid he wouldn't get away? He had, though. He ran down the side street and disappeared. How had he done that? Gary hadn't been that far behind him. There had been two cars leaving the parking lot, going out the back way. Would it be helpful to try to find the drivers and ask if they'd seen anything? No. Gary had already said he couldn't flag them down and didn't know who the drivers were, but he could see enough to know neither was wearing a clown mask. Could he have hidden in another car? That was possible. If he ducked down behind the seat . . .? She'd ask Gary if he'd looked in any parked cars. Even if they figured out where he'd gone, that didn't tell them who he was. If they could just find out who Victoria had made clown costumes for . . . Her copies of Victoria's ledger sheets were on her desk. She'd get them and take another look. Maybe something would come to her.

The cat and Millie followed her into the guest bedroom that doubled as an office. The cat sat in front of his mostly empty food dish and meowed. Loudly. Insistently. His water dish was also empty.

'At least you got out of my chair,' Mary told him. 'Hang on a minute. I'll get you taken care of.'

She put the pages on the dining room table before she filled the cat's dishes. She watched him a minute then motioned to Millie. They snuck out of the room and carefully closed the door.

'There. We can have our chair back.' But it wasn't her big chair she wanted right then. She spread the ledger sheets out on the table and went through them. She was sure they had been right. The columns were neatly drawn, but the entries weren't always completely legible. The large C that they thought stood for clown costume was clear, but the notation opposite Pamela's wedding dress wasn't. It said WD, but the ink was smeared. The entry under it was easier to read but wouldn't have made sense if it hadn't been opposite KK. Krissie. Pamela's only bridesmaid. Both dresses were marked PIF. That could mean only one thing. BD had to stand for bridesmaid dress, but what was the G for? Green? Yes, Krissie's dress was a lovely shade of soft green. Only, what did V mean? The kind of material or something else? Veil? Not for the first time, she wished Victoria had kept more extensive records instead of these cryptic initials. She followed her finger down the column. If she could figure out who some of these other people were, maybe she could also figure out who had ordered a clown costume.

The next set of initials had a small sketch instead of initials describing the garment. It looked like a child's dress with puffy sleeves and a large bow on the back. Mary could just make out the initials FG and another G. Flower girl and the dress would be green as well? The owner's initials she thought she recognized. Rowena White, Luke's niece. She'd heard she was to be the flower girl. Had Victoria made all the bridal party dresses? Evidently. How had they not sent them home with Pamela when she and Krissie picked up their dresses? No matter. She'd make sure they got them.

Next one down was Luke's mother's initials.

That proved it. Only, where did she go from here? There

were three pages of people who wanted garments made and that was just in the last couple of months. She looked them over again, trying to figure out the dates. It appeared it signified the date the order was ready.

So. There were four large Cs. When had they been delivered? All done at least a week ago. All different initials for the owners but not for the garments. All were marked PIF and all had a check mark by them. Did that mean they were all picked up? She shook her head. She had no idea how to identify the owners of the costumes. MG, KN, TT, and PC. Did she know anyone with those initials? She did, but that didn't get her any further. The people that immediately came to mind weren't the kind of men who would walk into a bank and shoot someone. At least she didn't think so. It seemed to her there wasn't enough information in this little notebook for her to go on but for Victoria either. Where were the measurements? All dressmakers took measurements. How about addresses and phone numbers? Shouldn't the dates for fittings be entered someplace? If Victoria had all that information, where was it? She closed her eyes, trying to see the room she and Pat had explored. What had they missed? The computer. There was a laptop on the little desk where she had found the notebook. That had to be where Victoria had all the detailed information.

Why hadn't she thought of it while they were there? The cat, of course. She'd been distracted by him and by the wedding dresses. Then, when she found the notebook she forgot all about the computer. She'd thought they'd found what they needed. In a way, they had. Only, it was only part of it. Even if she could go back and get the computer, she wouldn't know what to do with it. It was probably password protected and she had no idea how one got into someone else's computer records. But they might be important. If she was right, those records could give them the names they needed. She'd ask Dan. Surely someone at the police station knew how to break into someone's computer. In the meantime, what should she do? She had no idea how long it would take to get into that computer.

She was fresh out of ideas. No, she wasn't. Joy. She had

been in the park all day and had taken over for Mary that
night. She must have talked to a lot of people, seen a lot of
costumes. Maybe she'd seen and recognized someone dressed
as a clown, one with balloons on his costume. It wasn't much,
but it was a start. She'd talk to Joy in the morning. Feeling
more optimistic, she finished the last of her quiche, put
the plate in the dishwasher, and, with Millie sitting close beside
her in their now-free large chair, turned on *Masterpiece
Mystery*.

TWENTY

J oy wasn't home. Mary left a message, wondering where
she could be at eight thirty in the morning, but it didn't
matter. Joy would call her back when she could, and, in
the meantime, she was going to introduce Zoe to Robbie. His
parents had called back last night. They were willing to give
it a try. They told Robbie a dog was coming to visit but hadn't
mentioned that the dog might come every day. They'd take it
one day at a time, at least for now. Mary was finishing her
coffee, standing by the kitchen sink, when the doorbell rang.
Millie, of course, was there first, barking a warning this was
private property, then, in delight, when she saw who stood
there.

'You sound a lot fiercer than you are.' Janelle and Zoe
entered. She was dressed in her police uniform, complete with
the heavy belt hung with equipment Mary could only guess
at. She did know the thing hanging on Janelle's hip was a gun,
and the long wand was what they used to call a billy club.
Other than that, it just looked heavy. So did the jacket Janelle
wore. Fall was finally here, and winter wasn't far behind. Mary
wondered if she'd still need her tinted glasses when the sky
was overcast and her allergies were cleared up. She had
them on today, but the sun was bright, even if the day wasn't
especially warm.

Janelle handed Mary Zoe's leash with obvious reluctance.

'I hope this works out. I know my mother wouldn't approve of this, but toward the end she didn't approve of a lot of things. Do you have my cell phone number?'

'No.' Mary looked around. The cat was in her office, and she wasn't sure she wanted to let it out, but it couldn't stay in there forever.

She opened the door and the cat walked out, inspected them all, especially the dogs, then walked directly to Mary's chair and, graceful as a ballerina, leapt into it. He sat facing them, as if daring anyone to unseat him. Mary sighed and went in search of a pad and pen. Janelle stood in front of the chair, having what looked like a staring contest with the cat. The cat seemed to be winning.

'All right,' she told Janelle. 'What is it?' She wrote it down and nodded. 'I don't think we'll need to get in touch with you, but just in case. By the way, can you tell me where your mother got the dog? I believe there are several organizations and Robbie's parents thought they'd like to talk to the people there, get some idea of how to handle the dog, what commands Robbie should use, what to expect, that kind of thing. I think that seems a good idea, don't you?'

A startled expression passed over Janelle's face, but as quickly as it had come, it disappeared. 'If the boy likes the dog, it might be better if I spend some time with him tonight, teaching him what he needs to know. It's not hard. He'll pick it up fast. Why don't you text me their phone number and I'll call them later this morning. Right now, I have to go or I'll be late.'

Surprised, Mary had no choice but to agree. 'I'll tell them.' She barely got the words out of her mouth before Janelle was out the door. Wondering what she was going to be late for, Mary went back into the kitchen to get Millie's leash and her purse. She wondered if Janelle realized Robbie was the son of Mike Gallagher, one of the other officers on Santa Louisa's small police force. Oh, well, it didn't matter. What did was getting Zoe over to Robbie Gallagher's. She wanted to have some time with them to see for herself how this was going to work out. She also wanted to talk to Nancy. About Robbie, yes, but also about Troy Turnbull. If she remembered right,

Troy's wife was a close friend of Nancy's. Both girls were in their late twenties and had gone to high school together. Nancy was bound to have an opinion about Troy, and maybe some actual information. She might feel like talking over a cup of coffee while they watched Robbie and Zoe get to know each other. She felt more and more she needed as much information as she could get about Troy.

It took no encouragement at all to get the dogs out the back door and into the car. In a matter of moments, they were on their way.

TWENTY-ONE

Zoe seemed a little hesitant as they stood on the porch, waiting for the door to open. Millie didn't. She had been here before, several times, and she liked visiting Robbie. Or, maybe it was because Robbie often had crumbs on his shirt front. Millie was fond of crumbs, and Robbie was fond of having her sit on his lap. Mary hoped he would be as fond of Zoe.

Nancy smiled as she opened the door. 'Robbie's been waiting since dawn. A new dog visitor is a big thing.' She stepped onto the porch and half closed the door. 'Mike and I searched on the internet last night. Service dogs like this one can help a boy like Robbie go to school. He's doing find here, and I like homeschooling him, but he needs friends. He needs to try to do some of the activities the other kids do. If a dog can help him do that . . .' Tears appeared. She wiped them off with a vicious gesture. One escaped and ran down the side of her nose. She ignored it.

So did Mary. 'Let's go in and see if they like each other.'

Millie preceded the rest of them into the house, stub of a tail straight up, certain of her welcome. Mary and Nancy followed more slowly, Zoe by Mary's side, looking around, seemingly assessing where she was. Until they reached the living room. The dog stopped and stared at Robbie in his wheelchair. Mary stopped as well. What was the dog doing? Every muscle in her body seemed to have gone on alert. She glanced at Mary then once again at the boy. Millie was beside his chair, waiting to say hello, but Robbie seemed as intent on Zoe as she was on him.

'Are you Zoe?' he finally said.

The dog's tail began to wag, slowly, then a little harder, and she took a step forward. Again, she looked up at Mary.

'Are you waiting for permission?' she asked the dog. 'Go, go to him.' Mary pointed toward Robbie and dropped Zoe's leash. The dog started toward the boy, moving slowly, head slightly down.

'Dear God in heaven, have I done the right thing?'

Mary couldn't tell from Zoe's body position if she was in attack mode or just what she was going to do. Her tail had stopped wagging and her gait toward the chair was slow and deliberate. Surely she wouldn't . . . she didn't. She stopped in front of the chair, sniffed Robbie's legs gently, moved closer, and nudged his hand, then sat and put one front paw in his lap. She didn't move when he threw himself forward and enveloped her in a huge hug.

Mary heaved a sigh of relief.

Nancy, still behind her, gasped. 'Oh, he's leaning forward too far. He's going to fall out.'

She started forward, intent on catching her son, but Zoe was way ahead of her. The dog was on her feet, leaning in on Robbie, carefully and slowly letting him hold onto her for balance, almost pushing him back in his chair.

'I've never seen a dog do that,' breathed Nancy. 'She kept him from falling.'

Mary hadn't either. She hadn't known it was possible. What else could the dog do? Evidently, a lot. Zoe was as close to the chair as she could get, looking into Robbie's eyes. If it was possible for a dog to smile, this one was doing it.

'I like Zoe.' Robbie still hung onto the dog.

'She likes you, too.' Mary could feel her eyes mist but was determined to act as if this was an every day visit. 'Look, Millie came to visit you as well. Say hello to Robbie, Millie.'

Millie, who had been watching the interchange between

Robbie and Zoe with apparent interest, inched closer to the wheelchair and licked Robbie's fingers. Zoe carefully put herself between Millie and the boy, not growling, not threatening, just between them, and she sat down.

'Mike and I read about this last night. The dogs go on duty and don't go off. Zoe seems to have decided Robbie is hers to take care of. Amazing.'

There was awe in Nancy's voice mixed with what Mary thought was happiness and hope. Mary wished she shared the hope. Janelle was only lending them the dog, so they couldn't get too attached. Only Robbie seemed to already have, so did Nancy, and they had only just met Zoe. Had she made a terrible mistake? She didn't think so. If Zoe worked out, they could apply for a dog of their own. If money was a factor, she'd make sure they got it. In the meantime . . . 'Has Robbie had breakfast? We could go into the kitchen and chat a bit while he eats.'

'Can Zoe have some too?' Robbie had a sippy cup in a cup holder on his wheelchair, and he tried to pick it up. 'She can have some toast. Millie, too.' The cup almost made it to his mouth but the excitement of having the dog seemed to exaggerate his palsy. His hand started to shake, and the cup went flying. Zoe didn't miss a beat. She was on her feet, dragging her leash behind her, and on top of the cup. She picked it up gently, turned, and went back to Robbie. The dog held onto the cup while placing it in his hand, and only let go when she knew he had it. Mary thought Nancy was going to break out into tears any minute. She wasn't so sure she wasn't as well. Time for a distraction.

'I don't suppose you have any coffee left?' She turned to face Nancy, who picked up on the cue.

'I just made a fresh pot. Why don't we all go in the kitchen? Robbie, take Zoe and show her where the water dish is, can you do that?'

'Sure.' He put his chair in motion. Zoe stayed glued to his side.

Millie watched this with what looked like confusion, but she followed Mary and crawled under the table when Mary pulled out a chair.

They talked about Robbie and the dog for a few minutes while they sipped their coffee. Nancy told Mary what they'd learned about service dogs on the internet and how she hoped they wouldn't confuse the dog. 'Did Janelle give you the name of the organization Zoe came from?'

Mary shook her head. 'She said she'd help you with some of the basic stuff when she picks Zoe up tonight.'

'Oh.' Nancy looked puzzled but didn't say any more. They watched the boy and the dog for a few more minutes.

Finally, Mary said, 'I've been meaning to ask you, how is your friend, Ashley? Isn't she about ready to have that baby?'

'Ashley Turnbull? She's fine. She's due next month. Why?'

A good question and one Mary wasn't sure how to answer. She certainly couldn't explain to Nancy about the initials and Victoria's logbook, but maybe she could ask about a costume. 'Oh, I've been thinking about them. I was in the Yum Yum and Ruthie said Troy had a new job. I hope it works out for him. Ashley was teaching school, wasn't she? Will she go back after the baby is born?'

'She may have to. They want to buy a house but can't on what Troy makes. Mike doesn't make that much, either, but we got lucky. His grandmother left him some money, and we used it to buy this place. I don't know what we would have done otherwise. He's fixed it so Robbie can get around fine in his chair. We couldn't have done that in a rental.' Worry lines briefly crossed her face. 'It still isn't easy. I had to quit work when Robbie was born, then we had Cloe . . . sometimes it's a struggle to make the payment, but it's worth giving up other things to have this house, in this neighborhood. It's a wonderful place for the kids to grow up.'

'He's done a great job.' Mary looked around the neat, clean kitchen. There was a high chair without a tray pushed in at the opposite end of the table, and one end had a lowered table attachment a wheelchair could fit under. The door to the hallway had been widened and she could see a small ramp built over the sill to the door leading outside. Mike had thought of everything. 'Was Robbie able to make it to the park for Halloween? Did he have a costume?'

'He sure did. He went as a clown. So did Mike.'

Mary almost choked on her coffee. Initials flashed through her mind. MG was one set. No. It wasn't possible. Mike wasn't a candidate even for suspicion. He was a great father and, from what Dan said, an exceptional police officer, one he was eyeing for promotion. Mike would never dream of doing such a thing. But they needed money. Nancy had as much as said so.

'Did you make their costumes?'

Nancy laughed. 'I made Robbie's, he's not particular, but Mike had Victoria make his. She wasn't really that expensive and he claimed he'd wear it every Halloween so we could justify the expense. He doesn't very often spend money on himself, so I didn't say anything. Cloe wore an old bunny costume of Robbie's. Next year, when she's three, I want to get her a Disney princess costume.'

'I'm sure she'll love that.' Mary set down her coffee cup, wondering what to say next. Somehow, asking if Nancy knew what Troy wore for Halloween seemed out of the question. She needed to go. She needed to think. She needed to talk to Dan. And, she smiled as the idea came to her, she needed to get her oil changed. It was just possible that Eduardo, who owned Safe Auto, would know if Troy had a clown costume. The worst that could happen is she got an oil change a little early. She pushed back her chair. Millie crawled out from under the table and Robbie tore his attention away from Zoe to smile at Mary. She smiled back and turned to Nancy.

'Do you have Janelle's cell number? No? I'll leave it with you. If you need some help, with commands or anything, just give her a call.'

'I think we have the basics down pretty good.' Nancy pushed back her own chair. 'I can't thank you enough for arranging this.'

Mary looked at Robbie, who had one hand resting on Zoe's head. That hand was still, no sign of the palsy that often afflicted him. Maybe this would work out.

'I hope you have a successful day.' Privately, Mary was shook to her core. She needed to think. 'Let me know about tomorrow morning, what you and Janelle decide. I don't know her schedule, but maybe she can drop Zoe off on her way into the station.' She hesitated, gave Nancy a hug, something that seemed to catch Nancy off guard.

Mary thought she was going to say something but a dark-haired, blue-eyed, almost-three-year-old walked into the room, holding a stuffed animal who she seemed to be talking to. She stopped, looked at Mary, then Millie, and caught sight of Zoe. 'Puppies. Two puppies.'

Mary turned to Nancy. 'She's a smart one. You've been working with her a lot?'

'It's easy. She picks things up quickly. We're going to try to enroll her in preschool next year. If Robbie can go to school and Cloe is in preschool, I may be able to go back to work at least part-time. That would help a lot.'

Mary nodded. She and Millie started toward the front door. She looked back at Robbie, Zoe tight by his side, and felt herself shudder. The joy on that child's face. She fervently hoped nothing happened to shatter it.

TWENTY-TWO

D an was asleep. She knew that because the nurse who'd struggled to take Dan's vital signs yesterday stood in the doorway barring Sean Ryan from entering.

'I don't care who you are. He overdid it yesterday and paid for it by being in pain all last night. The doctor upped his pain medication and added something so he could sleep, and that's what he's going to do. Sleep. You can talk to him maybe tomorrow, but, for now, he's off limits.'

Mary could tell by the redness taking over Detective Ryan's ears he was furious. Sean Ryan wasn't used to not getting his way.

'Is he all right?'

Ryan wheeled around at the sound of her voice. Mary ignored him.

So did the nurse. 'He moved that arm too much yesterday. I knew we should have kept it in that sling a little longer, but that man insisted he was doing fine.' She smiled slightly and shook her head. 'He can charm the birds right out of the trees when he puts his mind to it, but then the next moment, he can be a royal pain in the you know where.' She glared at Ryan. 'I've got him back in the sling so the arm can't move, and he's going to stay that way.' She turned to Mary. 'He should be awake this afternoon, when the meds wear off. Mrs Dunham is coming back then. You want her to call you?'

Mary shook her head. 'I'll give her a call later. I just stopped by to see how he was doing. I'll be back tomorrow.' She nodded at Ryan and started back down the hall, but Ryan took hold of her arm.

'I need to talk to you.'

She stared at him then at his hand still holding her arm. She didn't bother to hold back an angry glare.

He dropped her arm immediately. 'I'm sorry. I didn't mean . . . Can we talk for a minute? There's a waiting room over there.' He indicated a group of plastic chairs grouped around a low table in an alcove down the hall.

She tried not to grind her teeth but couldn't think of a legitimate reason to refuse. 'Just for a minute. Millie's in the car. I lowered the windows some and it's not hot but still, I don't like to leave her.'

She walked down the hall toward the chairs, leaving him to walk behind, chose a chair, and sat. He pulled out one opposite but let a minute or so go by before he spoke. He didn't look at her. Instead, he sat, an elbow on each knee, hands clasped together between his knees, staring at the floor. She waited.

Finally, he looked at her. 'I think we've ah gotten off on the wrong foot. I don't want to antagonize you, or anything, but this isn't an easy case, and everyone in this town is outraged and wants it solved. If I seemed pushy, I'm sorry.'

That cost him something, but why had he done it? He wanted something, she was sure, but what? She was about to find out.

'Dan, Chief Dunham, he said . . .' Ryan hesitated again. 'I was making a big mistake if I didn't ask you for help, that you were a better detective than the two of us put together.' The look on his face said he didn't believe that for one minute.

'He said you know just about everyone in town and they all talk to you. So, I wondered . . .'

Ahh! He wanted information. She had some, but she was a long way from ready to share it with him. She was sure he'd already badgered Troy and everyone he knew and must have gotten nowhere. She wasn't going to have him badgering Mike and his family. Mike wasn't the only one who had a clown suit, besides possibly Troy. There were two other names on that list. But Ryan was mumbling something. She bent down to listen.

'I know you've been talking to people.'

'Dan told me to keep out of this one.'

'Yeah. He said you were the one who figured out who murdered the pet store owner and almost got yourself killed in the process. I guess there were others, too. He said you'd already figured out some things, like those initials, and the bank teller had identified the material as the same as what the clown she saw was wearing. That suggests Victoria made the one the killer wore, and that was more than we've done so far. He said I'd do well to work with you. So . . .'

Ryan seemed to be in pain. He leaned forward again, letting his hands dangle, and took a deep breath before he looked directly at Mary. The expression on his face clearly said he didn't want to work with her, but if she had information he wanted, needed, he'd swallow his pride, at least for a little while, until he had enough to make an arrest. Mary almost sympathized with his dilemma. Almost. Not enough, however, to pass along the very little she knew, and she wasn't about to share any suspicions she might have formed. She'd wait and talk them over with Dan when he was able to listen. In the meantime, she'd hear Ryan out.

'What exactly do you have in mind, Detective?' She tried to keep her tone neutral, even if inside she wasn't neutral at all.

He seemed at a loss to explain. Maybe he didn't really know what he wanted. But he needed help, and he knew it. 'If you find out anything that seems to point to someone, anything at all, I'd like you to come to me. I'll take it from there.'

'What do you mean by anything?'

He still seemed at a loss. 'Maybe someone saw someone in a clown costume or overheard something or . . .?'

In other words, he didn't want to work with her, didn't want to bounce ideas off her, and certainly didn't want to listen to hers. He wanted her to become the neighborhood snitch. That she wasn't prepared to do.

'If I should come across anything I think you need to hear, I'll be sure to give you a call.' She wondered if she had just lied to the police. She was sure he would like to know about Mike's costume, but too bad.

She pushed her chair back and stared to rise, but Ryan reached out and put his hand gently on hers. She stiffened, but he didn't take hold of her.

Instead, he said, 'I really do want to work with you. I know people are going to tell you things, and I don't want you to get yourself in trouble.' He gave a rueful little laugh. 'Dan Dunham would have my hide if he thought I let you get shot.'

She gave him a grim little smile in return. 'I assure you, Detective Ryan, I have no desire to be shot, or shot at. If I hear anything you need to know, I'll give you a call. Right now, I need to get back to my dog.'

He let her walk away without another word, but she didn't relax until she reached her car and sat in the driver's seat, Millie trying to climb into her lap in her joy to see her. Mary looked at her hand, which rested on the steering wheel. It was trembling. Not because she was scared, at least not really. She certainly didn't want to get shot but didn't think there was much danger of that. There was more danger of getting the wrong person accused of murder in the zeal of the police, and the people in the town, to find whoever had committed this senseless crime. She couldn't believe it was Mike. However, he had a costume made by Victoria and his family needed money. Nancy had as much as admitted it. She supposed having a 'special needs' child was expensive. She wondered how their insurance worked. There wasn't time to wonder about that now, besides it was none of her business. What was, or at least what she was going to make it her business to find out was who belonged to those remaining two sets of initials and to find out if Troy could be a real suspect. If not, then she'd have to start looking for someone with his initials, and she wasn't too sure where to start. Maybe eliminating Troy should come first.

'Millie, we're about to get our oil changed.'

TWENTY-THREE

M ary drove through the open gate in the chain link fence that surrounded a battered-looking brown building displaying an almost equally battered-looking sign that proclaimed 'Safe Auto'. She stopped in front of the small office that adjoined the four auto bays. They were all full.

She opened the car door and, holding Millie's leash a little tighter than necessary, walked into the office. A tall, thin man with a huge handlebar mustache stared at her, no expression on his long face. His expression didn't change when he leaned on the counter and looked down at Millie.

'Mrs McGill, Millie.' He waited.

'Mr O'Hare,' Mary said, equally expressionless.

Eduardo O'Hare liked formality. He called everybody but his closest friends by their last name and expected the same courtesy. He wasn't an easy man. His hair-trigger temper had gotten him into trouble, and in jail, on more than one occasion, but he also was a genius with cars. He knew them all, had a library of manuals on the care of almost every model made, as well as an up-to-date computer system. He could diagnose and fix almost any car and if he couldn't, he'd tell you why and what to do. Taking his advice was a good idea for a lot of reasons. He trained his workers himself and expected a high standard of workmanship. That he had hired Troy said a lot.

'I think we're due for an oil change.' Mary looked around, trying to see if she spotted Troy. She didn't, but then the only two men working were both hidden from view, one because he was under a car with only his feet visible, the other effectively hidden behind large goggles as he leaned over the open hood of a car.

Eduardo O'Hare turned to his computer, tapped in a command, scrolled down, read something and nodded. 'You're actually a little overdue. I think we sent you an email.'

Heat crept up Mary's neck and around her ears. She felt as much as heard the accusation in his voice and it reminded her of being scolded by her father. He had never spanked her. He never needed to. That implied reprimand and disappointment she hadn't behaved as he expected was enough. It irritated her profoundly that Eduardo had the same effect on her.

She determined to ignore him. 'Do you have time today?'

Eduardo shook his head. 'Full up. Couldn't get to it until early evening and I need to close on time tonight.' He scrolled down a little more. 'How about day after tomorrow? Ten o'clock?'

It was phrased as a question, but it really wasn't. Eduardo was always overbooked so you took the time he offered. Other appointments could wait. She nodded and took out her phone and entered it in her calendar.

Eduardo almost smiled. It was hard to tell under the mustache and it disappeared before Mary could be sure. 'Mrs McGill, I heard you were in the bank when the robbery occurred. How is Chief Dunham?'

'Thank you for asking, Mr O'Hare. He's still in the hospital but is going to be fine. He may even go home in a couple of days.'

'I'm sure Mrs Dunham would like that. I'm sure the whole department would. The man they have taking his place is nothing like Chief Dunham.'

Mary had been about to leave but Eduardo caught her attention. He must be talking about Detective Ryan. 'Have you met him? The man taking Dan's, Chief Dunham's, place?'

It wasn't hard to tell, even under the mustache, that Eduardo was furious. 'He came in here yesterday, flashing his badge, demanding to talk to Troy, who was working on a car. We had a deadline, so I asked this detective if I could be of help. He wanted to know where Troy was Halloween late afternoon. I told him he was here, working. We didn't close that night until six. He accused me of lying. I do not lie, and I told him so. Then I asked why he wanted to speak to Troy, did they think he had done something wrong? Troy does have a temper, but he is getting better at controlling it. He must. He is going to be a father. This Ryan told me it was none of my business and that he wanted to talk to Troy. I found Troy for him, and they went into the office, there.' He pointed to a small cubicle glassed off from both the waiting room and the auto shop. 'Troy looked very white when he came out and claimed he had no idea what it was all about. The man wanted to know where he was Halloween afternoon and asked him several times. He told him the same as me, here, working on a car till six. The man is rude, and I will never work on a car of his. He is not welcome in my shop.' He closed down his computer and started to turn away. 'Please tell Chief Dunham we are all praying for him to get better and hope it will be soon. I will see you in two days.'

He left. So did Mary. She sat in the car for a few minutes, going over what she had just learned. Troy had an alibi. A waterproof alibi. Which meant he probably didn't have a clown costume. It also meant the initials in Victoria's book weren't his. Whose, then, were they? Four people had bought a clown costume, one of those people had robbed the bank and committed murder, and they only knew who one of them was. Mike Gallagher. Was he guilty? Mary hoped not. Who were the other three? Right now, she had no idea, but she was going to find out. She wondered if she and Pat had missed something in Victoria's shop, other than the computer. They had spent a lot of time on wedding dresses and the cat. The cat, who was probably even now sitting in her reading chair. They had come across the little notebook almost by accident. More likely, the computer was their best bet. Someone had to get into that thing and see. Mary knew almost nothing about computers, at least nothing about breaking into one. She also felt she couldn't go into Victoria's shop and take it. Even though she had the shop key she didn't have permission to remove the computer. Drat and blast! Dan would get himself so worn out he needed to sleep right when she needed to talk to him. What should she do now? Millie whined, put her front feet on the back of the passenger side and gave a sharp bark.

'You want to go home? You probably need water. All right. We'll get a little lunch and I'll try to think what we need to do next.'

TWENTY-FOUR

The cat seemed pleased to see them. He jumped down from what was now seemingly his chair to greet them, winding around Mary's feet, purring loudly.

'You have to get out of the way,' she told him. 'You're going to trip me.'

The cat, still purring, unwound himself and headed toward the office, pausing to look over his shoulder and emitting a loud meow. Not quite sure what he wanted, she followed. His water dish was half full, and his dinner dish was empty. He sat in from of them and meowed again, louder.

'You must have had Victoria well trained.' She filled both dishes.

Millie sat in the doorway, watching. Mary didn't think she looked happy.

'I really don't like him best.' She bent down, picked up the little dog, and held her close for a moment. 'It's just that he makes more noise than you do. Come on. I'll give you a little lunch.'

She set Millie down, put a handful of kibble in her dish, checked her water, then turned to the refrigerator to see what she might make for herself. Nothing looked tempting. She reluctantly settled for a bowl of leftover pasta, which she put in the microwave, and heated up some coffee.

'What did we do before we had microwaves?' she asked Millie, who had finished her kibble and crawled under the kitchen table. Mary forked up a mouthful of the pasta, but it didn't make it to her mouth. She put it down and reached for the papers that had Victoria's records on it. She stared again at the initials. There it was. MG. Above it was the first clown notation TT, then further down, KN. The last one was PC. She put a check by MG. They knew who it was. But they didn't know where Mike was late Halloween afternoon. She put a line through TT. Even if Troy bought the costume, he had an ironclad alibi for the time in question. Who were the other two? There was only one way she could think to find out. She pushed the pasta aside and reached for the phone. It rang before she could pick up the receiver. The screen showed Joy's number.

'Joy? Mary. I need to ask you a question.'

'About what?' Joy was nothing if not direct.

'About Halloween in the park. Dan needs to know.'

'How is that poor man? The thought that someone could do such a thing . . .'

Mary hurriedly got the conversation back on track. 'He's better. He'll be on his way home soon, but it may be a while before he's back on the job.'

'Have you met that rude man who's taking Dan's place?'

'Yes, I have met Sean Ryan and no, he certainly isn't Dan. But this isn't about him, Joy. It's about costumes.'

'Do you mean the clown costume? What about it?'

'Yes. I need to know if you remember seeing anyone dressed like a clown in the park that day.'

'As a matter of fact, yeah.'

'You do? Who was it?'

'Mike Gallagher.'

Mary felt her heart sink. 'Did he have Robbie with him? Was Nancy there?'

'She was. She had the little girl. That child is sure cute. She had on a bunny costume. The little boy, Robbie, was dressed as a clown like Mike.'

'I'll bet she was a cute bunny. Joy, do you remember anyone else who was dressed as a clown?'

There was a long pause before Joy spoke again. 'That was the funniest thing.'

'What was?'

Joy hesitated again but finally said, 'There was this other clown right in front of me. I walked up behind him, was going to ask him what he'd done with Robbie. I couldn't see the kid anywhere. Well, it wasn't Mike. It was Paul Cummings.'

'Who is Paul Cummings and why did you think he was Mike?'

'Their costumes looked almost exactly alike. When he turned around I could see it wasn't Mike but from the back, I sure thought it was. You haven't met Paul yet? He's kind of new in town. Works for one of the wineries. Does Dan think Mike robbed the bank?'

'Of course not. In what way were the costumes alike?'

'They both had those silly balloons all over them. Why are you asking me all this?'

'Dan wants me to try to identify all the clowns that were running around that day. That's all you saw? I'll tell Dan, and Joy, thanks.'

Mary wasn't sure Joy bought her vague clown excuse, but it didn't matter. What did was they had the name of another of Victoria's customers. Maybe they did. But it sounded promising. Now, all she had to do was find out who this person was, where he worked, and why he might have wanted to rob a bank. Piece of cake. Sure. 'Millie, we have to find out something about Paul Cummings. Then we have to find out who KN and TT are.' She sighed. 'I know. It'll be hard, but we can do it. The man who shot Dan isn't getting away with this.'

She stared at her rapidly cooling pasta, but she didn't really see it. Who would know this Paul Cummings? Someone who worked in the wine industry, someone . . . Sabrina. Her great-niece. Her husband, Mark Tortelli, was a winemaker for Silver Springs and Sabrina ran the tasting room. She might know. It was worth a phone call. She hadn't seen Sabrina for a while. She and Mark had been out of the country and had only just returned, but she was sure they had gone back to work. She'd try the winery. She got the answering machine. Mary wasn't fond of talking to machines, but it seemed it was impossible to avoid them. She left a not-too-detailed message, asking only if Sabrina knew Paul Cummings and anything about him. She didn't leave a reason, just she would like the information. Discouraged, she hung up. No telling when Sabrina would return the phone call. In the meantime, what should she do? She didn't want to bother Dan, not today. He really did need to rest and nothing she had was urgent. Was there some way she could go about finding out who the other two initials really were?

The phone rang.

It was Ruthie. The last of the lunch crowd had left, her staff was cleaning the restaurant in preparation for tomorrow morning, and could she come look at the cat.

She certainly could.

'Cat, we may have found you a new home. How would you like to live in a restaurant, sleep in the back room, go home with Ruthie at night, and have really delicious snacks?'

Mary approached the chair where the cat had once again taken charge. He opened one eye. She stopped. Would he let her pick him up? Ruthie had been on her way when she called. She'd be here any minute. She'd like to meet her at the door with the cat in her arms, perhaps transfer him to Ruthie's. She reached out a hand. The cat didn't move. She laid it on top of his head and started to gently rub the spot between his ears. He leaned into her hand, so she rubbed one ear. A faint purr sounded. She let her hand run down the back of his neck and under his shoulder. The cat opened both eyes and looked at her but did nothing. So far, so good. She leaned over and slowly picked him up. To her surprise, he snuggled down in her arms and began his loud and rusty-sounding purr. The cat liked it. She stood still, wondering what she should do next when the doorbell rang.

Ruthie stood on the front porch, a smile on her face, a brown paper sack in her hands. She stared at Mary, then at the cat residing comfortably in Mary's arms. Her smile faded. 'Is that him?'

Mary's smile was forced. She nodded. 'Handsome, isn't he?'

'Not quite the way I'd put it. What happened to his ear?' Ruthie walked into the room and looked around. 'The special today was Irish stew. I thought you might like some for your dinner. Shall I put this in the kitchen?'

Still holding the cat, Mary led the way, Ruthie right behind her. Millie sat in the middle of the living room, looking dejected.

Drat and blast. This wasn't going well at all. Ruthie was obviously not impressed with the cat and now Millie was jealous.

'Thank you,' she told Ruthie. 'I love your Irish stew. I'll enjoy every mouthful. Why don't we go back in the living room and you two can get acquainted?' Still carrying the cat, who purred a little louder, she indicated the big chair. 'Sit down there. I'll put him in your lap and you can see what you think. He really is a nice cat.'

Ruthie sat, and Mary placed the cat in her lap. The cat didn't move for a moment, just stared at Ruthie.

'He likes having his ears rubbed.' Mary sat on the couch and Millie jumped up beside her.

Ruthie tentatively started to rub the cat's ears. The cat quit purring. 'What's his name?

Mary shrugged. 'I have no idea. I've been calling him cat.'

'He's got to have a name. Who would know what Victoria called him?'

'Probably one of her customers. Evidently, he had the run of the shop during the day. The only list of the customers I have is the one I told you about. By the way, Troy has an ironclad alibi for Halloween afternoon. He wasn't our clown.'

Ruthie nodded. 'I heard. Now, if that detective who's taking Dan's place will back off . . .'

'Ryan. Is he still worrying Troy?'

Ruthie nodded. 'The man has a one-track mind.'

The cat stood up, stretched, turned in a couple of circles, and lay back down on Ruthie's lap.

'Just making himself more comfortable. I think he likes you.'

'You think?'

Mary wasn't sure if the cat liked Ruthie or if he thought the chair was his and he was going to sit in it even if it meant sitting on her lap. But she smiled and nodded. Ruthie rubbed the spot between the cat's ears again and the purr started again. The cat seemed to relax.

Ruthie didn't. 'Janelle Tucker came in today. She said she'd let her dog – Zoe? – stay with Robbie Gallagher. Said she was going over there this afternoon, when her shift ends, to help him learn commands and things like that. She didn't seem very happy, though. Said it was her mother's dog and she didn't think her mother would approve. Why that should matter,

I can't for the life of me understand. Her mother's dead. But then, she was always devoted to her mother. I never understood that either.'

'Strange, but I don't remember them. What was she like? The mother, I mean.'

It took Ruthie a minute. She kept stroking the cat while she seemed to search for words. 'It's been almost twenty years, but there are some people you just don't forget. I don't like to speak ill of the dead, but I must admit, I didn't like her much. She was the type to always blame someone else for whatever happened. They used to come into the Yum Yum for lunch sometimes. The little girl loved our hamburgers. She was a sweet little thing and the husband seemed nice enough. But the woman was a constant complainer. It was a shame what happened to him but the grapes failing was his fault. Grapes need water. He had no idea how to irrigate them and wouldn't ask for help. It was too bad she got left cleaning up the mess he created but she made it worse by the way she complained about everything and everyone. She told me once about someone who took her parking place somewhere, don't know the details, but that was years before they came here, and she was still going on about it. Not my type of woman.' She took her hand off the cat's head and gently picked him up off her lap and set him on the floor. 'I need to go. I'll let you know about the cat.' She looked at him.

He turned his back on her and headed for the office.

Ruthie sighed. 'He has a mind of his own, doesn't he?'

'He's a cat,' Mary replied.

'Yes. He is.' She stared after the retreating cat for a moment then turned. 'Mary, I hope you don't think I don't like Janelle because I didn't think much of her mother. I do. She's a nice woman. Everyone on the police force thinks so as well. I hear she's working hard to help find out who did this to Dan and poor Victoria.' She grinned. 'And she thinks I'm a great cook.'

With that, she was out the door.

Mary had hoped this little meet and greet with the cat would have gone better. She'd hoped Ruthie would take him off her hands, but it didn't look as if that would be the case. Oh well. They'd find him a home with someone. He did seem to be a nice cat. She glanced at the clock with surprise. It was past Millie's dinnertime and getting close to hers. She called Millie into the kitchen, filled her dish, and turned to the package Ruthie had left. It smelled wonderful. Just the thing for a chilly evening. She'd make a small salad and put in one of those frozen rolls she'd bought and hadn't tried yet. But first, she was going to pour herself a glass of wine and turn on the local news. She wanted to see if they were still covering the bank robbery and if so, what they were saying.

She sipped her wine and let her thoughts drift. They were talking about high school football, a sport that had never interested her. She let herself think of the initials, of what she'd learned, or thought she'd learned, and what came next. She only half heard what the news anchor was saying and almost missed it. But the statement jolted her attention back to the screen. Local banker dead. Her breath almost stopped. Who . . . not Glen. It couldn't be . . . no. It was Chet Bradley who was dead.

TWENTY-FIVE

The clock radio clicked on, playing NPR's morning news program. The phone rang at the same time. Mary opened one eye. Seven thirty. Who would be calling her at this hour and how had she slept so late? She rolled over to pick up the phone to be met with an angry yowl. What on earth? The cat stalked out of the room as she answered.

'Hello?' She sounded sleepy she knew, and she was. She hadn't had a restful night's sleep.

Ellen's voice sounded as if she was fully awake. 'Did I wake you? I'm sorry, but I was sure you'd be up. Should I call back later? I'm on my way to a meeting, but I could . . .'

'No, no. I slept in a little but was awake when you called. What's up?' Mary pushed back the quilt and swung her legs over the side of the bed. This must be something important. Ellen wasn't calling to chat.

'Sabrina called. She said she and Mark are going out of town to a wine tasting or something and she was afraid she might not get in touch with you, so she left you a message. I have no idea what she's talking about, but you probably do. She said under no circumstances get involved with Paul Cummings. He's a liar and a crook. Evidently, he worked for them in the tasting room for a short time, but he managed to steal from the cash register and she thinks he got away with probably a pallet of wine. He worked for Briar Patch Winery as well, and they let him go because of something about a customer's credit card. They could never prove anything, but they were sure he stole it. She says keep away from him. So, how did you get mixed up with a man like that?'

'I'm not. Mixed up, I mean. I've never even met him. But, Ellen, he bought a clown suit from Victoria and he had it on Halloween night. It doesn't prove anything, but, given his reputation, it sounds as if someone needs to find out more about Paul Cummings.'

She could hear a soft, 'Ohhh boy,' over the phone. 'I take it you haven't told Dan yet.'

'No. I didn't know a thing about him until you told me what Sabrina said. I think I'd better tell him sometime today, though. How is he?'

'Better this morning, judging from how antsy he is, a lot better. Sleeping almost all day yesterday was good for him. The man wants to join the hunt and he needs to back off. I guess you should tell him but keeping him from getting out of bed and finding this Paul whatever his name is won't be easy.' She made a sound that sounded like a combination of a sigh and a grinding of teeth. 'Are you sure you don't want to tell Ryan?'

The noise Mary made wasn't too much different. 'He'd just go out and find Paul. Bring him in and badger the life out of him. That's what he did with Troy Turnbull, even after Eduardo O'Hare told him that he had been under some car until six Halloween night. We don't know if this man is guilty. We don't know anything. Yet. Dan can't do anything himself, but he'll know how we should proceed. Or even if we should.'

'I'm sure he'll think more needs to be known about Paul.

OK. Go talk it over with him. I'll be in to see him about lunchtime. If you can make it then, we can all talk it over. Right now, I've got to run. See you later.'

'Wait. Ellen, did you hear about Chet? Do you know what happened?'

Mary caught her before they were disconnected. 'I don't know much. Someone said they think it was a heart attack, but that's not for sure. Evidently, he'd been up all morning and was fine. The nurse put him back in bed after lunch and when she went in to check on him later, he was dead. Poor old guy. He got lucky. At least, he didn't have to suffer. Gotta run.' The line went dead.

Mary thought again about her Samuel. He hadn't suffered either, but he'd also missed out on a lot of years, ones they would have shared. A tear formed, but she brushed it away. There was nothing she could do about how Sam died, but she could feed Millie and the cat. Then she could call Ysabel, Reverend Les McIntyre's wife, and see if she knew when the funeral was going to be and if Mary's hospitality committee was supposed to arrange for the reception after the service. Chet had been a long-time member of St Mark's, so there was no doubt his funeral would be there and Les McIntyre would conduct it.

It took several rings before Ysabel picked up, and she sounded a little breathless.

'Are you all right? You sound out of breath.'

'Is that you, Mary? I am. I was helping with the preschoolers and had to run to get this. Are you calling about Chet?'

'Yes. I heard about it on the news last night. Poor old Chet, but at least he didn't hang on for months, dying by inches. He really hadn't had a life for a while now.'

'No, he hadn't.' Sadness was evident in Ysabel's voice. 'But he's not going to go to his final resting place for a while yet. We just got word there's going to be an autopsy.'

'A what? Why? He was an old, senile, sick man. Why do they want to do an autopsy? How does his family feel about that?'

'Evidently not too good, but the police have ordered one.'

'What police? Why?'

'I don't know why. You know that detective that's taking Dan's place while he's in the hospital? Ryan, I think his name is. He ordered it. We have no idea when the funeral is going to be, but we might as well get it planned. It's going to be a big one. Chet was a well-known man in town and, until the last few years at the bank, a highly respected one. The reception after the burial will be well attended. Do you want to call a meeting of your committee?'

Mary didn't say anything for a minute. The autopsy information had surprised her, but she agreed with Ysabel. They needed to get started. 'Yes, I think we need to. But first, I think I need to talk to Nora and their daughter, Mary Beth. I assume she's either already here or on her way. Doesn't their son live in New York or some such place? I imagine he must be on his way as well. I'll find out what the family wants and then we should have a meeting as soon as possible. What dates do you have open?'

Mary heard what sounded like paper rustling on the other end of the phone and a little heavy breathing.

'How about Saturday around one? That should give you time and nothing is going on at the church on Saturday. Pamela and Luke's wedding is two weeks from Sunday, and that's the next huge thing we have scheduled, right after that is the Thanksgiving dinner for the homeless. I assume your committee is on top of that?'

'Yes. All of our donations are being double-checked and we'll start collecting the nonperishable items next week. This year we're not going to use the church's dishes. I expect about two hundred or so and we just can't keep washing that many plates. Our committee is meeting' – she paused to check her calendar – 'late Monday afternoon. Saturday will be fine. About one? I'll send out an email this morning and I'll stop by to see what I can do for Nora.' She took a deep breath. She knew how Nora must be feeling about now, and it wasn't good. 'Even when you know it's coming, it's never easy. I'll get back to you and confirm everything later this afternoon.' She hung up but didn't move for a few minutes. She stared out the kitchen window, wondering why the police thought they needed an autopsy. Feeling confused and more than a little uneasy, she turned to find two animals sitting side by side, staring at her.

'You both ate, or are you wondering what's wrong? I wish I could tell you. I also wish I could tell you what I'm going to do, besides going to see poor Nora.' She thought for a minute. 'Maybe I should stop by the police station and have a chat with Agnes. She might not be much of a front desk person, but as a fount of information, she's the best. It's not always correct, I know, but sometimes she comes up with something useful. Yes. I'll do that. Then on to see Dan.'

Millie cocked her head as she listened to Mary. The cat simply sat.

'Millie, you come with me. Cat, you'll have to stay here. You'll be fine. We know who owns two of those clown costumes, but we don't know who bought the other two. You might give that some thought while we're gone.'

The cat got up, stretched, turned, and walked into Mary's bedroom and jumped up on the bed. Mary sighed and headed for the shower.

TWENTY-SIX

The lobby of the police department looked deserted. Only Agnes was there, sitting behind the front desk, reading a paperback romance novel. Mary briefly wondered how many of them she got through in a week. 'Hi, Agnes,' she said.

Agnes quickly stuffed the book under her desk then sighed in relief when she saw who stood there. 'Hi, Mary. Millie, you look darling.'

The dog did look cute. Mary had replaced the bows Millie had on after her last bath and she hadn't taken them off yet. She wagged her stub of a tail at Agnes.

'What are you two doing here?'

'Stopped by to say hello. I'm going to see Dan later this

afternoon and wondered if there was anything you thought I should tell him?'

Agnes looked blank. 'About what?'

'Oh, how the investigation is going. That kind of thing. He's not taking to lying in bed well. I don't think he's very happy with the reports he's getting. He said to ask you.'

'Ask me what?'

Mary felt the twinge of irritation Agnes always created start to creep over her. *Patience*, she reminded herself. With Agnes it was always patience. 'What everybody is doing. Are there any new leads?'

Agnes gave a knowing nod, not that Mary thought it meant she knew anything, but maybe. 'Everybody is doing about what you'd expect. Gary is beating himself up because he didn't stop those cars, the ones that drove out of the library parking lot. They might have seen something. I don't think they did. The robbery and the clown have been all over the TV. If whoever they were had seen something important, you can bet your bottom dollar they'd be in here. That new girl, Janelle, she's trying, but she doesn't know anyone in town so she's not much help. But she is taking over the routine stuff so the guys can try to find leads to follow. That Ryan just keeps yelling at everyone to do better, but he's floundering. No one's getting anywhere. That blasted clown just up and disappeared.'

Mary had almost forgotten about the cars leaving the parking lot that afternoon. 'Why is Gary so upset about the cars who drove off from the library?'

'He thinks he should have stopped them to get a statement. One was some guy in a pickup, wearing a cowboy hat. Around here, pickups are a dime a dozen. Says he thinks the other driver might have been a woman, but she was turning into the street when he got there and he only caught a glimpse. Says he yelled, but neither of them stopped. He was afraid the clown was getting away, so he started searching through the parking lot. Now he thinks he should have run after them, or called it in. But it doesn't sound to me like either one of them even knew the bank'd been robbed.'

Mary understood why Gary hadn't stopped them. Both the

pickup and the car were going out the back exit, onto Elm Street, probably to avoid all the commotion in the park, and it could be they didn't know a thing about the robbery. They would have wondered about the sirens, though. Even if they hadn't stopped, one, or both of them, should have come forward. However, if they hadn't seen anyone, like a clown, maybe they didn't feel the need. Gary was lucky Dan wasn't running this show. He would have gotten the back side of Dan's tongue for not having tried harder to stop those cars. However, he hadn't so it no longer mattered. 'Janelle is settling in well?'

'Nice kid. Yeah, she's doing all the small stuff, like she was out at Shady Acres with Mike yesterday, just going through the motions. Seems one of the old dears' purse went missing. I guess she was having a hissy fit, saying it was stolen. Wanted the police. Janelle went, but they'd already found it. Someone picked it up by mistake in the lunchroom. Today, she's on patrol and, since we're shorthanded, she's out there on our mean streets by herself.' Agnes laughed heartedly. 'She says she should have her dog with her, but I guess she's let little Robbie Gallagher have the dog during the day. Darned nice of her, I'd say. Guess she was her mother's dog, and it seems her mother's stuff is important to her. She was telling me she brought all her things with her, not clothes, but furniture, dishes, pictures, that kind of thing. You don't see many kids so dedicated to their mother like that nowadays.'

Mary thought it sounded a little odd, but maybe she didn't have any dishes of her own. Agnes was given to exaggeration, she wasn't going to pursue it. She was more interested in the people in the cars. Was Ruthie right? Could the clown have been crouched down in one of them? 'Gary doesn't have any idea . . .' was as far as she got.

There was a commotion in the back hallway and Janelle walked in.

'Agnes, I need you. I brought in a prisoner and we need to book him.' She paused as she caught sight of Mary and Millie. 'Oh. Hello, Mrs McGill. Sorry about the interruption.' She turned back to Agnes. 'I've got him in interrogation room one. I'll bring him up front so you can get the paperwork started, but I'm not taking his handcuffs off until one of the guys get back. I had the devil of a time getting them on him. Can you see if we can get someone back here?'

'Sure.' Agnes fiddled with the radio that had been spitting out unintelligible static the whole time Mary had been talking with her. 'I think Mike is close. I'll call him.' She held one half of large headphones up to her ear. 'Who you got and what did he do?'

'Paul Cummings. This time we caught him trying to buy stuff with a stolen credit card. One that had gone missing at the last winery he worked for. Tell Mike to hurry.'

Paul Cummings. The one who had a clown costume made by Victoria, who had worn it Halloween night, who had been suspected of several small thefts from at least two wineries. Who could very well be their bank robber. Should she tell Janelle? She certainly wasn't going to tell Agnes. No. She needed to talk this over with Dan. He would know what to do. She quickly made her excuses to Agnes and Janelle, but they were both intent on the task before them. She and Millie slipped out the door.

'Things are getting complicated,' she told Millie. 'You're going to visit Furry Friends while I go see Dan, and don't even think of bringing home another cat.'

TWENTY-SEVEN

'Thank goodness you're awake.'

Dan sat in a chair with the sliding tray table over his legs, holding a coffee cup somewhat precariously with his right hand. There was a notebook stuffed with papers spread out on the tray and a scowl on his face. 'Blast that woman. I don't think she's ever heard of staples, nor of paper clips. Hi, Mary. Pull out that chair over there and tell me what's going on.'

'I will in a minute, but first, why is Chet having an autopsy?'

'You make it sound as if he's having his appendix out.' Dan

lifted the coffee cup to his mouth with care. 'I had no idea it was this hard to function with only one arm. This damn shoulder better heal, fast. I'm sick of all this.'

'Be grateful you're alive and tell me about Chet.' She pulled the chair close to the bed opposite him and settled herself.

Dan set the coffee cup down on the tray, tried to get the papers that were spread out back in the notebook, gave up, and finally looked at her. 'Where did you hear about the autopsy?'

'Ysabel. She says we can't set a date for the funeral because of it but we can start to plan. It's going to be a big one.' She waited, but Dan kept looking at the papers and didn't say anything. 'Why are you doing an autopsy?'

He finally looked up. 'This stays with you.'

She nodded.

'It appears he may have been smothered.'

'What?' Mary could barely get the word out. She'd been afraid of something like this when she heard about the autopsy but still, the shock was huge. 'Why would someone do that to Chet? An old man, already dying? I don't understand.' She took a breath and steadied herself. 'How do you know that?'

There was deep sadness in Dan's voice and on his face. 'His eyes. All the blood vessels had hemorrhaged. It could have been from natural causes, but the nurse that found him doesn't think so. Only one way to find out for sure, so that's what's going to happen.' He looked at her and, before she could ask him another question, said, 'And I don't know who or why. We're waiting on the results to see how to proceed, but, in the meantime, I've got someone over at Shady Acres asking questions. You and your committee can go ahead with your planning. I'll let you know later about dates. Now, what do you have to tell me?'

She edged herself a little forward in her chair, wiggling until she had both feet firmly on the floor and placed her purse squarely in the middle of her lap. 'I know who two of the sets of initials belong to.'

Dan stared at her for a minute then started to laugh. 'Of course you do. Don't tell me how you know, at least not right now, just who they are.'

'You're not going to like one of them, but I think he's innocent. The other one is a real possibility, but I didn't want to say anything to Janelle in front of Agnes.'

Dan stopped laughing. He stared at her for a minute then shook his head. 'Explain.'

'One of the costumes was sold to Mike Gallagher. He wore it to the park Halloween night. Robbie, his little boy, had a clown costume as well, that his mother, Nancy, made. I don't know where he was that afternoon, but I know for sure Mike had one, because Nancy told me.'

Dan looked a little sick. He leaned back and closed his eyes. 'Who's the other one?'

'Paul Cummings. He's—'

Dan's eyes opened wide. 'Paul Cummings? Who works at Silver Springs Winery?'

'He used to. Sabrina let him go. Now he works . . . somewhere else. But right now, he's in your jail.'

Dan almost shot out of the chair. 'He is? Why?'

'I'm not sure, but it has to do with a stolen credit card. Janelle brought him in, but I didn't want to tell her, about the clown costume in front of Agnes. Actually, I wanted to talk to you first before I said anything to anybody.'

She thought Dan might get up and walk, or trot, or run out the door, but he restrained himself. Instead, he asked in a somewhat strangulated tone, 'I'm almost afraid to ask this, but how do you know Paul Cummings has a clown costume made by Victoria Witherspoon?'

Mary told him about how Joy saw Mike in his costume Halloween night, pushing Robbie in his chair, then later mistook Paul for Mike because they had identical costumes.

Dan kept shaking his head. 'I assume Ryan knows nothing about this.'

'I haven't told him.'

Dan leaned back and stared at her. 'I may hire you to train a couple of my people in how to run an investigation.' He thought for a few more minutes. 'OK, I'm going to discreetly try to find out where Mike was the afternoon of Halloween. I can't see him doing anything like that, especially going back that evening in costume with his kids, but we need to clear him or look at him harder. As for Paul Cummings, I'll talk to Janelle. Find out how she knew about the credit card, then we'll see if we can find out if he has an alibi for that afternoon. He's the kind that just might be brazen enough to turn up that night. What are you going to do after you leave here?'

'Go see Chet's family. See if they've thought about the funeral yet, what they want us to do. We usually do the food. St Mark's has a fund for that kind of thing, and I can arrange for the church flowers. I imagine O'Dell's will be the funeral home. I want to see how she's holding up and if I can do anything, bring over dinner or something.'

Dan almost smiled. 'Of course that's what you're going to do. Give the family my condolences.'

Mary made no move to get up. 'There's one more thing.'

Dan raised his eyebrows. 'Oh? What?'

'Victoria had a laptop. I saw it on her desk, but after I found the notebook, I forgot about it.'

'A laptop? You think . . .?'

'I think it's possible. The notebook doesn't tell us all the things she would need to know, like measurements, addresses, phone numbers . . .'

'Full names.' There was no grin on Dan's face now. 'Mary, I need you to pick up that computer.'

'What? Me?' That sounded unwilling, but that was the way she felt. She didn't mind helping the police, well, helping Dan, but she wanted to get back to Millie. She'd also left the cat roaming free in the house, and that thought made her nervous. He hadn't done one wrong thing, at least not so far, but he did like to jump on things, like the kitchen counter. But if Dan thought it was important, well, she'd do it. 'What do you want me to do?'

'I want you to go to Victoria's shop and pick up that laptop. Please do it before you go see Nora. You do still have the keys, don't you?'

Mary could only stare at him. 'You want me to do it right now? Why? What am I supposed to do with it after I get it? I don't understand.'

Dan moved around, pushed a pillow that had slid out from behind his back more or less where it belonged and muttered under his breath. 'Think about it. You may not be the only one who thinks Victoria might have, and probably did, keep all her records on her computer, and one of those clowns has a strong interest in making sure his name doesn't appear anywhere in them. Victoria's shop has no alarm system, and I'll bet the locks on her door wouldn't keep out a determined two-year-old. I want the computer out of there and someplace safe.'

A cold chill ran up the back of Mary's neck. 'That hadn't occurred to me, but you're right. Except, how would the clown know we know Victoria recognized him because of the costume?'

'It's all over town. Evidently Tammy from the bank told her mother we thought the clown had his costume made by Victoria but all we have to go on are some initials. The mother told her bridge club, who told someone at the beauty shop, and who knows where it went from there. Ellen heard it at her office, and I understand it was the central topic of conversation at the Yum Yum today. According to Janelle, everyone was speculating who the initials belong to, even though no one knows what they are. She came in to ask me about it. Says everyone in town seems to know about it but her and what should she do.'

'What did you tell her?' Mary's voice was faint, but this was news she wasn't prepared for.

'Not much. Just that we were trying to identify them. She knew about Troy but evidently didn't know there were other people we were trying to find. I'll need to tell her to be sure to keep Paul locked up, and I'll have to tell Ryan about the clown suit.' He grinned. 'Paul is in for a difficult afternoon. First the credit card then possible murder. Enough to give that young man one enormous headache. Wish I could be there to help it along.'

From the look on Dan's face, Mary thought Paul Cummings should be grateful Dan wouldn't be. 'What am I supposed to do with the computer when I get it? Keep it?'

Dan nodded. 'Yes. First, we don't know if Mike is involved and I see no reason to spread the word that the computer is no longer in the shop. Second, I don't think there's a single person on our miniscule force who has the expertise to break into it if its password protected. I doubt she has too many protections on it, or that they're complicated, but still, we need someone who can get into it. I'll take care of the legal part but arranging that could take some time. Take it home. I'll send someone for it as soon as I can. I'm going to call Judge Watkins after you leave. I need a court order to get the information, and I want it where it's safe in the meantime. Will you do it?'

Mary gulped but nodded her head. She started to say something but was interrupted by Janelle walking through the open door of Dan's room.

'What's he got you doing now?'

'Another little errand.' Mary managed to laugh, but she was shaken by the thought of going into Victoria's shop and removing the computer. Why, she wasn't sure, but she was. This was one time she could really use Millie. And Millie was coming with her. She would stop at Furry Friends before she went into the shop. She wasn't a guard dog, but she'd tried to protect Mary once before and she could sure bark and growl when she needed to. Speaking of dogs: 'How did Robbie and Zoe get on?'

'Beautifully.' The look on Janelle's face wasn't one of pure joy. 'I haven't seen that dog so happy in a long time.' She sighed. 'I'm glad she found a job but I do miss her.'

Mary smiled and gathered up her purse. 'I'd better get going. Need to pick up Millie and then I'd better see how Nora is getting along. I know they didn't expect to keep Chet around much longer, but still, it's always hard.'

'Nora?' Janelle raised her eyebrows in question.

'Chet's wife. This is going to be hard on her. Neither of their children live in town anymore, but we'll help her get through it. We just need to know when the body will be released. Autopsies always seem to take so long.'

'Autopsy? They're going to do an autopsy? Why?' Janelle whirled around to stare at Dan. 'I hadn't heard that.'

'They always do one when they aren't quite sure of the cause of death. He seemed fine yesterday, then someone went to check on him. I guess he was supposed to be taking a nap, only he was dead. This one shouldn't take long. Mary, I'll keep you up to date. You emailed your committee yet?'

She nodded. 'We'll meet Saturday at the church to plan as much as we can.' She smiled at them both, turned, and walked out the doorway.

TWENTY-EIGHT

Mary pulled into the parking lot behind the row of businesses and stopped in the back of Victoria's shop. There weren't many cars at this end of the lot. The other end, where the beauty shop and the candy store were, was almost full. But they had open back doors. The shops at this end kept their doors closed. Mary wanted to go into the shop, get the computer, and get out without seeing or talking to anyone. Not that Dan had scared her. Of course, he hadn't, but it seemed prudent not to advertise what she was here to do. She hitched her purse under her arm, opened the door for Millie to jump out, keys in hand, and approached the back door of A Stitch in Time. She had inserted the key when she heard her name called. The keys dropped to the ground.

'Oh, I'm so sorry. I didn't mean to startle you. Here, let me get them.' Kyle Nevins, the only male hairdresser at Snip and Curl, knelt, picked up the keys, and handed them to Mary.

'I called out because I wanted to remind you of your appointment tomorrow. I know Lucille always sends out an email, but people don't always check them. I hope I didn't frighten you.'

He had, but Mary took a deep breath and let it out slowly. She tried to smile. 'Oh, no. I didn't see you.'

'I was getting ready to leave. It's a short day for me. I see you're going into Victoria's. Is there something I can help you with?' He glanced at Millie, who sat close to Mary's legs, looking at him with no expression, and took a step back. 'This must be the famous Millie everyone talks about.' He wiggled his fingers at the dog but made no attempt to touch her.

Millie made no response.

It took Mary a second to collect her thoughts. She wasn't about to tell anyone what her errand was, not even Kyle. 'Thanks, but no, I came to pick up the flower girl dress for Luke and Pamela's wedding. I think it's done. They'll need it . . .' She beamed at him and dangled the keys from her hand, hoping he'd go away. 'We already rescued her wedding gown and Krissie's dress. It's going to be a nice wedding.'

Kyle looked skeptical, but he nodded. 'Yes, we're doing the hair for the whole wedding party. I'm sure the wedding will be lovely. Well, if you're sure I can't help . . .'

Mary smiled and shook her head. Kyle nodded and headed toward a bright yellow Smart car parked just down from hers. She'd seen it around town but didn't know it was Kyle's.

'How do you like your little car?' she asked his retreating back.

He turned and smiled. 'Love it. Great gas mileage. Easy to park. Glad they finally made it over here. Guess they're all the rage in Europe.' He unlocked the driver's door, climbed in, and started the engine. With a wave in their direction, he was gone.

Mary and Millie stood for another minute, staring after him, then Mary gathered herself and turned back to the door. It opened easily. 'That little car looks like a clown car, don't you think?'

Millie didn't answer. Mary hadn't thought she would.

'He couldn't possibly have a dog with that car. It's way too small. Come on, let's get that computer and, while we're here, we might as well get the flower girl dress, too.' She stopped and turned back to the door. 'Wait.'

Millie obliged.

'I'm going to lock this.' She wasn't sure why, but she didn't feel comfortable knowing the door would be unlocked and they would be upstairs. 'I don't know what you're so nervous about,' she chided herself. 'No one knows you're here, and no one's been trying to get in here, either.' She decided to get the computer first, then there were a couple of other things she wanted to look at. Calling Millie, she started up the stairs.

The laptop lay on the desk, just as she remembered. Nothing

appeared different. Nothing was out of place that she could see. Heaving a sigh of relief, she told Millie rather grumpily, 'How we're supposed to collect the laptop, the keyboard, the mouse, and the cord, I don't know.' Did they need the keyboard? Or the mouse? The laptop didn't need a separate keyboard, but it seemed Victoria had used one, probably because it was easier to type on. But she did need the charger. She lifted the closed laptop and immediately put it down. It wasn't especially heavy, but it was bulky, and the cord was long and unwieldy with no place to wind it up. There were carrying cases for these things. Did Victoria have one? Yes. Under the desk. She pulled it out and, with relative ease, stuffed both the laptop and the cord into it. The mouse and the extra keyboard went in as well. Then she opened all the desk drawers looking for paper files but found none. The same bills and other mail were still on the desk. The drawers held paper and other office supplies but no files. Feeling more confident, she zipped the case shut and she and Millie went back downstairs. Mary set the case by the back door. Millie looked at the closed door expectantly, but Mary told her, 'We're not finished yet. There's something I want to check.'

She went to the rack that held the finished garments, flipped through them until she came to the small green dress she was sure was for the flower girl and the dark green dress with Luke's mother's initials. She laid them over the computer case and she and Millie went into the main room. It was dim. The closed blinds let in little light. She flipped on the switch and walked over to the large cutting board and pulled out the rolling cabinet that held the patterns. The clown pattern was the first one she pulled out. 'Just as I thought. The costume is two pieces. The pants have elastic in the waist, at least that's what it says on the instructions, and the top pulls on over the head. The ruff goes on . . . Hmm. It must have a tie of some sort or it wouldn't stay put on the shoulders. Yes. Well, there goes that theory.' She stared at the pattern once more then pulled out one of the pieces and laid it on the table. 'This is the front of the top and it isn't a solid piece. So how . . .?' She studied it a minute then pulled out another rolling tub, this one with drawers marked 'thread', 'needles', 'hooks', 'zippers', 'decorations' and other things. She opened the one that contained zippers and started to go through them. She pulled out a long, wide zipper already mounted on an even wider piece of tape and dangled it up toward the light. There was a large round silver ring attached to the pull that immediately caught the light.

'I was right.' She sighed. 'A front zipper.

'She made one costume with it. I'll bet the other three costume tops pull over the head, just as the pattern calls for, but the one the robber had on was zipped. It was the silver ring I saw sparkle that day. Only, I don't think this helps us much in finding out who wore it. But it may clear Mike. I wonder if Dan can get a warrant to search Paul Cumming's place. The evidence against him is thin, but we know he has a costume. If his has a zipper, that could be damning. Come on. We've still got to go see Nora. Maybe there's something we can do for her.'

She replaced the pattern piece and the zipper and rolled the tubs back under the table, then snapped Millie's leash back on her collar. She paused only long enough to find the computer case under the dresses and grasp it by the handle. She unlocked the back door, looked both ways to make sure no one was in sight, then walked to her car. Millie went onto the back seat, the dresses and computer into the trunk. She went back, locked the door, then tried the lock to be sure it held. Satisfied, she got in the car and headed for the Bradleys'.

TWENTY-NINE

'Is this where we turn?'

Millie sat in the front seat with a clear view of the long driveway they had turned into. She declined to answer. She was too busy watching the ground squirrels run for cover at the sight of them.

'Yes. That's their mailbox.' Mary drove slowly up the long gravel drive to the two-story farm-style house that sat on top of the hill. The view, as they passed through the grove of old oaks and heavy shrubs to arrive at the top, was spectacular. Chet and Nora had bought this land when parcels like this were cheap, before the wineries had appeared, along with hordes of tourists. Santa Louisa had been a sleepy little agriculture town back then. The house was no mansion, but it was large, comfortable, and had been designed to take advantage of the view. You could see the whole town from here, along with the many vineyards that increasingly dotted the hillsides. Mary had been here many times over the years, and she never failed to pause to admire the view. Today the front door opened almost before she and Millie were out of the car.

Nick, their oldest son, stood there, smiling. 'Mrs McGill, so good to see you. My mother was asking when you'd show up. Please, come in.'

Les and Ysabel McIntyre sat side by side on the long sofa that faced the front window. Nora sat in one of the large easy chairs covered in a bright flowered print. Its cheerful cover was in sharp contrast to the bleak look on Nora's face. That she had been crying was obvious. Her red swollen eyes spoke loudly of her distress, as did her uncombed hair and the rumpled look of her housedress. Nora was normally an immaculate woman who never had a hair out of place, even when gardening. Today, she didn't seem to notice. But she noticed Mary.

'Mary. You came, and you brought Millie.' Nora reached her hands out to Millie, who walked over and sniffed them. Nora moved over and patted the chair.

Millie looked up at Mary, who nodded and dropped the leash. The little dog jumped up beside Nora and put her head in her lap. A ghost of a smile appeared on Nora's face as she started to stroke the dog, and Mary thought her breathing seemed less ragged. Mary backed up and took the chair on the other side of the low table that separated them. Nick took the high green wingback that anchored the grouping.

'Mary, Les says we can't set a date for the funeral because the police want to do an autopsy. They haven't said a word about it to me. Don't they usually have to ask? Have you seen Dan Dunham? What does he say?' Nora stopped stroking the dog and seemed almost to plead with Mary for information.

Mary wasn't sure what to say. The police didn't have to get permission if they suspected a wrongful death, but how would she say that to Nora? Evasion was the only thing she could think of. 'I think there are a lot of reasons for doing one. Chet was old and had dementia. I suppose the coroner couldn't be sure of the cause of death, so they have to find out.'

That statement wouldn't have satisfied her, and she thought Nora looked doubtful. Maybe if she embellished it . . .? 'They did one on Samuel when he died. The heart attack was sudden, and he hadn't had any heart problems that we knew of.' What she didn't say was she was asked. If this autopsy showed natural causes, then Nora need never know something much more unpleasant had been suspected. That Chet had been smothered would be almost more than Nora could bear, and she didn't want to be the one who explained it to her. However, the fact that Mary's husband had been autopsied seemed to calm Nora.

'Oh.' Nora resumed absently scratching Millie's ears.

Millie rolled over, inviting her to move on to her stomach.

'Well, I guess they know what they're doing. But the whole thing . . . we knew he wasn't going to make it much longer, but this was so sudden. I had been to see him, not that he knew who I was.' She left off scratching Millie again and squirmed around to reach a pocket in her dress and pulled out a rumpled-looking tissue and started to dab her eyes.

Millie took the hint and jumped down, dragging her leash behind her.

'Mother, while Mrs McGill and Reverend and Mrs McIntyre are here, perhaps we should make some plans, or at least tell them what you'd like. I know it's hard, but we have to at least choose a funeral home.'

They all turned to look at him in surprise.

'I assumed it would be O'Dell's,' Les said. 'Aren't the O'Dells old family friends?'

'They retired but their son took over. Of course, they'll do it. I suppose I have to choose a casket?' Nora started to dab her eyes again.

Nick got up to sit on the arm of his mother's chair. He slid an arm around her and gave her a gentle hug. 'Not right now, you don't. We'll wait until my sister Mary Beth gets here.'

'This is so unreal.' Nora resumed dabbing. 'One minute he's here, the next he's gone. He'd talked to that young police-woman. I don't know what they said. I walked up as she was leaving, but she smiled at me.'

A policewoman? 'Was that Janelle Tucker?' Mary pushed Millie, who had jumped up beside her, over a little and leaned forward in her chair.

Nora shook her head slightly. 'I don't know her name. Only that she was there. Something about someone's missing purse.'

Yes. That's what Agnes had said. But why was she in Chet's room? Or was she? He often sat on the big front porch in his wheelchair. Many of the elderly patients did. 'Was she youngish, in her thirties, with a small brown hair bun?'

'Yes. She talked to all the people on the porch.'

'Janelle Tucker? Mother, wasn't Tucker the name of that woman whose husband died on his tractor? The one Dad was going to have to foreclose on because his grapes all dried up?'

Nora leaned against him and didn't answer for a moment. 'I remember the fuss but not the woman's name. It could be, I suppose. But that was a long time ago.'

'They had two daughters. I remember the oldest one. She was pretty cute. Could this Janelle be one of them?'

'She is.' Mary had to smile. She must have been more than cute for Nick to have remembered her after all these years. 'She's the younger daughter. The mother died. Janelle worked for a police department in southern California, and when this job came up, she decided to come back and see if the town was as nice as she remembered it as a child. Happy memories, she told me. We've grown a lot since then.'

'We have, indeed. How nice that Janelle has happy memories of her childhood.' Les glanced at his cell then at Mary and nodded in a way she knew meant let's get this show on the road. Leave it to Les to politely but firmly get them back on track.

'We have indeed,' Ysabel said. 'Grown. Would you like the church committee to take care of the reception after the funeral?

There will be a lot of people. Chet was a popular person in town. He was one of the reasons we've grown and grown so nicely.'

That brought a smile to Nora's face, or almost a smile. 'He was a good man and he loved this town. I think he'd like it if the church hosted the reception. We'll have something small at home later.'

'Is there anything I can do for you right now?' Mary pushed herself out of the chair and reached for her purse. 'I'd be happy to bring you dinner. Are you expecting out-of-town relatives? Can we help with that?'

Nick threw up his hands in a 'no' gesture. 'Food is already pouring in. The kitchen table is full of bowls of I don't know what, there are salads and casseroles, and someone sent a ham. There are three coffee cakes and I counted six pies. We do not need food. My sister will be here later tonight. I'm picking her up at the airport. After that, I'm not sure whose coming. Dad's brother won't be able to and . . . well . . . we'll see. If we need help with any of that, I'll let you know and, Mrs McGill, thank you.'

Les and Ysabel got up as well.

'We'll contact O'Dell's. I'll leave word with the police to please keep in touch with us. This man who's taking over for Dan isn't nearly as cooperative as Dan is, but I'm sure it will all work out.' Les took Nora's hand and gave it a light squeeze; Ysabel gave her a hug. 'If there's anything we can do for you tonight, please let us know. One of us will contact you in the morning. Nick, give our best to your sister. Les will announce to the congregation Sunday morning. We'll let them all know as soon as we have a date and we'll pray for all of you.'

That last sentence startled Mary. Today was Friday, tomorrow Saturday. How had she managed to lose track of time so completely? She also gave Nora a hug, shook hands with Nick, and they were out the door.

'Mary, wait.' Les put a hand on her arm as she was about to open the car door. 'What was all that about the autopsy? Do you know why they're doing one?'

'Just what I told Nora,' she said evasively.

Dan had said their suspicions were confidential, but she

wouldn't want to betray a trust, even if it hadn't been spelled out. However, this was Les and Ysabel. She sighed. They waited.

'All right, but for now this doesn't go any further.'

They both nodded.

'Evidently they think someone might have smothered poor old Chet.'

Ysabel sucked her breath in with a hiss. 'Oh, no,' she whispered.

The sorrowful look on Les's usually pleasant face deepened. 'Why? Why would someone do that to an old man?'

Mary felt about as miserable as Ysabel looked. 'I have no idea. It's so odd. First the robbery of what used to be his bank and now this.'

'You think they might be connected? How?'

'I have no idea, but it doesn't feel right. Maybe he did die of natural causes. They don't know, so, before anyone says anything, especially to the family, I think we should wait for the autopsy report. I hope they get it out soon.'

'Yes,' Les said, his tone grim. 'Let's hope. We'll see you Sunday.'

It wasn't a question. They all knew Mary would be there, overseeing her welcoming committee, making sure there would be coffee and baked goods at the fellowship meeting after the service. Right now, she was going home to try to find a hiding place for the computer. She also wanted to take her shoes off, pour herself a glass of wine, and think. That these two episodes weren't connected didn't seem possible, and what the connection might be was starting to murkily make its way through her mind. She checked to make sure Millie was in her place on the back seat and started down the driveway and down the hill, Les and Ysabel right behind her.

THIRTY

Mary stood in the middle of the kitchen, holding the computer case, looking around. Millie sat by her side. The cat wound its way through her legs purring loudly.

'Where am I supposed to hide something like this?' she said aloud to no one in particular.

Dan hadn't exactly asked her to hide the computer, just to get it out of Victoria's workshop, but the idea someone who had already killed once might want it made her nervous. She didn't think someone would break in looking for it. No one knew she had it, but she felt uneasy.

'Where am I supposed to put this thing? Under my bed? That's the first place I'd look if I was the robber. Under the sofa?' She walked into the living room and looked at the sofa. Not a chance it would fit under there. The hall closet? That was hardly hiding it. She couldn't put it in the clothes hamper or the dryer. Could she?

Now she was getting silly. Dan only wanted the computer in safekeeping until he could get a search warrant or whatever he needed. All she had to do was keep it safe. She walked over to her desk and set the case down beside her desktop monitor and stared at it. What if she took it out of the case and set it up on her desk as if it belonged to her? Like *The Purloined Letter* Mr Poe made so famous. She had no more than taken it out of its case and set it, open, on the desk than the doorbell rang. Should she answer it? Maybe she'd pretend she wasn't home. But Millie had already announced loudly that they were. Trying not to trip on the cat, who rubbed against her legs purring his rusty-sounding purr, she answered the door. It was Mike Gallagher in his police uniform, smiling at her.

'Why, Mike. What a surprise.' She started to smile, but alarm bells went off. 'Is everything all right? Is this about Robbie?'

Mike nodded. 'It's about Robbie, and he's fine. At least, for the time being, but I'd like to talk to you.'

'Of course.' She opened the door wider, grabbed Millie by the collar so she couldn't jump on him, and motioned for him to enter.

'Come sit down. Millie wants to say hello and it will be easier on you if you're sitting.'

Mike laughed and did as instructed. Millie immediately ran over, sniffed his legs, then offered him her ears for scratching. He obliged.

Mary took the big chair. The cat jumped into her lap. Accepting the inevitable, she moved him over a little. 'What about Robbie?'

Mike left off scratching Millie's ears. He stared past Mary into her office, to where the laptop sat on her desk. 'Robbie's becoming dependent on that dog. It's only been two days, and he not only adores her but she seems to give him confidence to try things we haven't been able to. Even therapy hasn't gotten him to try to take a step, for instance, but if Zoe is beside him, he will. Then he's overjoyed because he did it.'

'That's wonderful.' Mary beamed at him, delighted to hear her plan seemed to be working.

Robbie had the help he so badly needed, Nancy was better able to cope with both Robbie and a toddler, and Zoe had a job.

Only the look on Mike's face said something was wrong. 'What? What's wrong?'

'Nancy and I are scared Robbie is getting too attached and if the dog doesn't stay, well, he'll go into a tailspin. I don't think Janelle wants to give the dog up, even if she doesn't need her. Something about Zoe being her mother's dog. We wondered if we could get Robbie a dog of his own. I understand they're free. We wouldn't be able to do it otherwise. Our insurance doesn't pay for all the therapy and only part of the doctor's bills, so there isn't much left to pay for a dog. But if we could keep Zoe, even if only on a part-time basis, it would be best. We thought maybe you could talk to her, find out what her plans are, or at least where Zoe came from. That dog is amazing, but I don't know if it's the dog or the training or both. Anyway, I don't want Robbie hurt.' His fingers seemed to tighten around Millie's ears as he looked at Mary. 'I don't know what to do. Janelle said she'd be out of town this weekend and asked if Zoe could stay with us. Of course we had to let her because Robbie was overjoyed, but we're afraid things are getting out of hand.' His rapidly blinking eyes told more than the slight tremor in his hands as he let go of Millie's ears.

'Why don't you talk to her?' Mary tried to put that as softly as possible, not wanting him to think she wouldn't do what she could. 'You work with her. Wouldn't that be best?'

Mike shook his head. 'I really like Janelle and she's a good cop. I wouldn't want to put her in a bad situation, thinking she had to do something she didn't want because we work together. But if we could at least know what she's thinking . . . anyway, if you could feel her out some way?'

Mary wasn't sure she knew how to do that, but since this had been her idea, she had to try. 'Janelle's out of town? When will she be back?'

'Late Sunday. She's on the schedule for Monday morning. She won't pick up the dog until Monday afternoon. If you could talk to her then, see if we can work out something on a long-term basis, that would be great.' He gave Millie a final pat and stood. 'If not, we'll have to discontinue Zoe's visits. I'll look into getting him a dog of his own, but he's crazy about this one.' He looked past her into her office. 'Two computers? You really have joined the digital age. My mom won't even use a cell phone. I guess you need two with all the events you run.' He gave the office another hard look before he turned back to her. 'I can't thank you enough for all this.'

'Don't thank me yet. I'll talk to Janelle Monday and we'll see what happens. In the meantime, let Robbie enjoy his weekend with Zoe and quit worrying. We'll figure out something.'

'Lately, worry seems to be my middle name.'

Worry didn't appear to be the only emotion on Mike's face or in his voice. Anger, frustration, even despair seemed equally evident as he walked out the doorway. Mary closed the door behind him, then stood, staring at it. She was afraid Mike was stretched to the breaking point. Had putting Zoe and Robbie together been a bad idea? She hoped not. The dog certainly gave Robbie a reason to try. Would another dog do the same thing? Was there a possibility Janelle would give Zoe to Robbie? Mary thought she just might. She'd seemed pleased this afternoon they were getting along so well and had admitted the dog needed a job, but there was something odd about that conversation. Another thought was more troubling than Robbie and Zoe. What would Mike do to help his son? How far would he go? Could he really be the clown who robbed the bank, not meaning to hurt anyone, and found himself boxed into a corner? He was a trained policeman. He knew how to use a gun and wouldn't fall to pieces easily. At least not during the event. He'd fall apart afterwards, when the enormity of what he'd done had time to eat at him.

She walked back into the living room and sat on the sofa, where Mike had sat. The laptop on her desk was in full view, the empty carrying case beside her chair. Had Mike realized it wasn't hers? How could he? Lots of people had a laptop and a desktop computer. He'd seemed pretty interested. He'd stared in the room before he left as he adjusted the holster . . . his gun . . . his gun. What kind of gun had the robber used? Mary knew nothing about guns. Samuel hadn't hunted, and neither of them had felt the need to have one for protection. Not in this small town, where everyone knew everyone else. In large part, they still did. If the gun used was one a policeman might have . . . another thing to discuss with Dan.

She walked into the office and stared at the computer. This little closed black box might hold the answer to all their questions, but it also could put someone behind bars for the rest of their life. She wasn't afraid to keep it, at least not very, but the desire to protect its contents suddenly became overwhelming. What could she do? *The Purloined Letter*. Of course. Why hadn't she thought of it before? She picked up the office phone and dialed.

THIRTY-ONE

The beauty shop was almost empty. Even at nine on a Saturday morning, Mary had expected to see more women in there, but she was relieved. Her hospitality committee meeting to plan Chet's funeral was scheduled for one, and she had to go home and pick up Millie before then. Millie didn't like to be left alone for very long. She'd take her frustration out on the sofa pillows. The cat didn't seem to care one way or the other. Although it was a much nicer cat than she'd expected, she hoped Pat Bennington was having some luck finding it a home. Her wandering thoughts were interrupted by Lucille, owner of Snip and Curl.

'You've left it too long again. You're beginning to look like a poodle. Sit down.'

Lucille was right. She had left it too long, but things kept happening. Like the Halloween in the Park event and the bank robbery. They tended to make her forget about her hair. But it was time for it to come off. Lucille swirled the protective cape around like a matador and swiveled the chair around so Mary's back was to the mirror and she faced the empty station on the other side of the room.

'For heaven's sake, what's all that?'

The station's counter was piled with balloons. Not fat, round ones but long, skinny ones twisted into odd shapes. Some were all one color, others were a combination of colors that didn't always complement each other.

'That's Kyle's latest project. He should have taken them home last night, but he didn't, and he hasn't shown up this morning. That young man is getting more scattered by the day.'

Mary's chair twisted, and she faced the mirror, but not for long.

'Let's get over to the shampoo bowl before someone beats us to it.'

Mary looked around. There was only one other customer

in the place, and her hair dripped water which Eva, the new girl, was drying off with a towel. However, she heaved herself out of the swirling chair without falling over the foot rest and settled down, her head over the shampoo bowl.

Lucille immediately started asking questions. 'How's Dan? I hear he's going home today. Is that true? Sure hope so.'

Mary's head was showered with warm water immediately followed by shampoo and strong fingers that started rubbing into her scalp.

'AGGGGG.' It was all Mary could say. It was hard to answer questions when you were upside down over a shampoo bowl. However, it didn't seem to matter as Lucille had more questions and didn't bother pausing for an answer.

'Do they have any idea who that clown was who shot Dan and Victoria? I can't believe they can't find him. How can someone disappear dressed like that in a public parking place? He had an accomplice. That's what I think. He jumped in a car and huddled down in the back and his accomplice drove off as if nothing had happened.' Fingers dug into Mary's scalp, then warm water again. A towel was wrapped around Mary's head, and she was sitting upright in the chair, feeling a little out of breath.

Lucille helped her into the swivel chair, dried her hair off, tossed the towel to one side, and began to comb. 'I suppose you want it the same as always. One of these days I want to comb it over like this, maybe do a little bang, sort of feather in the sides . . .'

Mary shook her head. 'My hair is happy the way you always cut it, and so am I.'

Lucille sighed and began to snip. 'Is Dan really going home today?'

'If he is, I haven't heard about it. The doctor said maybe. I know he's better. He's demanding reports on everything his people do.'

Lucille smiled – a rather mirthless smile. 'Bet that sticks in Sean Ryan's craw. He can go back to San Louis Obispo and never come back, for all I care.'

Mary jerked her head around in surprise. 'Why? What did he ever do to you?'

Lucille moved Mary's head back where she wanted it and resumed snipping. 'Nothing to me. He was rude as rude can be to Kyle, who does most of the men. Kyle's good, just ask any of the guys who come in, but not mister ego on two legs. Kept critiquing Kyle, pointing out each hair, not giving him a chance to finish anything. He almost had Kyle in tears, rage, or frustration. I don't know which, but he sure had him rattled. I almost took over, but Kyle finished, and the guy looked great. Then he didn't tip him. What a jerk.'

She swung Mary around once more and started doing something to the back of her head.

Mary stared at the balloons. 'What is Kyle doing with those balloons? They look like something out of a child's nightmare.'

Lucille laughed. 'You got the child part right. Kyle's decided he needs a part-time job and thinks that being a clown for kids' birthday parties would suit him fine. He's trying to learn how to make balloon animals. That pile over there is as far as he's gotten. That, and practicing his pathetic jokes on us. He's going to bore the kids to death unless he has them on the floor laughing at his pathetic animals. He even got himself a clown costume but, of course, no bookings. I hope he never gets one. I like Kyle. He's a good guy, but as a clown in front of a dozen little demons? It won't work. He's good at what he does here. He needs to stick with it.'

Mary hardly felt Lucille swing her around again or heard the blow dryer. She barely looked in the mirror when Lucille handed her a hand mirror and turned her so she could see the back. She nodded, claimed it was great, but was in a daze as she paid her and walked out. She sat in the car for several minutes, thinking. Kyle had a clown suit. His initials fit the last suit Victoria had made that they hadn't identified. Kyle wanted to be a birthday clown. Really? Lucille was right. The kids would eat his lunch. Kyle was nice enough but intense, and he had no sense of humor. He wasn't spontaneous, and she was sure he couldn't do a prat fall. If he did, he wouldn't get a laugh. Did he have the nerve to rob a bank? Why would he do it? Did he have something against Chet? The more she thought about Chet, the more she was convinced if he was smothered, it was by the clown. Only, this time not in costume. Who of the people they thought might be involved were at or near Shady Acres yesterday? She wondered if she could stop by . . . no. Not without talking to Dan first. She had a lot of things to talk to Dan about, and one of them had to do with guns. She clicked on her cell, sent Ellen a text asking if Dan was going home and what time that would be, and then started the engine. She had just enough time to get Millie, eat a bite, and show up at her meeting.

THIRTY-TWO

M ary pulled into the garage and pushed the button to close the door behind her. She left her purse on the seat, took her keys, and opened the side door leading into her backyard. She was greeted by Millie.

'What are you doing here?' She gasped as she stared down at the wiggling dog. 'I left you in the house. How did you get out?' Filled with trepidation, she pushed the side door wider and stepped into her yard.

The cat sat on the top step of her back stairs, obviously not happy. He yowled loudly at the sight of her. The door into the kitchen was closed. She had left it closed, but both animals had been in the house. How had they gotten out? Only one way she could think of. She'd had an uninvited visitor. Was the person still in the house? What should she do?

She stood by the gate, staring at the door, frozen with indecision. It had to be the clown. He knew she had Victoria's computer. How? Who could have known? Mike knew. He had been here last night and had stared at it. How he could know it was Victoria's, she had no idea, but he had been interested. Who else? Kyle. He had seen her in the parking lot behind Victoria's shop. She'd told him she was picking up dresses, but it wouldn't take much imagination to realize dresses weren't the only thing she was after. It certainly wasn't Paul. He was still in jail, at least she thought he was. He'd have no way to know she'd taken the laptop out of the shop. He probably didn't even know who she was. She hadn't known him. As for Troy, well, he had a solid alibi, so he didn't seem likely. Right now, who wasn't the question. Was someone still in her house? That was the question. Maybe she should grab Millie and head for the police station. Or she could call 9-1-1 and have someone come out. That made the most sense. Only, what if no one had been here? Maybe she'd accidently locked the animals out. She had been in a hurry. Could that be possible?

If she walked up the stairs and someone was still inside, would Millie bark a warning? Lassie would have, but she wasn't sure about Millie. Maybe if she made a lot of noise, banged on something, spoke loudly and hoped whoever it was had left or would leave. She took a deep breath, marched up the stairs, opened the door, and slammed it shut, then opened it again and hollered at the top of her lungs, 'I can't believe I locked you both out. Come on, I'll get you water.'

But she didn't step in. She listened quietly. If someone was here, would they try to get away? She fervently hoped so. Was that a click? The lock on the front door? She remembered turning the dead bolt last night. Could that be the intruder leaving? What should she do? Go into the living room and check? Look out the window and try to see someone? Or stay where she was until she knew the coast was clear? The cat made the decision. He didn't stay in the doorway. He wound himself around Mary's legs and started to meow loudly, wanting something and making sure she knew it. Any other sound, like the front door closing, was drowned out.

'Shhh,' she told him, but he meowed louder.

Millie wasn't much help. Evidently tired of sitting in the doorway, she pushed by Mary, entered the kitchen, and headed for her water bowl. She gave no sign that someone might be in the house.

'I can't stand here,' Mary announced to the room at large. She got no answer. She took a deep breath and entered the kitchen, leaving the door slightly ajar in case she needed to make a hasty exit. As quietly as she could, she inched her way across the floor to the door leading into the dining area and peeked around it, keeping herself flat behind the doorjamb. She wasn't sure why, but she'd seen it done on the TV police shows, so there must be a reason. She'd ask Dan, but there were a lot of questions ahead of that one, and the dining room appeared empty.

Sliding herself around the jamb and into the dining room, she craned her neck to investigate the living room. It also appeared empty. So did the office. Also, the bathroom and her bedroom. She began to relax. No one was here. Someone had been, though. Her clothes hamper lid was up. Someone had tossed her soiled laundry back in with abandon. Her blue pants were on the floor behind it. The hairs on the back of her neck were beginning to tingle, but she continued to look around. Someone had looked under the bed. The small rug she kept beside it was almost all the way under. It hadn't been this morning. Had they been in the office? At first glance, it didn't look disturbed. Her desk looked the same as she'd left it. The computer was silent, her printer still on the small filing cabinet, the drawers closed. So were the desk drawers, and none of the furniture appeared to have been moved. Except her mother's old chest of drawers, the one with the hard-to-open bottom drawer, which was slightly askew. The drawers were deep and wide, a perfect place to hide a laptop, only she hadn't. She hadn't opened that drawer in ages. Someone had and hadn't been able to close it all the way. Something else caught her eye. The closet door. She kept her coats and winter shoes in there. She kept a lot of things on the two shelves above the clothes rack, and she kept the door closed. Only, it wasn't. You had to look closely, but it hadn't quite caught. She took a deep breath, then another. Someone had been here, looking for something, and there was only one possibility.

She wanted to sit down, to think about this, but she had to check the front door. She saw the dead bolt pulled back before she got to it. That it had been locked when she left, she was sure. She locked it every night and hadn't opened it that morning. Someone had left that way. No point in looking out the window. Whoever it was had long gone, but she did anyway. The street was empty. Locking the dead bolt once more, she walked over to her chair and dropped down. Luckily, the cat wasn't in it. What should she do? Call the police? No. Nothing was taken, and she'd have to explain what she thought the intruder was looking for. She needed to talk to Dan before she did that.

Go to her meeting and act as if nothing had happened? Probably, but could she pull it off? She looked at her hand resting on her knee. It shook when she tried to pick it up. Deep breath. Take another one. Think. Someone had been in her house, looking for the computer. Who? Someone who knew she had it, and that it might, probably did, have the names of Victoria's clients, full names, information on what they bought, incriminating evidence. The killer would want that evidence. Badly. Who knew? Only one person leapt to mind. Kyle. He had seen her in the back of Victoria's shop. She had told him she was going in to get dresses. He knew she would be at the beauty shop this morning, and he hadn't shown up for his morning appointments, who, according to Lucille, had left in disgust. Kyle, who had a clown suit, a counter full of twisted balloons, and a desire to be a birthday party entertainer. Kyle, who was always short of money. Her knees felt too weak to carry her, but she had to get up.

Wait. What about Chet? Why would Kyle want to kill him? Was he even at Shady Acres yesterday? She didn't know. But she could find out. Vanessa Butterworth was head administrator of Shady Acres and a member of St Mark's hospitality committee. She would be at the meeting which was scheduled to start – Mary glanced at her watch – in ten minutes. If she hurried, she wouldn't be too late. Weak knees forgotten, she hurried into the office, picked up the folder marked 'Hospitality, St Marks' off her desk, called Millie, and headed for the back door. Millie ran on ahead, eager to get in the car. Mary paused to make sure the cat was in the house, then did something she rarely did. She locked her back door.

THIRTY-THREE

'Where have you been?' Exclamations came at her from all sides. 'We were getting worried. Are you all right?'

'For heaven's sake, I'm only seven minutes late,' she told Ysabel.

'I know, but you're always early. What happened?'

Feeling slightly irritated and more than slightly shook, she took a breath before answering. She didn't want to snap anyone's head off. These were good people who were concerned. She was, too, but for different reasons. 'I was at Lucille's Snip and Curl and then I had to pick up Millie. Took me longer than I thought. Have you started?'

Ysabel shook her head. 'No. You have the folder. We thought we'd wait. But everyone's here.'

Mary's committee of eight was seated around a large round table on folding chairs, full white coffee mugs in front of several of them. Mary took a seat and Ysabel put a full cup in front of her. She smiled her thanks and opened her folder. Millie crawled under the table and put her head on Mary's shoe.

'All right, everyone. O'Dell's will do the funeral. They'll take care of the incoming flowers. We'll do the church flowers, as usual, and Nora has asked us to provide the refreshments after the graveside ceremony. We will have to come back here. There's no way we can get all the people who will be at this funeral into their house.'

'We couldn't get them up the driveway, either.' That from Ray Fisher, who knew Chet's family well. They had grown up together, been in Kiwanis together, and raised their kids together. Ray had almost gone off the driveway into the ravine below one dark night and hadn't forgotten it.

An assenting murmur went around the table, and Mary went on. 'Here's a sample menu we've used before. Pass it around and then let's see what everyone thinks.'

Everyone had seen it before and knew what worked and what didn't. Ideas were offered and approved or ignored. They all agreed this time disposable plates, cups, napkins, and silverware would be used. The budget was checked, assignments for different jobs made, and a date for a follow-up meeting discussed.

'Do we have any idea when the body will be released?' Ysabel asked.

That question was addressed to Mary, but she didn't have an answer. She didn't have an answer why they needed an autopsy, either.

'I hear that San Louis detective whose taking Dan's place has been questioning that poor kid Troy Turnbull. Why would he think Troy would shoot up a bank?' Hank Fielding finished his coffee and set the mug on the table with a small bang.

'Troy has an alibi,' Mary said.

Everyone looked at her, but no one said anything until Mary Kate Reardon said, 'I heard they arrested Paul Cummings.'

'I thought they arrested him for stealing a credit card.' Lulu Edwards looked confused.

Mary marveled, not for the first time, how fast news, or gossip, traveled in her small town.

'That, too,' Mary Kate said. 'But he has a clown costume. Someone, I forget who, saw him Halloween night. I don't know if he did it or not, but whoever did was dressed as a clown, and I hear Paul Cummings was fired from at least two wineries because he was caught stealing.'

Speculation went on for another few minutes, the time was noted, chairs were pushed back, and people started to disperse.

Mary also got up. She edged closer to Vanessa Butterworth. 'Have you got a minute?'

Vanessa looked at her curiously and nodded. 'I'm not quite finished with my coffee. What's up?'

That was what Mary wanted to ask Vanessa, but she was going to have to edge around what she wanted to know. She sat back down. Millie, who had raised her head in preparation to leave, lowered it again.

'I heard you had an incident out there on Thursday before they found Chet dead.'

Vanessa glowered and set her mug on the table with a bang. 'Norma Wilson. Remember her?'

Mary nodded guardedly. Norma was hard to forget. She'd tended to have hysterics at the drop of a hat when she was a young woman raising her three children, and age hadn't improved her. 'What did she do this time?'

'Left her purse in the dining room. It wasn't the first time she'd done it, but usually one of the aides spots it and returns it to her before she falls apart. This time, no one could find it. So, of course, Norma demanded the police. I felt like a fool calling them, I knew it would turn up, but it was the only way to calm her down. Two of them showed up. Mike Gallagher and a new officer, Janelle something. Nice lady. She helped search the rooms for the purse, but it was Mike who found it. In Elsie Carter's room. She'd picked it up, meaning to return it to Norma, but had fallen asleep instead.' Vanessa looked at Mary and shook her head. 'All that fuss for absolutely nothing.'

A chill ran down Mary's spine. Mike had been at Shady Acres, searching in patients' rooms, about the time Chet had been smothered. If he had been smothered. Why would Mike do that? Why would anyone? Maybe she was wrong. Maybe Chet's death and the robbery weren't connected. Maybe Chet just up and died. But she didn't like it. Any of it. There was something she wasn't seeing. Maybe . . . 'Vanessa, do you know Kyle Nevins?'

'Why, yes. His mother lives in the retirement wing. She plays a mean hand of bridge and runs her regular foursome like a third-world dictator. She runs Kyle like that as well. He visits her on a regular basis. When she doesn't have a bridge game going, of course. Why?'

Mary wasn't sure why, and Vanessa's answer didn't help her much. 'Was Kyle there on Thursday?'

Vanessa was silent for a moment. 'I don't know. Visitors don't have to sign into the resident's wing. I see him often, though. He has lunch with her sometimes, but I don't remember him that day. But, Mary, Thursday was crazy.' She looked at the clock on the meeting hall wall. 'I've got to go. I have a staff meeting in half an hour. Is there anything else? I think I know what to do to get ready for the funeral.'

Mary didn't doubt for a minute that Thursday had been crazy. She smiled at Vanessa. 'No, nothing. Thank you and, Vanessa, I'll be in touch when we get a date for the funeral. It should go smoothly. It's not like we haven't done this before.'

Vanessa laughed, nodded, and hurried out of the room, her cell phone already up to her ear.

Mary sat for a moment, thinking. Finally, she pushed back her chair, picked up her mug and Vanessa's, and put them in the commercial dishwasher. 'Millie, I have no idea what's going on, but I do know I'm missing something. Dan's apparently coming home today.' She looked at her watch. 'He's probably there now. I think we're going to pay him a visit.'

Millie trotted after Mary as they left the room.

THIRTY-FOUR

Dan was home and he had company. Sean Ryan and Janelle Tucker were there. Ryan was talking to Dan, who was propped up in his recliner, a blanket over his knees, Janelle standing by, holding a notebook and pen. Morgan lay beside the chair, and Ellen was hovering around behind him, trying to wrap a shawl around his shoulders. That wasn't working out too well.

'I'm fine,' he said. 'I don't want a shawl.'

'You just got out of the hospital.' Ellen tried one more time to drape it over his shoulders.

'The hospital didn't think I needed one. They were quite content to wrap me up in plaster and tape, some of which they let me take home.' He sounded a little bitter, but he reached up and patted his wife's hand. 'Ellen, thank you but I'm fine.'

Ellen gave up and greeted her aunt. Millie greeted Morgan. No one even noticed the ginger cat who sat on the bookcase in front of the complete works of Charles Dickens, which suited Jake, the cat, just fine.

'Sean was telling me they think they have a good case

against Paul Cummings. They got a search warrant and found the clown suit.' Dan waved Mary toward a chair.

Sean Ryan frowned. Evidently, he didn't approve of Dan bringing Mary up to date.

She didn't care. They'd need more than the costume to convict Paul Cummings. 'Did you find the gun also?'

'No.' Janelle quit writing in her notebook. 'We sent the costume to the lab to see if there's any evidence of gun residue. We couldn't find any trace of the money or the bag, but we will.'

Mary thought Dan didn't look convinced. He would be less convinced when he heard what she had to tell him, but she had no intention of talking to him with Ryan there. He seemed fixated on Paul Cummings, who probably should go to jail for something, but not necessarily for murder. So, she changed the subject.

'I had a committee meeting this morning. We've done the preliminary planning for Chet's funeral and will finalize everything when you give us a date. Any news yet?'

The look of disapproval Ryan gave Dan would have made a lesser man run for cover.

Dan ignored him. 'Nothing yet. Besides, I can't see a connection.'

Janelle quit writing and stared at them. 'You think there's a connection between the bank robbery and that man who died at the nursing home? You said he'd been gone from the bank for years. How could there be a connection?'

'There isn't one,' Ryan said, not bothering to hide his annoyance. 'According to what I've been told, he'd been in a serious decline for a long time. How could he be connected to a bank robbery?'

A valid question and one to which Mary had no answer. Just a feeling, which she didn't think Ryan would appreciate. However, they had four suspects and not one of them had a connection to Chet, either now or in the past. She had to admit, even to herself, that faint nagging feeling was probably completely wrong. But Dan's answer made her wonder.

'He may not have been, but don't forget there was evidence he'd been smothered. There had to be a reason, and I don't think there's a homicidal maniac running around Shady Acres smothering old people. Let's see what the autopsy says.'

Janelle looked a little pale when Dan mentioned autopsy. It was a terrible thought, an old defenseless man smothered to death.

Ryan didn't look as upset. He looked irritated. He turned to Janelle, and the expression on his face changed. The smile he gave her, and his tone of voice was friendly. More than friendly. 'You ready to go, Janelle? It's past lunchtime. Maybe we can get a quick bite before we go back to the station.' He checked his watch. 'I think we've brought Chief Dunham up to date.' He turned to Dan. 'Is there anything more we can tell you?'

Dan glanced at Mary then addressed Ryan. 'No, that was a pretty thorough report. It doesn't sound as if we have enough on Cummings to charge him with murder, but you can hold him on the credit card charge. See if the DA will indict. I'll see you in the morning, then, and if anything new turns up, let me know.'

Janelle closed her notebook and started for the door. Mary caught a look at the hand that held it. There was a large bandage across the back.

'Oh, Janelle. What happened?'

Janelle started, looked at her hand, and then at Mary. 'I had an argument with a rose bush and lost.' She laughed. 'It's fine.'

Mary nodded.

Ryan turned quickly to follow Janelle, reaching out as if to take her arm. A question from Dan stopped him.

'Sean, I forgot to ask. How's your wife? That new baby keeping her pretty busy, I expect.'

Ryan started, as if he'd been hit with an electric cattle prod. Mary saw him jerk.

He turned back to Dan, his face a mix of emotions. Mary thought fright and possibly embarrassment were mixed with a lot of irritation. 'They're both fine. Thanks for asking,' he said in a frozen tone.

'Glad to hear that,' Dan said. 'New babies can be stressful. See you in the morning.'

No one said anything until they heard the front door slam.

'That was interesting,' Ellen finally said.

'I didn't know he was a new father,' Mary added thoughtfully. 'He didn't look happy when you reminded him.'

'Yeah,' Dan said. 'I don't suppose he was. But babies are stressful, and sometimes young fathers get a little . . . well, let's say they like to remember their bachelor days. Janelle is a good-looking woman. Ryan's at a stage in life where a man can get tempted. Doesn't hurt to be reminded what's important.'

Mary almost laughed. Ryan had been reminded. But if she'd read the expression on Janelle's face right, he wouldn't get to first base. He probably wouldn't get out of the batter's box.

Ellen picked up another point. 'You think she's good-looking? I guess, if you like the leggy skinny type.'

Dan reached up with his good hand and found hers. He pulled her around the chair and slid his hand up around her waist. 'She's a sexy woman, even with those tinted glasses she wears, but she can't hold a candle to you. Not in any way.' He gave her a pat.

She dropped a kiss on his head.

Mary said, 'Janelle is a good-looking woman, what we used to call handsome. She's tall, but she doesn't impress me as a particularly strong woman. I wonder why she chose police work.'

'Her mother told her it would be a good job with good benefits. Said she could help bring people to justice. Evidently Janelle agreed. She went through the Los Angeles police academy and that's no easy feat. I'm not entirely sure why she chose to come back here, but I'm glad she did. She has a good head on her shoulders.'

Mary nodded. Interesting but not relevant to what she had to say. 'Let's get down to business. I have some things to tell you.'

'I figured you did. Shoot.'

Mary thought he might have phrased that better. 'Someone broke into my house this morning while I was at the Snip and Curl. Also, I think I know who belongs to the last set of initials.' She paused to let that sink in.

Ellen gasped a little.

Dan's hand clutched the side of the chair so hard his knuckles turned white. 'Who?'

'Who broke into my house or who do the initials belong to?'

'Both.' That came out through clenched teeth.

'I don't know who was in the house, but I can guess. I think whoever it was wanted Victoria's computer. The last initials belong to Kyle Nevins.'

'Kyle Nevins. Who cuts hair?'

'Kyle . . . you're kidding.' Ellen shook her head in disbelief. 'Kyle wouldn't hurt a fly. Literally. I watched him shoo one away in the beauty shop one day. Lucille wasn't so sensitive. She wacked it with a towel. Kyle is nice to everyone.'

'Why do you think Kyle is one of Victoria's clowns?' Dan looked more curious than surprised.

'I don't think. I know. He bought the costume because he's decided to become a birthday party clown. He's learning to make animal balloons but, judging from the ones I saw at the shop, it's a steep learning curve and he hasn't climbed up it very far.'

Ellen gave a snort of laughter. 'Kyle, a clown? That's funny, but Kyle isn't. He's great with hair, though. What gave you the idea . . . Lucille. Is that where you got all this?'

Mary nodded. 'That and I saw the balloons. Anyway, we know he has a clown costume and his initials fit the last set. I also learned that his mother is in the residential section of Shady Acres and he visits her regularly. I don't know for sure if he was there on Thursday, but he would certainly know his way around. He could have smothered poor old Chet. Another thing. Kyle knew I had Victoria's computer. He saw me going into the shop yesterday. I told him I was going to pick up dresses, but it wouldn't take much of a leap to know I might be, and probably was, picking up the computer, not if you were the clown and already worried about what might be on it. He also knew I had an appointment at the shop this morning, and he showed up late.'

'You think he was the one who broke in? How do you know someone had been there?' Dan didn't sound dubious, only thoughtful.

Mary described what she'd found, and Dan nodded.

'The computer, he didn't get it?'

Mary's smile was complacent. 'No. I'd removed it to a much safer place.'

'Where?' Ellen's eyes sparkled with curiosity.

'Somewhere safe. I'll tell you both where when Dan gets whatever he needs to get to have someone hack into it.'

'I'm working on that.' Dan seemed no less curious than Ellen, but he didn't press Mary. At least not on the location of the computer. 'I think you and Millie should come visit us for a few days.'

Mary knew what he meant, but she had no intention of complying. 'I'm visiting you right now.'

'You know what I mean. What if this person breaks into your home again and you're there?'

'That person is likely Kyle, and he won't be back. He knows the computer isn't there.'

'Why would Kyle murder Chet and why would he rob the bank?' Ellen detached Dan's arm from around her waist and headed for the kitchen. 'Talk loud. I'm going to make coffee.'

'Good idea,' Mary called after her. She returned to Dan. 'I don't know why any of them would want to kill Chet or rob the bank. Well, that's not exactly true. I know why Mike might want to. Rob the bank, I mean. They need money. I guess their insurance doesn't pay for a lot of the therapy Robbie needs, and it's putting a strain on them. In every way. But I can't see Mike resorting to something like that.'

Dan didn't say anything for a moment. 'I didn't realize his insurance didn't cover everything. He should have come to me. I've been thinking he was ready for a promotion. Maybe I can speed that up. But not if he's the clown. Then he gets to go to jail for a long time.' He started to chew on that thought.

Mary gave him another. 'If Chet really was smothered and it links to the robbery, we're down to two suspects. Mike and Kyle. Paul Cummings was safe in jail when Chet was killed, and Troy Turnbull has an alibi for the robbery.'

'There's been a slight hitch in that alibi.' Dan smiled a mirthless little smile. 'It seems Eduardo O'Hare, from the garage, was out picking up a broken-down car that afternoon. He was gone for over an hour, about the same time as the robbery. He came back into town after it was all over and heard about it from Troy and some of their clients. There's no one to say Troy didn't put on his clown suit after O'Hare left, zip over to the bank, which is literally around the corner, perform the robbery, and somehow ditch the clown suit and return back to work before Eduardo returned.'

Mary sucked in her breath. That changed things. 'If it was Troy, he would have been on foot. Where did he change out of the clown costume?'

'Good question. One that has no answer yet. There's no sign of a gun or any trace of the money or the bag. To date, no answers to any of those things. Just that he could have.'

'He could have. So could any of them. I assume Troy is back in first place on Sean Ryan's potential suspect list, with Paul Cummings next. But if Chet is a victim, then Paul is out.'

'You seem determined to involve Chet.' Ellen set a mug of coffee in front of her aunt, put another one by Dan's good arm, and sank down on one end of the couch with her own.

Jake, the cat, jumped up in her lap, eyeing the dogs as if he dared them to intrude. Neither of them did. Jake purred, settled himself down and Ellen began to rub his ears with her free hand.

'Why are you so certain Chet's death is murder and the same person did it?'

'I've been thinking about that.' Mary picked up her own mug, watched the steam rise above the lip, touched it to her tongue, and abruptly set it back down. 'The robbery was planned meticulously. The clown costume ordered early on, the clown mask and the shoes probably obtained online. Those shoes, by the way, sure didn't interfere with him running down the street. That also had to be planned. Glen believed he knew when the cash drawers were refilled, so he had to know they would be at their lowest level. He also had to know the bank wouldn't be crowded, that it was a slow time. All that took a lot of planning. It also makes me wonder why he chose that time. It would seem the money wasn't all that important.'

She paused, waiting for comments. Ellen nodded.

Dan stared at her and shook his head. 'I don't suppose you'd like to head up my crime-scene unit, would you?'

Mary ignored that. 'I keep asking myself why someone would rob the bank when the cash drawers were at their lowest. This happened after the noon-hour rush and the drawers wouldn't be filled again until mid-afternoon, before the going-home rush. He must have known that. So, I think there was a personal reason he robbed the bank.'

'Personal reason? What personal reason?' Ellen quit rubbing Jake's ears and stared at her aunt.

Jake protested. She started again.

'Revenge,' Dan said with a sigh as he punched the button on the arm of the chair. It straightened up. So did he and his feet hit the floor. 'We considered that when we thought Troy might have done it. Now we're back to that idea.'

'How would that include Chet?' Ellen asked.

Mary thought Ellen had a good point. 'Could Troy have thought Chet had something to do with him not getting the loan?'

Ellen frowned and set Jake on the floor. 'I don't see how. Chet hadn't had anything to do with the working of the bank for . . . six years?'

Dan agreed.

'I also don't see how robbing a bank is revenge. Banks aren't people. You can't take revenge on an institution.'

'You're right, of course, but maybe someone wanted to cast doubt on the safety of the bank? On its good reputation? Or . . .?' said Mary.

'Or maybe someone was just pissed off and couldn't think of any other way to get back at the bank. Or the people who run it.' Dan wiggled around in the chair and tried to get up.

'Where are you going?' Ellen was on her feet, alarm on her face. 'What do you need? I'll get it.'

'You can't. I need to use the bathroom, and I don't need help. But thanks for the offer.' He kissed her lightly on the cheek and, more slowly than Mary would have liked to see him move, he started for the hallway.

Ellen seemed to hold her breath as she watched him go, only letting it out when the bathroom door closed.

'He's fine,' Mary said. 'He's doing better than I expected.'

'Most of that is sheer will. He doesn't like being laid up,

and he doesn't like having someone else run his department. I know he's going to do too much too soon, but I don't know what to do about it.'

'Let him alone. This one is personal, and he's not going to rest until we know who shot both him and Victoria. But his staff seems to be trying to do whatever they can. I was surprised to see Janelle, though. I thought she had the weekend off.'

'I think she's going somewhere late this afternoon and will be back Sunday night. She goes off-duty today around five. She's turned out to be a good addition to the force. Dan says she's had great training and she's smart. He hopes she stays around for a long time.'

Mary nodded. Dan came back into the room. She smiled at him but watched carefully as he eased himself back into the chair. His left arm still wasn't functional. It wasn't as taped up as it had been, but it was still in a sling that held it close to his body. She could see that it put him off balance and he wasn't pleased about it. He muttered something she couldn't quite catch as he lowered himself down in his chair, resting his weight on his right arm.

'There's one more thing I need to tell you before I go,' she said.

'Oh?' Dan cocked one eyebrow.

'What?' Ellen leaned forward a little, expectation on her face.

'You know I went to Victoria's shop yesterday. Something had been bothering me, and I wanted to see if I could find an answer, so I looked at her patterns.'

Dan looked blank and Ellen puzzled. They nodded at her to go on.

'The clown costume is in two pieces. Three, really. The pants, the top, and the ruff are separate. The top is designed to be pulled on over your head. Three of those costumes pull on, one zips up the front.'

'What? How do you know that?'

'It's the only thing that makes sense. The clown wouldn't have wanted to take the time to struggle out of a pullover top. He needed to get out of it fast. So, he had his made with a zipper. I found what I think was what Victoria used. It's a heavy one with a large silver ring. I saw it flash in the sun when the shooter came out of the bank that day. I held this one up to the light and it did the same thing.'

Ellen leaned back against the sofa pillows and laughed. 'Of course. Why didn't I think of that?'

'I wondered but wasn't sure until I looked at the pattern.' Mary looked at her niece with skepticism. Ellen had no interest in sewing. She doubted if she even knew how to thread the sewing machine. 'I looked at the pattern carefully. It's been altered.'

Dan looked at her, obviously confused. 'Why do we care if she made a top with a zipper and a ring?'

'Two reasons. First, the day of the robbery, when the clown stopped, and I thought he was going to shoot me and Millie, I saw the sun reflecting off something on the top of the costume, up by the neck but not covered by the ruff. I didn't pay any attention to it, but I do remember it. I think it was the ring attached to the zipper. Second reason, no one else had any reason to have Victoria alter the pattern. I kept thinking how the clown could have disappeared so fast. Maybe he didn't. I think our clown wanted a zipper so he could get out of the costume fast. The pants are made with an elastic waist, but it would take more time to get out of the top if you had to untie it from behind and pull it over your head. I think this one was designed for a quick change.'

Ellen leaned forward and rested her elbows on her knees. 'Makes sense, but does it get us any further?'

'In a way. If, for instance, Ryan finds that Troy had a clown costume but it has a pull-over top, it helps to exonerate him. Or Paul Cummings. They've already found his. If it was a pull-over top, he probably didn't do it. Not full proof, but it's helpful.'

Dan nodded. 'It would be that. Unfortunately, the only costume we've actually found was Paul's.'

'But we know who the other three people who bought them are.' Mary felt she had to make her point if for no other reason than they had to start eliminating people. 'We know Mike has a costume, but we have no idea how it's made. We also know Kyle has one. Somehow, we need to get a look at both.' She sighed. 'We don't know if Troy has one, and I'm not sure how we find out.'

'Can you get a search warrant or something?' Ellen looked from Dan to Mary, evidently seeking an answer.

Mary didn't have one.

Dan ran the fingers of his uninjured hand through his hair, making it stand on end. 'It's interesting, but not even close to being enough to get a search warrant for any of them. We'll have to find another way. Besides, there are other things involved. Like Chet.'

Mary had started to her feet, Millie right beside her. It was time to go home, but there was one thing Dan had said that she couldn't seem to shake. 'You said it might be someone who was mad enough at the bank to take a sort of revenge by robbing it, even if it wouldn't really hurt the bank. A sort of symbolic revenge. Do you really believe that?'

Dan sighed deeply. 'I don't know. But the points you made earlier are valid. It could be someone who thinks they can get back at the bank this way, and, frankly, Chet fits into that mold.'

'What about Glen?'

'Glen.' Dan stared at her.

Ellen gasped. 'Do you think Glen might be in danger?'

'Danger? Glen? I never thought of it before this.' Dan's expression changed from startled to thoughtful.

'Dan.' Ellen got up to stand beside him, leaned over him, and squeezed his good arm. 'Do you really think this stupid clown would try to harm Glen? For revenge? For what? A loan they couldn't get? I can't believe it, but should you warn him?'

'Warn him against what?' Dan sounded dubious and a little dismissive, but his brow was furrowed. 'We don't have a shred of evidence that the motive for this robbery was some weird kind of revenge. It's all theory, just like Chet's death is. We don't really know anything right now except we have four people who had clown costumes made by Victoria. We can't even prove the costume this robber wore was one she made. That material isn't available only in Santa Louisa. No, I don't think there's anything to warn Glen about. We'll keep looking

His chances of no one noticing him were good. Most people were asleep at this hour of the morning. Mike was here, in this room and certainly not acting like he'd just tried to kill someone. On the other hand, what better alibi could he have than trying to solve the case?

She shuddered. She didn't want it to be him. Mike didn't seem the type to carry a grudge, but he was a policeman. He had a gun and knew how to use it. He was also strong. It would have taken no time at all to smother poor old Chet. He had been there, at Shady Acres, when Chet died. She didn't want it to be Kyle, either. Such a harmless man and so talented with hair. She wondered if he was asleep in his bed or if he was putting away a clown suit that zipped down the front. Why would he shoot out John and Glen's front window? Or kill Chet? Or rob the bank? They needed to find out more about Kyle.

Thank goodness Paul Cummings was in jail. At least they could rule him out. Couldn't they? 'Dan, is Paul Cummings still in jail?'

It was Mike who answered. 'The little rat made bail. But the case against him is solid. He'll be back in soon. If he doesn't flee, that is.'

Ryan didn't look happy Mike had relayed that news. He addressed Mike in clipped tones. 'Have you contacted forensics?'

Mike nodded. 'Just got a text. They're on the way, but they have to come from San Louis Obispo. It'll be a while before they get here. Why don't I have a look around outside? Probably nothing to find, but it can't hurt.' It was obvious he addressed this last to Dan.

Dan looked at him for a moment then nodded. 'Be careful you don't stomp on something that could possibly be evidence.'

'I'll be careful, but unless he left a cigar butt or something, there won't be much to find. It's nothing but sidewalk out there, and as for the grass, we haven't had a drop of rain for a month.' He nodded to Dan and walked out the front door.

He walked down the few steps, out to the sidewalk, and slowly started to walk around the area where the clown must have stood, looking back through the window that was no longer there, then down at the sidewalk, then back into the street. Mary wasn't sure what he was doing, but he seemed to know.

She sighed and spoke to Ellen. 'Let's get that glass cleaned up. Mike was right. One of these dogs is going to get glass in their paws if we don't.'

'I'll help.' Pat Bennington turned toward the kitchen. 'Where do you keep the brooms?'

'Pat, we need to get going. The dog's fine, but we've got a whole hospital of them who will need attention starting' – Karl looked at his phone and sighed – 'in a couple of hours.'

'We can manage,' Mary told her. 'You and Karl go on. Ellen won't leave here until Dan does anyway.' What she didn't say was she had no intention of leaving right away, either. She needed to ask Dan a few questions and didn't want to do it in front of Mike or especially Ryan.

'Well, if you're sure . . .' Pat yawned and then laughed. 'All right. I'm glad we could help a little, though. See how Taffy gets through the night. And for heaven's sake, stay safe.' She hugged John, who stood beside her, then held her arms out to Glen, who gave her a big squeeze and a peck on the cheek.

'Thank you, both, it's not every vet who makes a house call at three in the morning,' Glen said.

Karl grinned. 'It's not every client who calls us at that hour to come treat a dog who was shot. Glad she wasn't. Glad you weren't either.' He slapped Glen on the back and he and Pat walked out the door.

The broken glass was gone and, upon Dan's instructions, placed in a large trash bag by the time the forensic team arrived. They didn't have much to do. The bullet had come from outside and there was nothing out there to point to who had fired the shot. Besides, John was adamant he had seen the clown and there was no reason not to believe him. They dug the bullet out of the mantle, took the trophy and the trash bag full of broken glass, why Mary didn't know, and left. Ryan stated, rather grouchily, that he and Mike would also be leaving. He would need statements from both John and Glen in the morning. He told Dan he would report any new developments, nodded to Ellen and Mary, and they also left.

Dan looked at Ellen then at Glen and John. Glen sat on a

small denim striped chair with graceful carved arms, John had plopped himself on the floor, legs outstretched, Taffy asleep on his lap. They both looked haggard.

'OK,' Dan sat up as straight as he could, 'go over this for me again. Start from when you drove into your driveway. Did you see a car parked on the street anywhere?'

John and Glen looked at each other and both shook their heads.

'You parked in the garage, is that right?'

Another nod.

'Then what happened?'

'Nothing out of the ordinary,' John said. 'The dogs were all over us. We got them settled then Glen made tea and we took it into the living room, thinking we'd be ready for bed when we finished. Glen said, "Let's see if we can see the moon, it's full tonight," and he went to pull the curtains back. He stood looking out the window and almost immediately the shot happened. I don't know how the bullet missed him, but he jumped back and fell over Taffy. It took me a second to realize what had happened. Then I jumped up.'

'Yelling, "Taffy, are you hurt?"' Glen put in. He grinned at John and leaned over and touched him on the shoulder. 'We know who counts around here.'

John smiled back at him and squeezed his hand. 'I figure you can take care of yourself. Anyway, Glen was winded but not hurt, but Taffy kept whimpering and she wouldn't get up, so we called Karl. Then we called the police.'

Mary turned to Dan. 'Shouldn't they go someplace else tonight? What's left of it, anyway? Do you think the clown will come back?'

'I strongly doubt it.' Dan squirmed around then stood up. He walked back over to the fireplace, looked once again at the hole where the bullet had been, then turned to look out onto the street. 'I think it would be a good idea to close those drapes, though. You'll need to get someone out here to fix this window first thing, but I think you'll be all right the rest of tonight. Let's talk about this clown.'

John and Glen looked at each other then back at Dan. 'All right. What are we supposed to talk about?'

Dan sighed, reached over and seemed to adjust the sling with his good hand, looked around the room, then back at the chair where he had spent the last couple of hours. He sighed again and settled himself back down in it. 'I don't suppose we could have some coffee? You two might have had caffeine overload, but I'm feeling in need of some.'

John scrambled to his feet, much to the displeasure of Taffy.

Ellen immediately got to hers. 'I'll fix it. I think Dan wants you here. Just tell me where the filters are.'

'Second cupboard on the left. Mugs are in the same cupboard. Coffee is in the fridge.'

Ellen left, and everyone looked expectantly at Dan. Mary wondered how much he was going to tell them. Evidently, a lot.

'We think we have four plausible suspects, but nothing that can help us make an arrest. We're working on a theory, which I'll tell you about later, but for now, here's our list. Troy Turnbull.' He raised his hand to interrupt Glen, who was about to object. 'Turns out his ironclad alibi wasn't so ironclad. He could have done it. Next, Paul Cummings.'

Glen made a rude noise but didn't follow it up with a comment.

Dan waited a second and went on. 'Mike Gallagher.' He waited, watching both faces. He didn't have to wait long.

John drew in his breath with a whoosh. 'Mike would never do something like this. Rob a bank, shoot two people, try to shoot Glen, never.'

Dan looked at Glen, whose brow furrowed. He looked more worried than angry.

'Who's the fourth one?' he asked Dan.

'Kyle Nevins.'

John burst out laughing. 'Kyle? He wouldn't know which end of a gun to fire. Besides, he'd probably faint at the thought of trying to rob a bank or shoot at us from the street. Kyle just doesn't—'

'Kyle has been trying to take over his mother's money for years,' Glen interrupted. 'She's in Shady Acres, but she's perfectly capable of managing it. She's perfectly capable of managing him as well. The first time Kyle tried was when she went there to live, right before Chet Bradley "retired". He approached me about it again a few months ago. Said she was failing. I said he had to get a court order, there was nothing I could do, and suggested he talk to a lawyer. He didn't like that. What he did do, I don't know.'

That was a piece of news that effectively shut down the conversation. John and Dan stared at Glen, almost in disbelief. Mary was sure she felt her heart skip a beat. Could Kyle really have done such an awful thing? He was the type to be vindictive. Bullied as a child by his schoolmates, bullied at home by his mother, getting back at the bank and Glen who wouldn't do as he wanted might have made him angry enough to try a stupid stunt like rob the bank. But murder Chet? Shoot at Glen? It was good she was sitting down. She felt a little lightheaded.

Ellen walked into the room bearing a tray with five mugs of coffee, a sugar bowl, and a cream pitcher. She set it down on the coffee table and looked around. 'What's going on here? You all look as if you just lost your best friend.' She paused. 'You haven't, have you?'

Mary took her mug and stirred a little cream into it. 'Not yet.'

'What does that mean?' Ellen handed a mug to John, who passed it to Glen, and took one for himself. She put cream and sugar in another one and handed it to Dan, then perched on the end of the sofa with her own and looked around the room. 'What did I miss?'

'Not much.' There was more than a trace of sarcasm in Dan's voice. 'Just that three of our four suspects have a motive for all this. Or sort of a motive. Only one person has a motive for all three events, if we include Chet, but then, we have a lot to learn.'

'Which one doesn't have a motive?' Ellen took a sip and fanned her mouth. 'McDonald's can't hold a candle to you guys when it comes to hot coffee. Let me guess. Paul Cummings doesn't. He could have robbed the bank, but why would he go after Chet and Glen? He doesn't seem the type to plan the way that robbery was, either.'

Glen heaved a loud sigh and set his mug on the table. 'Paul

Cummings just might have another motive for robbing the bank. I canceled his account and refused to cash a check for him. He was fuming mad and said he'd get even, if it was the last thing he ever did. I'm afraid I didn't pay any attention to him then, but I'm sure thinking about him now.'

John looked at Glen, his mouth half open as he stared. 'It sounds as if you've managed to piss off half the town. First Troy because he couldn't get a house loan, then Mike . . . what did you do to Mike? Then Paul Cummings and trying to push Kyle off on some lawyer. That's a pretty good score.'

'I didn't do anything to Mike. I was able to make them a house loan because they had a good down payment and good credit, but it was still tight. They want to take out a second to pay some doctor bills, but that won't happen until Nancy can go back to work. They know that. They weren't happy, but they understood.'

John passed the mug back and forth between his hands, not seeming to pay any attention to the swaying coffee. He would if it spilled, but Mary was too busy thinking about what they'd learned to be concerned.

'That means we're down to two?' Mary asked.

'It means we don't know enough. About the suspects or anything. If Chet was murdered, it changes a lot. We also need to be certain the bullet the clown fired at you tonight' – Dan motioned to Glen – 'matches the one that killed Victoria.'

'Do you know what kind of gun it is?' Mary knew next to nothing about guns except what she read in her beloved mysteries or on TV, but she did know about matching bullets.

'A Glock. Same kind I have. It's the favorite gun for lots of police.'

'Do a lot of your policemen carry one?'

'Just about everyone. And, yes, that includes Mike. Even Janelle has one, and Gary.' His expression changed to one of distaste. 'I guess we could somehow commandeer Mike's gun and test it, but I'm not sure how. The only possible shred of evidence we have on him is he has a clown costume.'

'Isn't that enough?' Ellen got up off the hard arm of the sofa and dropped onto the seat beside Mary.

Millie climbed into her lap.

Ellen began to absently stroke her ears. 'Can't you bring Kyle, for instance, in for questioning under the guise of talking to everyone who Victoria made a clown costume for? Can't you also ask to see the costumes? If they say no, you can take the next step, but if they say yes and either have an alibi or their costume slips over the head, well, then you can cross them off. Can't you do that?'

It took Dan a minute or so to answer. 'Yes, I can do that, but there are several reasons I don't want to, at least not right now. First, I want to do the questioning. Second, if I bring one of them in for questioning and he's not the one, I don't want word to get around I'm looking at all the people who had clown costumes made by Victoria. The word is already out that we're looking for people with certain initials who we think have a costume. If we pull in one for questioning, everyone in town would know we had a suspect. If I got the wrong person, the real clown would have that costume in the trash heap faster than you can say Jack Robinson. We know he hasn't ditched it yet, and I need more information before we can start to narrow this down.'

'What kind of information?' Ellen asked in strangulated tones. 'This guy is nuts. He may plan on attacking Glen and John again. I think you need to do something now.'

John looked as if he approved of that idea.

Glen didn't. 'I think Dan's right. You've narrowed it down to four people. Now you need to find out more information on those four. I'll help in any way I can.'

'I'm sure you will.' Dan's voice was grim. 'Being shot at isn't much fun. There's nothing more we can do tonight. And, just to make Ellen happy, Gary Pinardo is out there, across the street in the bushes, standing guard. He'll be there until sunup. So, you two go get some sleep. Ellen and I will as well, and Mary, you and Millie go on home. We'll get together tomorrow and see what we can work out.'

Just what they could work out, Mary didn't know. But she was tired, so was her brain, and maybe a little sleep would help it. Maybe it would help them all. However, a glance at her watch told her she wouldn't be getting much. It was already after five, and she had to be at the church no later than nine to help set up for the fellowship meeting after the service at St Mark's.

She turned to John and Glen. 'Are you sure you two will be all right? Is there anything you need?'

It took a few reassurances, but she finally followed Dan and Ellen out the door, Millie right at her heels.

'Where is Gary?' Ellen stood by the driver's door, looking across the street. The home stood well back from the street. The landscaping was lush, thick with trees and bushes. It was also completely enveloped in shadow. The sun wouldn't be up for a couple of hours. There was no sign of Gary. At least there wasn't until suddenly a figure appeared from behind a bush. Mary might have missed it altogether, but it waved a white handkerchief at them, then sank back out of sight. Gary was on duty. With a small sigh of relief, Mary and Millie started for home.

THIRTY-SEVEN

Mary sat in the pew later that morning, only half awake. Even after a long shower and two cups of coffee, she could feel her head nod and her eyes start to close. Les was giving an inspiring sermon, she was sure, but she was glad there would be no test later. She would fail for sure.

At last it was over, and the congregation filed out and made their way to the church hall, where coffee, juice, and donuts awaited. Maybe a little activity and some fresh air would clear her brain. She busied herself with making sure platters of donuts were kept full and cartons of milk were supplied for those who wanted them, already opened for the children, with a straw inserted. The same with the juice containers. Pinching those open had ended in more than one milk or juice war. The adults, as usual, broke up into groups, but the main topic in all of them was the shooting last night. Neither Glen nor John had appeared this morning. Nor had Dan or Ellen. Mary wasn't surprised. If she had been able to think up a good excuse, she wouldn't have either. However, she was here, and Millie and the cat were, no doubt, having a nice nap on her bed.

The crowd was beginning to disappear. She was making the rounds, picking up coffee mugs, used napkins, and empty milk containers when she saw her. Janelle. Surprised, Mary stared at her. She looked different out of uniform. Janelle had on gray wool pants that hung smoothly over slim hips and a maroon long sleeve shirt of a silky material tucked into them held by a slender black belt. It looked as if she'd added shoulder pads, which surprised Mary. Women didn't much wear them anymore, but it probably kept the material in place. Janelle turned to her and smiled.

'I didn't know you went to church here,' Mary heard herself say before she could stop herself. It sounded rude but surprise took over before she could stop her tongue.

Janelle stood beside one of the round tables, looking around. She started toward Mary. 'I don't but thought I might like to. I know you belong and thought I'd find you here, I've been looking for you.'

'I thought you were out of town.' Mary shoved a handful of napkins into the big trash can. 'Is everything all right?'

'Detective Ryan called me this morning and told me about the shooting and asked me to come back early. So, here I am.'

'How did you get here so fast?' Mary wiped her hands on the dishtowel she'd flung over her shoulder and walked toward the kitchen, picking up several half-full coffee mugs as she went. 'I thought you were in Los Angeles.'

'No, just over on the coast.' Janelle gestured toward a table. 'Can we talk for a minute?'

'Of course.' Mary put the coffee mugs on the counter. 'There's some coffee left. Would you like some?'

Janelle shook her head, much to Mary's relief. She would have joined her, and right now, she felt she'd had enough caffeine. They pulled out chairs and sat. Joy was in the kitchen, wiping down the counters but out of earshot, and the other volunteers were packing up the leftover donuts and putting the few milk containers left in the refrigerator. They had the hall to themselves.

'What can I do for you?'

'You can give me some information.' Janelle's tone of voice was low as she, too, looked around. 'Chief Dunham called Sean, Detective Ryan, over to his house this morning, and they evidently had quite a talk. Chief Dunham has some theory that the bank robbery and the old man who died at the nursing home and the shooting last night are somehow connected. He also thinks Victoria Witherspoon made the costume the clown was wearing. Only no one knows who that is. Chief Dunham seems to think that information is on a computer she had. I'm here to pick it up.'

Janelle's lips were compressed into a straight line and her tone, while not exactly threatening, wasn't far from it. The hairs on the back of Mary's neck bristled, not unlike the cat. Had Dan approved this visit? It felt a whole lot more like Detective Ryan. 'Who told you to come accost me?'

'I'm not accosting you. I just need that computer.'

'I don't have any computer except my own.' That wasn't a lie. She didn't. She also had no intention of saying she had had Victoria's or what she'd done with it, at least not until she'd talked to Dan.

'But you were in her shop?'

'Yes. Pat Bennington and I were there to pick up Pamela's wedding dress and we got her cat. You met him the other night.'

The look of distaste on Janelle's face made it plain how she felt about the cat. 'I did. I don't like cats. I'm allergic to them. Did you see a computer while you were there?'

'I didn't know you were on the investigative team,' Mary said. 'I've been over all of this with Chief Dunham, and I'm sure he's shared with Detective Ryan, so I'm not sure what you're asking me for.' There was something about all this that didn't feel right.

Janelle's head jerked up, and she stared at Mary, then she removed her glasses, wiped her eyes with one of the leftover napkins on the table. She replaced the glasses and smiled, a faint and not very sincere smile. 'I guess I did come on a little strong. I'm sorry. This whole thing is getting on everyone's nerves, mine included. Evidently Chief Dunham talked to Detective Ryan early this morning. Said he wanted to bring him up to date. The chief said you have identified the people who bought clown suits from Victoria Witherspoon, or think you have, and are looking for a motive. Chief Dunham says all of them have had a run-in with the bank of some sort, and he thinks revenge against the bank might be a motive for all these episodes. That doesn't make any sense to me, but then, people do some strange things.' She watched Mary for a moment, as if waiting for a response. When she didn't get one, she continued. 'I'm not sure how revenge fits in with any of this, but I understand you were the one who discovered the initials in a notebook she kept, and you were the one who worked out who they stood for.'

'That's true,' Mary admitted slowly, 'but not all of them had a run-in with the bank. Mike Gallagher hasn't, according to Glen. I understand Glen refused to cash a check Paul presented to them, but I doubt that would have phased him much. It seems that young man has a history of trying to cash bad checks or get cash from someone else's debit card. I imagine the only thing he'd worry about was getting caught.'

'That leaves Troy, and somebody named Kyle Nevins. Is that right?'

'If indeed the clown really is wearing a Victoria Witherspoon costume.'

Janelle seemed about to say something, but Joy and her crew were ready to leave.

'Mary,' Joy called out, 'you and Janelle want any more of this coffee?'

Mary shook her head. 'No thanks, Joy. I'll clean the coffee pot before I leave. You all have done enough.'

'You sure? I can do it.' Joy sounded doubtful. She stared at Janelle as if she could be some dangerous criminal and Mary would be in grave danger if she left her.

Mary smiled a little at the thought. 'No. You run along. I'll do it and lock up. I have my key.'

Joy nodded, and she and her helpers walked out the door. Joy gave them one last long look as she let the door close behind her.

'You didn't want any, did you?' Mary motioned toward the

large commercial coffee maker and started to push back her chair.

Janelle shook her head. Mary sat back down.

'I was asking you about motive. You seem to have dismissed both Mike Gallagher and Paul Cummings. What motive could the other two have? Chief Dunham mentioned revenge. Revenge for what?'

'Janelle, are you investigating this with Detective Ryan? I didn't realize you were assigned to him.' Mary knew Dan had to bring Ryan up to date on what they had found out and what they thought, but why Janelle was questioning her, she didn't know, and it was making her uneasy.

A light flush ran up Janelle's cheeks. 'Not officially, but I have been helping him a little. I had some experience in Los Angeles with murder investigations.'

That probably explained it, but Mary still didn't feel right telling her what was no more than speculation on her part. 'Why don't you ask Dan, Chief Dunham, about that? I don't really know much about revenge and I certainly don't know why it might be a motive for someone to rob a bank.'

Janelle had leaned forward on her arms which she'd rested on the table as she peered at Mary. She leaned back, letting them drop to her sides as she stared at Mary through her tinted glasses. 'Revenge makes people do and say some odd things.' There was a sadness in her voice that Mary hadn't heard before. 'Maybe we're looking for someone who believes they were injured a long time ago. You know the people in this town. I don't. Do you think that's possible?' She stopped abruptly and tried to smile. 'Sorry. I didn't mean to ramble on, but we must find that computer. It may give us the clue we need to locate the shooter. We have a search warrant to search Victoria's shop and house. Maybe it's there. You didn't see it?'

Mary ignored Janelle's comment on revenge. It was her insistence on getting the computer that bothered her. 'Janelle, I wasn't searching Victoria's place. I was there to get dresses for a wedding and her cat. Good luck with finding it. When are you searching?'

'In the morning.' She pushed back her chair and stood,

looking at Mary. 'If you remember anything, you'll let me know?'

Mary nodded. 'By the way, have you picked Zoe up from the Gallaghers?'

Janelle seemed caught off guard by that question. 'No. She seems happy with Robbie and he seems to like her. She's a dog who needs a job and now she's got one. I've been thinking . . . I'll go over later today.'

Mary nodded again but said nothing more. It didn't seem the time to make Mike's pitch. Besides, Janelle might be thinking Zoe would be happier with Robbie. It would be great if she volunteered to give him the dog without Mary getting involved. However, if she didn't, well, she'd promised.

Janelle hadn't moved. She seemed to be lost in thought as she continued to stare at Mary, then suddenly she said, 'I'd better go. I assume you're going to see Chief Dunham today?'

Surprised, Mary nodded again. Dan was her nephew-in-law. Of course she was going to see him.

Janelle sighed faintly. 'Tell him . . . never mind. I'm sure Ryan told him everything we know. Thank you, Mrs McGill.' She started walking toward the doorway. Halfway there, she turned toward Mary as if to say something more, paused, her body tight as she stared at her, then she quickly wheeled around and went out the doorway.

Mary sat for another few minutes, trying to make sense of the conversation. Why had Janelle asked the questions she had? Was she really working the investigation? How much had Dan told Ryan? Most everything, she assumed. Ryan oversaw the investigation while Dan was laid up, but she didn't think that would last much longer. He didn't approve of Ryan's tactics and was sure Ryan wasn't getting the answers he needed. That business about the computer. Should she have told Janelle she knew where it was? No. However, she did need to know if Dan had his court order, or whatever he needed. David Black, from Mo Black's Computer Works was standing by, ready to try to pry out what information the computer had to offer as soon as she gave him the word. Maybe today. She got up abruptly, pushed her folding chair back under the table, and headed toward the coffee pot. As soon as it was clean, she was going home, picking up Millie, and heading for the Dunhams. She and Dan had to have a long talk.

THIRTY-EIGHT

Dan and Ellen had evidently gotten up late. Ellen was in a pair of much-used sweatpants and a baggy sweatshirt, her hair swept back in a ponytail. It looked like the pony had been galloping over the fields on a windy day. Dan had on a pair of plaid flannel pajama bottoms and a bathrobe thrown over his bad shoulder, his right arm in the other sleeve. It gave him a lopsided effect, as well as showing off his white bandages and a lopsided hairy chest. The hospital hadn't gone for the designer look when they shaved it.

Mary had gone home to get Millie before she came. She found her and the cat where she'd left them, on her bed, fast asleep. They'd arrived at Dan and Ellen's as they were finishing breakfast.

'It's been a busy morning.' Ellen poured her aunt a cup of coffee.

'Yes, it has been.' Mary snapped the leash off Millie's collar, so she could greet Morgan properly, and sat down in the rocking chair. 'I see Jake is still reading his way through Mr Dickens' works.'

Ellen laughed. 'It's his favorite spot. I don't know why. It isn't very wide, and there's no cushion. I keep thinking I should put a pillow or something up there, but I don't have one that will fit, and he doesn't seem to care.'

They all stared at the cat, who ignored them.

Mary took her first sip of coffee. 'I understand Detective Ryan came calling this morning.' She had taken the rocking chair because it was low enough that her feet hit the floor. She didn't set it in motion as Millie lay draped across her lap. 'How much did you tell him and what, if anything, did he have to tell you?'

'Not much, either way. They have no idea who the person was who shot up Glen and John's house, and if it was our clown, they have no idea where he went. I told him who you – we – thought the initials stood for and why. I had to tell him about Mike but made it clear he wasn't to start a heavy-handed interrogation of him, that we were sure he wasn't the one, but he latched right on to poor Kyle and seemed pleased there was a hole in Troy's alibi.'

'Did you tell him about the zipper?'

Ellen laughed. She had their breakfast plates in hand and was on the way to the kitchen, but she paused. 'You should have seen his face when Dan said a zipper might be evidence. A nice combination of shock and disbelief. Then when Dan told him it was you who came up with the theory, he really started to try to tear it apart. Let me put these in the sink.'

She was back almost immediately, waving the coffee pot in the air. Mary shook her head. Her stomach was already starting to protest on overdose of caffeine. Dan, however, accepted a refill.

'I think Ryan is afraid of you.' He grinned.

'Afraid! That's just plain silly.' Mary was shocked at the thought but secretly a little gratified. Ryan had been arrogant and not interested in anything she had to say. Maybe that meant he was finally listening.

'Actually, it's not.' The grin was gone. 'You're the only one who's come up with any actual evidence. You not only saw the guy, but you and Pat found the notebook and figured out what the initials stood for, and you found out who they all are. I think it scares the liver out of him that he hasn't discovered one single fact about this case.' He grinned again. 'I'm used to you.'

'Humph,' Mary muttered. 'Does that mean I don't scare you?'

Dan laughed aloud. 'It just means I'm used to you. I remember when you let me help bake cookies. You used to read to Ellen and me and made our birthday cakes. My mother was great, but she couldn't make a cake to save her life. You know pretty much everyone in this town, and they know you. That's an advantage he doesn't have and doesn't understand. Now. I have a piece of news for you.'

Mary brightened and leaned forward. She hoped it was good news.

'I got our court order. We can break into Victoria's computer. All you have to do is tell me where it's at.'

'The only place it could be. I took it to Mo Black's Computer Works. It's sitting on a shelf in the repair section, waiting for you to tell David to get started.'

Dan looked at her wide-eyed. Ellen quickly put her coffee mug on the table beside her as she almost doubled over with laughter. 'You've been reading Edgar Allen Poe again.'

'No.' Mary shook her head. 'But I was thinking about that story and thought the shop would be a good place. Besides, I put your name on the tag, just in case.' She turned to Dan, who grinned. 'So, what do we do next? Should I call David and tell him he has the go-ahead, or do you have to deliver a copy of the court order to him? How did you get it on a Sunday, anyway?'

Dan's grin got wider. 'It's a small town. Helps when you play poker with the judge.' The grin faded. 'Why don't you call David. Do you have his cell? Ask him to get started as soon as he can. I'll have the official document over to him in the morning, but if he can get on this today, it would be great. I have a feeling we're running out of time.'

'What? Why?' Mary exclaimed.

'Ryan has already started on our four suspects. It seemed he tried to get to Troy this morning, but he's at the hospital, waiting to become a father. While we were all at John and Glen's, learning that our clown had shot out their front window, Troy's wife was having labor pains. He's with her now. Ryan found him at the hospital this morning, pacing, in the waiting room. Ryan started by asking him if he had a clown costume. Dumb. Troy said he didn't know what he was talking about, why would he, and if he didn't believe him, go search his house. I don't know if Ryan arranged that or not, but if he did, I hope he got permission in writing.'

'I hope all goes well for them, but what about that makes you think we're running out of time?'

'Word had already spread around town the police are interested in anyone who wore a clown costume on

Halloween. We know Mike Gallagher has one, and my guys searched Paul Cummings's apartment for his. It doesn't have a front zipper, by the way. There is also no sign of a gun or a tote bag. That leaves Kyle, who must have already heard the news. If he's the one, he'll have that thing in the fireplace already, along with anything else that might smack of a clown.'

'Not necessarily.' Mary was trying to sort this out. 'Kyle would have no reason to. He's made no secret he has a costume. He's going to be a birthday party clown. Or at least try. He has a valid reason to have bought a costume. Does he have an alibi for last night? And, why on earth would he do a thing like that? It doesn't make sense.'

'None of this makes sense,' Dan stated firmly. 'We have four men who each had a clown costume on Halloween. Any one of them could have robbed the bank and shot Victoria and me, but there isn't one of them who have a motive, at least one we know of, to smother Chet or shoot out Glen and John's front window. I'm assuming whoever it was meant that bullet for Glen but missed. All three incidents are connected, I'm pretty sure, but how and why is beyond me.'

Ellen had been listening intently. She set down her coffee mug. 'What I don't understand is why a petty thief like Paul would have purchased a clown costume. It doesn't seem in character.'

A small unamused smile crossed Dan's face. 'It was in character, all right. They found more than a clown costume in Paul's apartment. Four wallets, all from people who had reported them stolen while they were at the park Halloween night. Also, a couple of credit cards that didn't belong to Paul, several cell phones, and a lady's handbag. Seems our Paul is an accomplished pickpocket. It's on his rap sheet, which is impressive. A clown costume that night was a great cover, and he made good use of it.'

'Which would give him a motive to shoot Victoria since he almost certainly bought his costume from her.' Mary took another sip as she tried to put all of what they knew into order. 'Maybe we were wrong about the robbery. Maybe Paul robbed the bank because there was almost no one in it and he was all right with not making a huge haul. But that doesn't explain why he would smother Chet or try to kill Glen.'

'It doesn't explain why Kyle would, or Mike either,' Ellen stated. 'Dan, are you warm enough? Your bathrobe has slipped.' It had. Dan yanked it back on his shoulder with his good hand. 'We're missing something. It almost has to be one of those four, but it doesn't fit.'

'Maybe Chet died of natural causes,' Mary put in. 'There just doesn't seem any reason for someone to kill him.'

'He was smothered,' Dan said, in what sounded almost like a growl. 'I got the autopsy report last night. Poor old guy. It didn't take long, but along with other evidence, there were bruises around his mouth, so someone pressed down hard. It has to be the same person, but why beats me.'

Mary sighed and moved over so Millie could jump down, being careful the chair didn't rock. 'You said Ryan was here this morning. Did he tell you he was going to get a warrant to search Victoria's shop? I know because Janelle came to see me. She asked a lot of questions, but what she really wanted to know was if I had taken a computer out of Victoria's shop.'

That got Dan's attention. 'No. I never mentioned a computer to him. Hmm. Maybe I've underestimated Ryan. Sounds as if they also don't think the initials are enough. That she must have kept more extensive records somewhere and that most people do it on a computer. What did you tell her?'

'That I didn't have it. She asked me if I'd noticed one while I was there, and I told her I was picking up wedding clothes and a cat. I hadn't paid much attention to anything else.'

Ellen let out a snort at that one. 'You didn't tell her about cutting off some material and showing it to Tammy? Or about hunting through her worktable, where you found the zipper and the clown pattern? Or how you and Pat went through all the dresses, looking for a clue and that's how you knew what the notebook with the initials in it was? Did she buy that?'

Mary could feel heat run up the back of her neck. Ellen was right. 'I didn't think I should tell her anything about the computer until I'd talked with Dan.' She squirmed a little in her chair, but Dan seemed to approve.

'I don't want anyone to get ahold of that computer until I

have a chance to look at it. The evidence we need to find out which one of our suspects is the guilty party may be on there.'

'You may end up just as confused as you are now,' Ellen said. 'Most likely, all you'll find is measurements, the names and addresses of the buyers, that kind of thing, and you don't need their measurements. You already have their names, thanks to my wonderful aunt.' She smiled at Mary, who smiled back.

'We may,' Dan said, 'and we may find that we can clear one of them. That would at least be a start. This heavy-handed stuff Ryan likes to pull gets you nowhere, in my opinion. There may come a time when it's necessary, but if I'm going to lean on someone that hard, I want heavy evidence to back me up. Go call David. Tell him to work his magic, then we'll see where we are.' He leaned back, readjusted his injured arm, and groaned. 'Ellen, I think I could use one of those pain pills about now.'

Ellen looked stricken but said nothing. She got up and headed for the kitchen. 'Be right back.'

Mary thought it was time she and Millie left. She was anxious to call David and she thought Dan needed to take a nap. He probably wouldn't if she were still there. She looked around for her purse and Millie's leash but, before she could snap it on her, Ellen was back, a pill in one hand, a glass of water in the other. She handed them to Dan, who tossed down the pill, drained the glass, and leaned back once more. Ellen motioned to Mary and they went back in the kitchen.

'He just won't quit. He was up half the night, couldn't get comfortable even with a whole bank of pillows piled up behind him, then Ryan appeared here early this morning.

'They went over everything for more than an hour. He doesn't approve of how Ryan is conducting this investigation and is itching to get back to the office and do it his way. But he's not ready. You can see that. He has me worried sick. That blasted clown, whoever he is. I'd love to wring his neck.' She walked over to the counter and picked up the coffee pot but didn't offer any to Mary. She just stood here, staring at the counter, trying to hold back tears, Mary was sure.

'He's going to be all right.' Mary walked over, took Ellen around the shoulders, and turned her around, placing the coffee pot back on the counter. She guided and gently pushed Ellen back to the table and got Ellen into a chair, handed her a paper napkin and pulled out a chair for herself. 'He really is, you know. Yes, I think he's doing a little too much, but there's no way to stop him, especially as he's not happy with Ryan. What we can do for him now is help him solve this. We need to find out who the clown is.'

'What more can we do? I'm fresh out of ideas.'

'The first thing is to get David going on that computer. It may not help, but we won't know until we look. In the meantime, I'd like to know a little more about Kyle and Paul. I can't see why Paul would have a motive to kill Chet or shoot up John and Glen's house, but since we know virtually nothing about him, except that he's a petty crook, there might be a connection. As for Kyle, we know he wanted the bank to do something they couldn't. Kyle's a little . . . different, but I never thought he was unhinged enough to do something like this, but he might be.'

'If he is, he can thank his mother. She's bullied him all his life, overprotected him to the point where he didn't have friends, didn't know how to make them. She got him financially tied to her as well. No wonder he wanted control of the money, such as it is, but I'm not sure he could handle it if he got it. He's finally making some money of his own, but his resentment of what his mother did to him must be huge. Maybe it spilled over to include the bank and those people who run it. I sure hope I haven't ruined Susannah's life like that.'

'You haven't, and you know it. A more grounded young woman would be hard to find.' Mary paused. 'Do you know anything about Paul?'

'Nothing but what the police know. He has a long list of petty crimes and has been in and out of jail since he was about twelve. He and his mother lived here briefly about eight or nine years ago, which would have put him in his early teens. I suppose something might have happened then but if so, I don't know what. I do know he got into trouble and his mother abandoned him to the tender mercies of the juvenile justice department.'

'How do you know that?' Mary felt a little shocked but also

a little sorry for Paul. Or, did he care? Mother/child relationships could get gritty sometimes.

'Dan told me. They pulled all his records. He left the area
after he got out of juvenile hall and went down south, where
he got into more trouble. Why he came back here, no one
knows.'

'We seem to have parent problems with at least two of our
suspects. I can't imagine Paul's rejection by his mother has
anything to do with what's going on here, but Kyle's problem
with his mother might.' She thought for a moment. 'Mother/
daughter relationship can be a bit tricky as well.'

'Are you thinking of mine with my mother? Your sister? I
love her, you know, but she's difficult. Always has been.'

'She's a strong-minded woman. Thinks she knows what's
best for all of us, but she's a loving woman. She wasn't who
I had in mind.'

'Who, then?'

'Janelle Tucker and her mother. She's told me a little about
her. They seemed to be very close, more so than most, but I
got a hint that life with her mother wasn't always a bed of
roses. That sometimes they had thorns.'

Ellen laughed but nodded. 'I got the same feeling. I was
waiting for Dan at the station one day several weeks ago when
she came in and we got to talking. She asked me about the
real estate office, wanted to know about Beau Chatsky. I told
her he'd died of a heart attack five years ago. She went on to
say her mother hated him, thought he was responsible for
selling them a piece of property that wasn't fit to grow grapes
on. I told her about the people who owned it now and how
successful they were with their grapes. That got her to talking
about her mother, whom I guess she adored, but she had a
peculiar childhood. It was just her and her mother. She was
homeschooled. Her mother didn't want her to date. She never
went anywhere without her until she got into the police
academy. Weird.'

'Very.' A little ripple of disgust ran through Mary. 'That
was no way to bring up a child.'

Ellen shrugged. 'She seems like a normal well-adjusted
young woman. Dan thinks she has the makings of a good

policewoman, so the mother must have done something right.'

'Maybe. She doesn't show much emotion, so it's hard to tell. Even with the dog. Zoe. Maybe I need to stop by on my way home and see how that's going. Anyway, I'll be on my way. I need to call David as well.' Mary pushed back her chair, dropped a kiss on Ellen's cheek, and picked up Millie's leash. 'Don't worry about Dan. He's going to be fine.'

She walked back through the living room, Ellen right behind her. They both stopped to stare at Dan, who had his chair pushed back, his feet up, and his eyes closed.

'I can tell you're both staring at me. I'm fine. I'm not asleep, but I am waiting for this damn pill to work. You two staring at me won't make it work any faster.'

'I'll call you later and tell you what David says.' Mary walked out the door.

THIRTY-NINE

Davidid Black said he'd start on the computer right away. Should he call her back or Dan?

Mary thought a minute, picturing Dan's face, not exactly writhing in pain but not as good as new, either. She had no idea how long this might take, but, just in case he got into it easily, she didn't want to have him wake Dan. 'Call me. I'll make sure he gets the info.'

'Will do,' David said in a cheerful voice. 'This is going to be fun. Let's hope there's something on there that will help.'

Mary hoped so as well. She pulled up in front of the Gallagher house. Mike's car was in the driveway. Good. They were all home.

Nancy opened the front. She looked as if she'd been crying. 'Oh, Mary. It's you. Come in, please.'

Resisting the impulse to reach out and take Nancy in her arms, she followed her into the living room. Mike stood in the middle of the room, his hands clenched at his sides, the tips of his ears bright red. With fury? It looked like it. Robbie was huddled down in his wheelchair, Zoe tight by his side. He looked as if he, too, would break into tears any minute.

'What's going on here?' Alarm bells were ringing loud and heavy in Mary's head. She wasn't sure what had happened, but it wasn't good. She needed to find out, now. 'What's happened?'

'Oh, Mary.' Nancy broke into tears again and couldn't go on.

Mike looked up and motioned her to sit down. He could barely get the words out. 'Sean Ryan and Janelle just left. They said I'm under suspicion for the bank robbery and for smothering Chet. All because I have a clown costume. They think I'm the one who shot out Glen's front window, too. I've been suspended. Me! Who does Ryan think he is? He doesn't have the authority to do this. He's conducting the investigation, not running our department.'

'Dear God in heaven, how stupid can one man get,' Mary exclaimed.

Dan was right. Ryan was so determined to get a culprit before anyone else, he forgot about evidence and good police work. He was flailing like a man going down for the last time, and he was going to take innocent people with him if he wasn't stopped.

'Anyone with a grain of sense knows you had nothing to do with the robbery or with Chet's death. Dan knows that and so do I, so don't worry. Dan will take care of this. Now, tell me what Detective Ryan said exactly.' She walked over to the sofa, sat down exactly in the middle and motioned Mike to come sit beside her. She wanted him to see she was on his side.

Reluctantly, he left his stance in the middle of the room and sat on the end of the sofa.

Nancy sat on the arm and leaned close to her husband. 'They wanted the clown costume Victoria made for him.'

'Did they just look at it or did they take it away?' Mary's money was on the latter. They probably hadn't found any powder residue on Paul's costume and thought they'd try Mike's. She wondered if they had Kyle's as well.

'They took it away and his gun as well.' Nancy had quit crying. She glanced over at Robbie, who hadn't moved, except to tighten his grip on Zoe. His eyes were wide open with fright.

'My dad never hurt anyone,' he proclaimed. 'He's the best dad in the world.' This last came out with a sob.

Zoe leaned up against his side and put a paw in his lap. He covered it with his hand.

Mary felt as if she was going to cry just watching him, but she didn't. She had to get this family over this unnecessary trauma. 'Tell me about the costume. Did it have a zipper down the front?'

Mike looked up in surprise. 'No. It pulled on over your head. Isn't that how they're all made?'

Not all of them. 'I imagine they're going to have it tested for gunpowder residue and the gun to see if it's the one used to kill Victoria and the one used last night. I know you're furious and rightly so but calm down. You'll be back on the force the minute Dan hears about this. You said Janelle was here? Did she say anything about taking Zoe home?'

Nancy dabbed her eyes with a tissue. 'She barely acknowledged the dog. Zoe got up and wagged her tail when she saw her but didn't approach her. Janelle looked at the dog, watched her stay right beside Robbie, but said nothing. She and that detective were all business. They wanted the costume and the gun and told Mike he was suspended until further notice.'

She turned toward Mike and put her arm on his shoulder so he had to turn to look at her. 'What are you worried about? You know what they're looking for and you know they won't find it. This is nonsense and it won't last long.'

'Is my dad going to jail?' There was no mistaking the fear in Robbie's voice or in the tremors in his hands.

Victoria, Dan and Chet weren't the only victims. The clown, whoever he turned out to be, had affected the lives of a lot of others. She thought of Ellen crying in the kitchen where Dan couldn't see her, of her terror the day he'd been shot. She looked at the anguish on Nancy's face and the confusion and worry on Robbie's, the hurt and anger in every move that Mike made. John and Glen with no front window but a load of worry of their own. Would he attack again? And Nora. A widow. Not that she hadn't known it was coming soon, but no one had expected Chet would be murdered. The violence of the act would leave a lasting impact on their family.

'No, Robbie. Your dad isn't going to jail. He has done nothing wrong, and he'll soon be back on the job.'

'Do you promise?' His voice sounded a little stronger but so young. So scared.

'I promise.' She sat a little straighter on her end of the sofa and addressed Mike and Nancy. 'You two need to pull it together. Your children need you.' She looked around. 'Where's Cloe?'

'In her room, asleep.' Nancy looked down the hall at the only closed door. 'At least I hope she's asleep. She usually takes a nap after lunch.' She sighed. 'She's been quiet for a long time. Much longer than usual. She might be playing with her Barbies or reading one of her books to them. I'm just glad she missed all this.'

Mary couldn't agree more. 'All right. Now, Mike, you were looking around the house outside last night. Did you come up with anything?'

'No.' He started to pay attention for the first time since Mary had arrived. 'There was no sign of anyone, but there were signs someone might have been in the bushes directly across the street. I couldn't be sure, but it looked like some branches were broken off and someone had gone through at least one of them. They would be in a direct line with where the shooter must have stood. I think he knew John and Glen were out for the evening and was waiting for them. I told Ryan about them but don't know if he followed through. I think John did see the clown, whoever he is, but it wasn't me.'

'I know that. Dan knows it as well.' Mary looked at Robbie and Zoe.

The dog had her head in his lap. He was fondling her ear. A look of almost peace was on Robbie's face. The reassurance Mary had given him about his dad seemed to have helped, but the dog's presence was what was important. She watched them for a few moments, wondering not for the first time if she'd done the right thing. These two had bonded in a way she had never seen between a dog and a person. Stronger, she thought, than her bond with Millie. No, that wasn't right. Different. Robbie was dependent on Zoe, and the dog knew it and reveled in taking care of him. Her relationship with Millie was more of a partnership, even if she did most of the caregiving, and she must admit, she also loved it.

It was time to go. Daylight was fading, and she wanted to get home before dark. Where the day had gone, she didn't know, but she wanted to sit in her big chair and sip a glass of wine while she thought about everything she'd learned, or thought she'd learned. After she got Millie's dinner, of course. And the cat's. She'd almost forgotten the cat. She hoped he hadn't decided to tear up anything.

She gave Robbie a kiss on the check, Zoe a pat on the head, and Nancy a squeeze and smiled at Mike. 'It's going to be all right. Just give us a little more time.'

FORTY

The house sat in darkness. It was only five, but daylight savings time had come and gone and Mary's backyard porch was hidden in shadow. The light from the garage helped but not enough. Mary was embarrassed to think she was afraid, but she was. Only a little, of course, but she found herself putting her car key between her fingers the way they had taught her in the AARP self-defense class she had taken. The door appeared to be locked. It was. Her key turned with a reassuring click. She opened the door slowly, ran her fingers around the doorjamb onto the wall and flipped the switch. Her kitchen shone with brightness. She took a deep breath and entered, Millie at her side. They were greeted by the cat, yowling he had been abandoned and where was his dinner.

Mary scooped him up and held him close, relieved that he seemed to be the only breathing thing in her house. 'I'm going to serve your dinner and Millie's right now.' But she would turn on the lights in the dining room and her room before she fed them.

There was no one in the house and no sign anyone had been there. Humming a little tune under her breath, she filled their dinner bowls. She watched for a few minutes as they ate, Millie attacking her food as if she hadn't eaten in a month, the cat looking his over, selecting the morsels he found tempting. She smiled, but her attention wasn't fully on them. The events since Halloween were foremost in her thoughts. The robbery, Victoria's death, Dan shot, then Chet, his death now officially murder, and Glen and John's shot-out window. There was no doubt in her mind the clown had meant to shoot Glen, and she was afraid he might try again. But why? How were all these things connected, because connected they were. On the TV crime programs she watched, they had a murder room. They kept a time line on a large chalkboard and had suspects' pictures pinned up sometimes with lines drawn between them and certain events. Maybe that was what she needed to do. List all the things that had happened and make a time line. Then see who fit into it.

Feeling slightly more hopeful, she got a lined notepad off her desk and a pen and pulled out a chair at the kitchen table. Fortified with a glass of white wine, she started with the robbery itself but put a line through that. She needed to start farther back. Where had she put her copy of Victoria's notes? There. On her desk. She would start with the dates of when the costumes were picked up. Or were those the dates they were ordered? She pulled out her calendar and started to trace the dates. They had to be the order dates. It seemed unlikely someone would pick up a Halloween costume in August, but someone might order one that early. Someone who was planning a robbery far ahead. She let her fingers run across the page to the initials. The first ones were TT. Troy? If it was him, he had planned far ahead. It didn't sound like him. Mike had ordered his mid-September. That seemed reasonable. But it also could indicate planning. The robbery had been carefully planned. What about the other two? Both around the first of October. Not exactly at the last minute, but that didn't leave Victoria a lot of time. They were simple garments to make,

so maybe . . . this wasn't getting her anywhere. She'd make
a time line of events. What she needed was to know where
everyone was at those times. How she was going to do that,
she wasn't sure. She didn't know where everyone was. She
decided to start with the events and underneath each put the
names of the people she knew were there or could have been.

She started with the bank robbery. Any one of the four could
have done it. Troy was supposed to have been at the auto shop,
but there was no one to verify that. Paul wasn't working at
the winery, so he could have robbed the bank. Mike was . . .
she had no idea where he was. On duty somewhere and Kyle
should have been at the beauty shop. She'd have to ask Lucille.
She made a note to herself, then started a new column topped
with Chet's name. That was easier. She knew Mike had been
at Shady Acres with Janelle. He could have smothered Chet,
but why? Kyle was often at Shady Acres, but she didn't know
if he had been there that afternoon. She would ask Vanessa if
anyone had seen him. Another note. As for Paul, she didn't
think he'd go unnoticed if he started prowling the halls.
Besides, as far as she knew, he'd never met Chet. Where did
that leave her? Nowhere helpful. There was also no way to
know who had shot at Glen, so she left the column under that
incident blank. Tapping her pen on the table in irritation and
frustration, she started to go back over everything that had
happened that she knew about. What was she leaving out? The
people who drove away from the library after the shooting.
She'd forgotten about them. Had either of them seen something? Gary seemed to think neither of them had on a clown
mask. He couldn't be sure, but did that prove anything?
Wouldn't the clown have removed the mask first thing? He
would have removed the whole costume as soon as possible.
That was presumably why he had his made with a zipper.
Ordering a zipper didn't seem to her something a man was
likely to think about. It was more likely a woman, used to
getting in and out of garments that presented a logistical
problem. But what woman would want to rob a bank, kill
Chet, and try to shoot Glen?

Janelle.

Now, why had her name popped into her head?

Mary laid her pen on the table, sat back, and stared at her list. There was something else, something she had noted at the time and had bothered her. What . . . after church services. Janelle. She walked away toward the doorway then turned back, paused, stared at Mary then hurried away. Something in the way she moved made her think of the clown. She shut her eyes and tried to picture the clown but what she heard was Tammy's voice. Shoulders. The clown had reminded her of John Lavorino. John had wide shoulders and slim hips. Maybe Janelle hadn't been wearing shoulder pads. She'd assumed the clown was a man. Why? Could he have been a she? No. Not possible. Only . . . they had never been able to understand where the clown had gone. What if he was a she, had zipped the clown top off as she ran, and pulled off the mask. She could have been in the car, innocently driving away when Gary ran into the parking lot. She was the one who had the costume top made with a front zipper for just that purpose. A fast way to change clothes.

Janelle could have been at the bank. She was a cool-headed woman, trained not to panic. She also had motive. A twisted, bizarre motive but maybe . . . Mary started another column. First, Janelle was devoted to her mother. They had lived together until her mother's death. She had been homeschooled after they'd left Santa Louisa and hadn't had much social contact until she had gone to the police academy. That all by her own admission. Second, her mother was the kind of person who always blamed someone else for any misfortune or mistake. Had Janelle's mother blamed the bank for their misfortunes? She had evidently thought they had bought a piece of substandard land, but someone else was producing excellent grapes. If a child heard all her life that someone had treated her family badly, had cheated them, would she want to take revenge? What had Janelle said? Revenge makes people do and say some odd things. Was Janelle determined to take her family's revenge after all these years? Impossible. The initials didn't include Janelle. They had identified all of them as belonging to a man. She couldn't be involved.

Mary thought about that. They weren't all positively identified. They had assumed Troy had a clown suit but didn't know for sure. However, that still didn't implicate Janelle. She was being ridiculous. Everyone liked Janelle. Dan thought she had great potential. She had lent Robbie her dog. That was certainly generous and thoughtful. There wasn't a shred of evidence that she was involved, just this wild suspicion. She stared at the list. All of the initials weren't all that clear. Either Victoria had a faulty pen that left blobs on the page or she had very bad handwriting. She looked closer, then held the sheet up to the light. There was a blob of some kind on the initials for TT. Mary pushed back her chair and headed for her office. There was a magnifying glass in her desk drawer. Muttering to herself that she was a fool, nonetheless she pulled it out and returned to the kitchen. The glass showed the T clearly. Only it wasn't a T. That small blob at the end was the foot of the T. The T was a J.

Stunned, Mary sat back and thought. Did anything else point to Janelle? The dog. No. But the cat. Victoria's cat. Janelle hated cats and Victoria's cat seemed to return the favor. Had the scratches on Janelle's hand come from a rose bush or from a cat who didn't want to go outside? Was it Janelle who had searched her house? Had she put the cat outside? Mary tried to remember any rose bushes around the house Janelle was renting. There were none she could remember. She knew the people who owned it and had lived there for years. They weren't gardeners. She'd been reading too many far-fetched mysteries. That was what her theory was as well. Far-fetched. Only, so many things fit. What should she do? Run it by Dan? She'd feel like an idiot if she did, especially if it turned out Janelle was innocent. She didn't know what to do.

The phone rang.

David told her the computer was successfully hacked. It had been easy. He thought it had information on it she and the police wanted and what should he do with it? She told him not to take it to the police department. He said he wanted to go home, and could she come and get it? He would stay at the shop until she got there if she came now.

Stunned, Mary agreed. She would look at the information on the computer before she took anything to Dan. If it pointed to someone else, she would never have to mention her wild flight of fantasy. On the other hand, if Janelle appeared anywhere on Victoria's records, then she'd voice her suspicions. She got up resolutely, grabbed her jacket off the hook beside the door, took down Millie's leash, and picked up her purse. 'Come on, let's go find out if I'm right or if I've gone insane.' She left the kitchen light on and, after making sure the cat was safely in the house, locked the door behind them.

FORTY-ONE

Mary walked out of Mo Black's Computer Works a little dazed and deep in thought. David had easily accessed Victoria's information and it changed everything. She wondered if it proved everything as well. She had to get this to Dan and right away. He could make the judgment on what they did next. Trying to balance herself, she prepared to cross the street to where she'd left her car. She'd deliberately parked it under the streetlight.

Even though it wasn't late, the town was dark and empty, except for the Watering Hole, which was down the street, and the light was somehow reassuring. She was irritated with herself for being so on edge but couldn't seem to help it. She shifted Millie's leash into her other hand, pushed the strap of her purse higher on her shoulder, and, clutching the handle of the computer carrying case in the other, started to step off the curb. She stopped. Someone was standing by her car. She couldn't make out who. The figure stood in the shadow just outside the circle of light, but someone was there, not moving. Waiting for her? Her heart started to pound, and she pulled Millie closer to her. What should she do? Knock on the Computer Works's door? David had left out the back by now. Try to slide out of the shadow created by the doorway and cross the street somewhere else? Impossible. Call for help? And say what? That someone was standing by her car and she was afraid. Of what? The decision was taken out of her hands.

'Mary?' A voice she knew called out to her. 'Is that you?'

Janelle. Dressed in her police blue, she stepped out of the
shadow to stand beside the driver's side door. 'Is everything
all right?'

'Yes, oh yes.' Reluctantly, Mary started across the street,
Millie trotting at her side, the computer case banging against
her other knee. 'I just picked up my laptop. David was so nice
to work on it for me on a Sunday, but I need it. All my
committee lists are on it.' She sounded flustered and she knew
it but couldn't seem to help it. 'What are you doing here?'

'I'm on patrol and saw your car. I thought I'd make sure
you were all right.'

There was a tone to Janelle's voice that didn't give Mary
comfort. She sounded calm, almost cold and forbidding.

'I'm fine. Millie and I will get along home, so if you don't
mind . . .'

She indicated the door that Janelle blocked, but she
didn't move, only stared at Mary.

'That's not your computer. It's Victoria's, isn't it? I heard
Chief Dunham tell you to get it the other day. I was right
outside his hospital room and heard everything you both said.
What did David Black do to it?'

A cold chill ran down Mary's spine. What did she do now?
'He didn't do anything. I need to go. Could you move, please?'

Janelle didn't. She stared at Mary, as if trying to make up
her mind about something. She looked different. No glasses.
This was the first time Mary had seen her without her tinted
glasses. The streetlight blared down on them, showing her
eyes to be blue, but the whites a dull red. Allergies. She had
said she had them to lots of things, cats especially. What
had Millie said? And Tammy? The clown had red eyes. She
wouldn't have had her glasses on under the clown mask. The
chill Mary felt got colder. 'Are your allergies any better?'

Janelle started, then smiled and leaned up against the car
door. 'Actually, they are. I think I may be allergic to dogs as
well as cats. Why?'

'It's the first time I've seen you without your glasses.' Mary
knew she was stalling for time. Why, she didn't know. In hopes
someone might walk by? She didn't know what else to
do. Janelle wasn't going to let her into her car. She had to do

something. They were at the end of the park, where the corn stalk maze still reigned. It was in deep shadow, it's opening hidden from view. If she could get close to it, maybe she and Millie could run along its dark side to the next street over. The police station was only two blocks from here. Would it be possible to get to it? Probably not, but if she could get someplace for a couple of minutes, maybe she could get to her cell. Call 9-1-1.

Janelle smiled and shifted her weight. 'You look nervous. Why is that?'

Mary shook her head. 'No, I'm not nervous. Why would you think that?'

Janelle took a step toward Mary and leaned forward a little, her feet slightly apart. 'Tell me something.' The coldness in her voice would have made a polar bear shiver. 'When did you figure it out?'

Mary hadn't expected that. She started to protest but didn't think it would do any good. Besides, she wanted an answer to a question of her own and admitting she suspected Janelle now wasn't going to put her in any less danger. She was in it up to her neck.

'You told me. In little ways, of course, but the only person who had a motive for everything that happened, the robbery, Chet's murder, shooting at Glen, was you. That was you in the car after the robbery, wasn't it? You were the one who had the clown costume made with a front zipper so you could get out of it quickly. Your initials were in Victoria's book. At first I thought the J was a T, but it wasn't. Both Minnie and Tammy said the clown had red eyes. Your eyes are reddened with allergies. You were driving one of the cars that left the parking lot that afternoon. Gary thought one driver was a woman but wasn't sure. You ripped off your mask and got out of the clown top and just drove off. Is that what happened?'

Janelle chuckled. 'That went off exactly as planned.' Her face darkened. 'I hadn't planned to shoot Victoria, though, or Chief Dunham.'

'I believe you,' Mary answered. 'What I don't understand is why? You took revenge on those people for your mother? Why?'

Janelle seemed to be looking at something over Mary's left shoulder, as if she was seeing something far away from Santa Louisa's city park.

'You'd have to have known my mother. She told me for years how awful this place was. When my father was in debt up to his eyebrows and the grapes were failing, the bank was going to foreclose. Mum had hysterics in the bank when she found out. She blamed Chet Bradley. He was bank president back then and the investment advisor. Said it was his fault, that the loan was onerous, that he'd conspired to make them fail. She went on about how she hated the bank people, the real estate people, the newspaper for how they'd treated them, how she needed to take revenge for my father's sake and for her own. Only, she never did. She used to say revenge is a dish best served cold. By that she meant you could go a long time before taking it. Revenge. She made me promise that if she died before she could, I would. I believed her. I came back here to make the people in this town pay for what they'd done to my family. You're a nice town. At least, you seem like one, on the surface. But you're all a bunch of small-town people who can't wait to take advantage of anyone new. I'll bet you all had a good laugh when my father died. That's what my mother said. You had to pay for that, to be punished. She didn't, couldn't, but I could. I have, and I'm not finished.' She stopped, rubbed her eyes with the hand not poised over her still-holstered gun, and looked at Mary, who had frozen in place with shock and growing indignation.

'I missed that banker, but I won't next time, and I still have the real estate person to make pay for his father's lies to mine. He may have died but his son is still there. The newspaper also needs to be punished for that awful obituary that made my father sound like a failure. Then I'll be on my way. I promised Mother I'd do it, and I will. I always keep my promises.' She glared at Mary. 'Now, the question is, what am I to do with you? That village idiot leading the investigation will never figure it out, but you did.' She laughed a little, then ran her hand over her eyes again as if they itched. 'You, Mrs McGill, are too clever for your own good.' She paused, and her expression hardened. 'First, hand me the computer, then we'll talk about you.' She reached down and loosened the flap on her holster.

Mary gulped. Janelle had no intention of letting her go but would she chance shooting her and possibly Millie in the public park? She took another look at Janelle's face. Probably she would. She had no idea what to do. She wasn't going to hand over the computer, but if she got shot, Janelle would take it anyway. She hefted the strap of her purse higher up on her shoulder as she frantically tried to think what her options were. There didn't seem to be any. She was conscious of Millie pulling on her leash and let up on it a little. What was the dog doing? Sniffing at Janelle's legs.

Janelle lifted one foot. 'What is that dog doing?' She pulled her leg up higher and leaned against the car to keep her balance, trying to avoid Millie, who walked between her and the car. The leash was behind Janelle's ankle, held tight as Millie strained to move forward. Mary saw her chance and yanked. It tightened against Janelle's leg, throwing her off balance. She slid down the car, trying to catch herself on the car mirror, instead almost falling on Millie, who protested loudly.

'Run, Millie!' Mary let go of Millie's leash, which unwound from around Janelle's leg as Millie frantically threw herself forward, trying to get free.

Janelle screamed and clung to the mirror, trying to get her balance. The screams seemed to frighten the dog even more. She shot off across the park, the leash flying in the air after her, toward the maze. It was their only chance. Mary followed, moving as fast as the banging computer case would let her. It wouldn't take Janelle long to be back on her feet. Mary, too, headed for the maze, hoping the shadow it cast would hide her enough. She needed to make it to the next street, where it was lighter and maybe held some people. Where was Millie? She couldn't see her. A black dog in a dark shadow. How was she supposed to . . .? There. Movement. That had to be Millie, but where was she going?

'Millie,' she shouted. 'Follow me.'

The dog paid no attention. Terrified, her flight instinct had taken over and she was running for all she was worth and suddenly disappeared. Mary glanced back. Janelle was on her feet and had started after them. Could she just leave Millie? No. She had to find where she had gone. She ran closer to the maze, out of breath and puffing badly. The dog was nowhere to be seen. She could, however, make out the opening to the maze. It was open. The boards that had been nailed across it were on the ground. Millie must have gone in. Should she? The running footsteps she heard behind her left no choice. She ran into the pitch-black maze.

FORTY-TWO

S he couldn't see a thing. She couldn't hear anything, either. Janelle must know where she was, but she hadn't come after her. At least not yet. Mary walked slowly forward, her free hand outstretched, hoping it would keep her from running into a wall. A mouthful of dried cornstalks wasn't something she could tolerate right now. Where was Millie? She didn't dare call out, Janelle might hear her, but she got more anxious with each step. Where was her dog? Something rubbed against her legs. She thought her heart would stop. Was it a rat? The something jumped up on her and whined. Millie. Thank goodness. She reached down and ruffled her ears then picked up the leash. They had to get out of here, but how? She kept moving forward, her arm outstretched, Millie close beside her.

Her hand hit something. It rustled. Cornstalks. She had come to the first split in the tunnel. Which way? She remembered someone saying always turn to the left. Was that right? She wasn't sure, but she didn't have much choice. They went left. Mary thought it was darker this way. Was that possible? She looked up. Black clouds were settling in at an alarming rate. The weather person had predicted the first rain of the season. It appeared he was right. The first drops started to fall. Just what she needed. Wait. Maybe it was. She and Millie walked down the black corridor a little way before she stopped. She set the computer bag down and rummaged in her purse.

Her hand hit her cell. She'd call for help. Praying it still had charge, she clicked the button. It was on. She had to hurry. She had no idea where Janelle was, and she and Millie had to keep moving, but she needed help. She held her breath as she dialed 9-1-1 and didn't let it out until she heard it ringing. *Pick up, Hazel, pick up.* It was Agnes who answered. 'Agnes, what are you doing there?'

'Hazel has a cold. Is that you, Mary? Is something the matter?'

'Yes. I'm in the corn maze and the clown is after me. Oh, Agnes, the clown is Janelle, and I think she's going to shoot me. Send help. Now!'

The line was silent. Finally, Agnes spoke. 'Janelle? The clown? You must be mistaken, Mary. Everybody likes Janelle. She couldn't be the clown. Besides, she's a woman.'

'I have no time to argue. She's in the maze. Send somebody now. She's going to shoot me.' She clicked off.

There was a rustling near where she and Millie crouched. Janelle. She was at the first split. Which way would Janelle go? Mary held her breath, trying to listen. Nothing. The faint rustle seemed to fade. Just then the rain let loose and drowned out any sound. But, if she couldn't hear Janelle, then Janelle couldn't hear her.

'Come on, Millie. Let's get out of here.' She flicked on the flashlight app and let it shine around the increasingly drenched cornstalk walls and down the path. She could just see the next division. She flicked off the light, picked up the computer bag and they started, her hand feeling their way along the cornstalks. The beat of Mary's heart drowned out the sound of the rain as it cascaded down the cornstalks and under the collar of her jacket. She ignored it. They had reached the next turn. They went left. She strained to hear sirens, cars, something that said help was on the way. Nothing. Somehow, the rustling of the dry leaves, the roar of the rain running down through the stalks was terrifying, but not knowing where Janelle was or if they were walking into a trap was worse. Were the boards nailed over the exit still in place? Could they get out? Where were the police? Had Agnes told anyone? She was protesting when Mary hung up. It was all too possible Agnes had shrugged and picked up her latest romance novel. If that was the case, Mary would have a few things to say to Dan about her when she got out of here. If she got out of here.

The computer bag was getting heavy. So was her purse. The strap dug into her shoulder. Her shoes were soaked, and rivers of mud were starting to form under her feet. Where was the next turn? She flicked on her flashlight, hoping Janelle couldn't see it. Up ahead. She hoped this was the last turn. The rain let up some. Enough that she could hear a new noise. Someone was crashing through the cornstalks. More than one someone. Voices called her name.

Relief washed across her in larger waves than the rain had. 'Here,' she managed to yell, hoping they'd know where 'here' was. She didn't.

More yelling. This time a woman's voice screaming invectives. Janelle? She didn't know. She was so tired, so wet, all she could think about was getting out of here. Suddenly, there was light, down where the path split. Someone running with a flashlight came along it, shouting her name. She managed to answer and around the corner came Gary, his heavy-duty flashlight illuminating the path.

She bent down and picked up an exhausted and muddy Millie and whispered in her ear, 'The Marines have landed. We're safe.'

FORTY-THREE

Mary sat in her big chair, in her flannel pajamas covered by her reindeer bathrobe, her now-warm feet encased in moccasin slippers. She'd stood in the shower she didn't know how long but finally had begun to warm up. She was exhausted but not sleepy. Millie sat beside her, also clean and presumably warm. Someone had given her a bath. She no longer had mud encased on her feet or bits of cornstalk caught in her hair. She smelled of Mary's best shampoo. Millie deserved every drop. If it hadn't been for her, they would probably both be dead.

Her living room had filled considerably while she was in the shower. Dan sat opposite her, dressed in what she thought were his pajama bottoms with a sweatshirt half on him and half off. His good arm was thrust into one sleeve, the other pulled over his sling. The effect was jarring, but she didn't think he cared.

John and Glen were also there, talking with Karl Bennington. She assumed John had called Glen after she'd been brought into the emergency room, much against her will. Other than being scared half to death, soaked with rain, and breathing in a lot of soggy cornstalk dust, she was fine. All she'd wanted to know was that Janelle was safely in jail and then get herself in a hot shower. Both wishes had finally been granted. She was sure Ellen had called the Benningtons. Pat was probably responsible for cleaning up Millie.

She sighed deeply and let her head fall back against her chair. Pat Bennington was in the kitchen with Ellen, fixing something. She hoped it wasn't coffee. She didn't need any more stimulant tonight.

Ellen walked into the dining room with a tray of mugs. 'Hot chocolate,' she stated with a grin, 'with an extra added ingredient.'

Mary glanced at the buffet, where she kept her wine rack and a couple of other bottles she rarely used. The brandy bottle was missing. She nodded at Ellen and smiled. Pat followed Ellen, carrying a plate heaped with brownies. 'Found these in the freezer. Hope you don't mind,' she said to Mary as she started passing them around.

Mary didn't mind at all. She could always make another batch. But she was getting impatient. She waited until everyone had a mug in their hands before she asked, 'Janelle is really in jail, isn't she?'

Dan grinned around a mouthful of brownie. 'I saw to it personally.'

'You went down to the police station?' Mary wasn't sure she liked that idea. He really wasn't ready for that, but it was reassuring to know he had taken care of it. 'What happened? Did she confess?'

Dan laughed. 'Absolutely not. She claimed she was trying

to save you. She had no idea why you and Millie had gone into the maze, but she was trying to get you out.'

'She's lying,' Mary replied tartly. 'She was going to shoot me, and probably Millie.' She laid her hand on Millie's head, who looked at her, then laid her head back down on Mary's lap.

'We know she is. I called David Black. He told us how to access the files and there it was. Janelle Tucker. Her size, her address, when she paid, and how much and, the most important thing, a special order. The top had a zipper all the way down the front.' His grin got wider. 'I've already gotten a warrant and have a team searching her house right now.'

'I think it's there,' Mary said. 'It was only last night she wore it when she shot at Glen. And, Dan, she would have tried again. She told me so.'

Silence descended as they absorbed that piece of news.

It was Ellen who broke it. 'OK, tell us how you figured this one out. Everyone thought the clown was a man. How did you know he was a she?'

'I didn't, at least not at first. It took much too long for me to put the facts together. It wasn't until today, after the service, that I realized. I saw Janelle from the back and thought she was a man. Then I went home, made a time line, and looked at motive. Janelle was the only one who had one, but the idea that she was taking revenge on the whole town still confounded me. Then I started adding up the facts. There were two people driving away from the library, even with all the sirens going off and the police cars starting to arrive. One was a pickup and the other a sedan. Gary said he didn't think either of them had on a clown mask and he thought a woman was driving the sedan. He wasn't looking for a woman. Gary saw no one else and no one has been able to figure out how the clown got away. Ruthie said she bet the clown had an accomplice and hid in the car while he or she drove away. That gave me a hint to what might have happened. Then Janelle was at Shady Acres when Chet was killed. She had scratches on her hand she said were from a rose bush. Her house has no rose bushes, but she hates cats. I think she got scratched the day she searched my house and put Millie and the cat outside. By the way, she knew I had Victoria's computer. She heard us talking that day in the hospital. She was outside the door, listening. Mostly, though, because she kept talking about her mother, how she thought she had somehow been mistreated while she lived here. I still didn't quite believe what I was seeing. No one would try to take revenge on a whole town twenty years later. I thought I had it all wrong. So, when David called me and said the computer was ready, I went. I wanted to see if it would confirm what I suspected or if I was going crazy. I was going to bring it to you' – she nodded at Dan – 'but Janelle was waiting for me by my car. She wanted the computer and had no intention of letting me go, either.' Mary shuddered a little and took another fortifying sip of the cocoa. 'If Millie hadn't tripped her, we wouldn't have gotten away.'

'Why?' Karl set his empty mug on the floor beside his chair. 'The bank? Chet? Then Glen? It doesn't make sense.'

'It does, and it doesn't.' Mary looked around the room at the waiting faces. 'You all knew a little about the motive. I just happened to run into people who filled it out for me. Unfortunately, I didn't put it all together early enough. I guess because we were all convinced we were looking for a man. A woman out to revenge her family's honor seemed so improbable.'

'Don't leave us guessing,' John said. 'Spill the beans.'

Mary laughed. It felt good to laugh. Too much tension for too long. But it didn't last long. This tale was far too sad. 'Janelle was her mother's favorite. At least she was the one who stayed with her after the sister married and moved away. She evidently didn't keep in touch. Janelle told me herself she was homeschooled and didn't have a social life until she went to the police academy. All her life, her mother told her how awful the people in this town had been to them, how they'd cheated her father when he took out the loan to buy his property, how the real estate people had sold him the wrong land, even how the local paper had not paid him enough homage in his obituary. She wanted revenge for all these perceived wrongs, but she never got past the talking stage. She made Janelle promise she'd take that revenge, kept telling her revenge was a dish best served cold. So, when she died, and

Janelle saw there was an opening on the police force here, she seized it. She would finally have her family's revenge.'

'Only it didn't work out very well.' Pat's voice was soft and sad. 'She's caused so much suffering for absolutely no reason, and, in the process, wrecked her own life.'

The room was silent once more. Finally, Mary said, 'Revenge. It's not a dish best served cold. That is stupid. It's a dish best not served at all.'

EPILOGUE

Mary sat in a pew in St Mark's Church, admiring the tubs of white roses mixed with winter greenery, the flickering candles, and the satin bows on every other pew, and sighed happily. It was a happy day.

Ellen sat on one side of her, Dan beside her. He wore a shirt and jacket for the first time since the shooting and looked good. Going back to work had agreed with him. Right after Janelle's arrest, he had thanked Detective Sean Ryan and sent him back to San Louis Obispo. He was back in charge and the whole force was happy. Janelle had been moved to San Louis, awaiting a mental evaluation and eventual trial for murder. Paul Cummings had also been moved to San Louis. Santa Louisa wasn't equipped to hold prisoners for long periods. Paul's trial for petty theft wouldn't be nearly as full of spectators as Janelle's.

She spotted Kyle sitting just behind the families, bursting with pride. He had done the hair for the whole wedding party. He had thrown away his clown costume, and his balloons, and was concentrating on what he did best. Hair. Mary had seen both Pamela and Krissie outside, and they looked spectacular. Kyle had finally come to terms with his talent. Good.

She saw movement coming up the side aisle behind her and turned in time to see the Gallaghers. Nancy had Cloe in her arms, the child looking like a little angel in her full skirted dress, tights, and black Mary Jane shoes. Exactly what a three-year-old should wear, in Mary's opinion, but it was the people behind Cloe that held her attention. Mike made his way up the aisle, walking behind his son. Robbie and his dog, Zoe, were slowly heading for a seat the usher had held for them. Robbie without his wheelchair, walking with his small crutches, braces on his legs, but walking. Zoe was tight by his side, matching her steps to his, glancing at him every other step, making sure he was steady. Mary thought she would break into tears, but she didn't. Something good had come of all this tragedy.

Even the cat had helped. After Chet's funeral and after Nora's children had gone home, Mary had asked Nora if she had ever thought about getting a cat.

'Oh, yes,' was her answer. It seemed Chet had hated cats, but she'd always wanted one.

Mary smiled. Nora and the cat bonded the minute they met. He now slept in Nora's favorite chair. She didn't seem to mind. She even called him Oreo.

A hush fell over the congregation. Luke and his brother took their places, Les stood on the altar in his cassock, his Bible in his hands as the organist played the first strains of 'The Wedding March'. The back doors of the church opened, and Luke's small niece started down the aisle. All heads turned to watch as the procession entered the church.

The wedding had begun.